THE SONGS OF THE KINGS

Nan A. Talese / Doubleday

NEW YORK   LONDON   TORONTO

SYDNEY   AUCKLAND

Barry Unsworth

THE
Songs
OF THE
Kings

PUBLISHED BY NAN A. TALESE
AN IMPRINT OF DOUBLEDAY
a division of Random House, Inc.
DOUBLEDAY is a registered trademark
of Random House, Inc.

Library of Congress Cataloging-in-Publication Data
Unsworth, Barry, 1930–
The songs of the kings : a novel / Barry Unsworth.
— 1st ed. in the United States of America
p. cm.
1. Iphigenia (Greek mythology) — Fiction.
2. Agamemnon (Greek mythology) — Fiction.
3. Greece — History — To 146 B.C. — Fiction.
4. Trojan War — Fiction. I. Title.
PR6071.N8 S66 2003
823'.914 — dc21
2002066845

ISBN 0-385-50114-5

PRINTED IN THE UNITED STATES OF AMERICA

April 2003

First published in the United Kingdom by
Hamish Hamilton, Ltd., London
First Edition in the United States of America

1   3   5   7   9   10   8   6   4   2

Book design by Jennifer Ann Daddio
Illustrations by Rafal Olbinski
Map copyright © Reg and Marjorie Piggott, 2002

For Aira with love and thanks

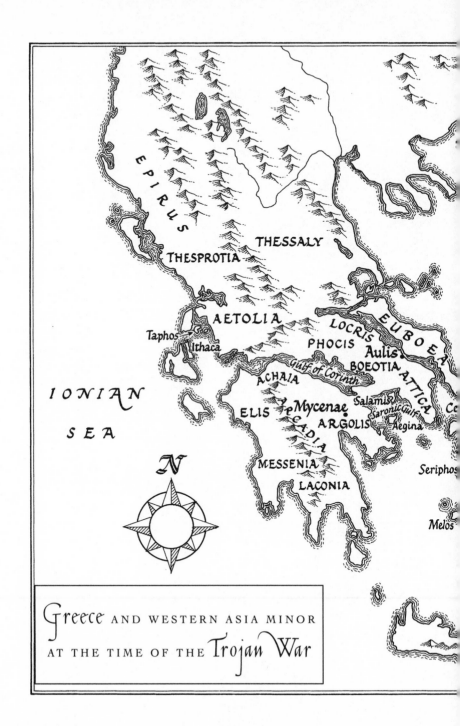

Greece AND WESTERN ASIA MINOR AT THE TIME OF THE Trojan War

THRACE

EUXINE SEA

PROPONTIS

Lemnos

.Troy

MYSIA

EGEAN

Chios

LYDIA

hareus Pt

SEA

CARIA

RETE

| 0 | | 100 | | 200 miles |
| 0 | 100 | 200 | 300 km |

THE

Eagles

OF

Zeus

1.

This was the sixth night. He had lain awake through most of it, listening to the wind, the body of the sleeping boy beside him, beset by fear at still not knowing the sender, fear of other failures that might follow from this. The strands of the wind he knew by this time; tensed in concentration, he imagined he could hold them apart, the shrilling high up among the bare rocks, the softer combing in the shrub lower down, the ripple of loose canvas from the tents. Even the very smallest sounds he strained to hear, random sobs and whispers, stirring of grasses, the faint scrape of displaced pebbles along the shore. A wind from the northeast, unheard of at this season, keeping the fleet trapped in these straits at Aulis, and the army with it, waking the men every morning to the unhappy knowledge of some god's displeasure. It came from the direction of Troy, where lay their dreams of conquest.

Six days and six nights with no sign of relenting, though the voices varied. The wind itself seemed to suffer in all its moods, even in its rages pleading to be quieted, to be soothed.

Then, early in the morning of the seventh day, came the summons from Agamemnon. He noted the time just as in those days of his power he noted all such things. Just before sunrise, the wind still there but quieter now, as if for the while exhausted after its riots in the dark. A time disputed between Hecate and Helius, when the world is between states. He was between states himself, as he also noted: neither inside the tent nor out of it, but cross-legged on a cushion at the threshold, watching his acolyte Poimenos, who was still half asleep, fumbling together a fire for the infusion of mint and honey he had been schooled to prepare. And he was neither clothed nor naked, being dressed only in a loincloth, with a piece of cotton over his shoulder as a shawl. These were things important to remember and interpret; not mortals but gods chose the times.

It was the chief scribe Chasimenos that brought the message, approaching from the rear, appearing suddenly, flanked by soldiers from the King's Guard. At midday, after the fight, Agamemnon would require the presence in his tent of Kalunas, I beg your pardon, *Calchas*, priest of Apollo.

He smiled saying this, glancing away with eyes so pale as to seem almost colorless in the narrow, bearded face. Calchas read the usual veiled contempt in voice and smile, the elaborate politeness, the stress upon the name, not his own, bestowed on him by the Greeks. Contempt too for his shaven face, his plaited hair, the smudges of kohl that would be still on his eyelids, the amulets worn as a bracelet, contrary to Greek custom. Asian priest of an Asian god without even a cult center yet established here.

All this was in the looks and the words—Calchas was practiced in reading such marks. But there was also the fact that this upstart diviner had been granted a shelter of canvas when most of the army spent the nights in the open, finding what cover they could; that he had a boy to share his tent and see to his needs; that he slept on a woolen mat, thickly woven; that he need not reply promptly to a messenger, even one of high rank. It was common knowledge that the King would make no decision, take no step, before Calchas had first scanned the auguries.

Chasimenos stood there waiting in his long-sleeved tunic of a palace bureaucrat. His smile had withered at the delay. "The King requires the presence of his seer," he repeated. The soldiers stood on either side of him, their long spears grounded, their faces heavy with ill humor at being given escort duties at such an hour, not much after dawn. It was early for the King to send; he would have had another bad night. Chasimenos had no need of an escort for such a small thing as this. But the habit of armed guards had grown in the days they had been there, waiting on the wind. Agamemnon himself never appeared without at least six. The diviner said, "Calchas will be honored beyond honor to kneel at the King's feet. May he live forever."

As he spoke he heard the small crackle of the fire, saw the smoke rise straight up in a thin plume. He felt a slight shudder within him, premonition of ill. These calms were dangerous, always brief, cheating the army with hope. There was some quality of danger too in this dawn summons to a meeting he had not been consulted about. Nothing of this showed on his face. He had known how to wait before answering, just as he knew now how to appear unaffected.

He had expected, the answer once given, that the other would quit his presence immediately—it was one he had never shown signs of liking, not even back in Mycenae, before they had set out. But Chasimenos remained there, and after a moment, in a tone he tried to make friendlier, said, "Which of them do you think will win?"

Now at last Calchas could permit himself to show some slight surprise. He was being solicited for an opinion as to who would live and who would die that morning, Stimon the Locrian or Opilmenos the Boeotian, due to fight a duel later on as champions of their respective tribes. "I have no ideas on the matter," he said, which was untrue.

"Opilmenos is the stronger and has more battle experience, but they say this Locrian is very quick."

Something in the tone of this suggested that the scribe might have a stake in the outcome. Calchas had heard from Poimenos, who came and went about the camp on various kinds of foraging expeditions, gathering gossip on the way, that the men were wagering on the result. Though what they could have to wager it was hard to see, they possessed nothing but their weapons.

Chasimenos was lingering still. "I thought that the god might have made it known to you," he said.

Calchas shook his head. "What does Lord Apollo care for the quarrels of men? Live or die, what concern is it of his? The gods will view the outcome with complete and serene indifference unless there is some offense we know nothing of, something done or left undone, said or left unsaid, which might weigh against the one or the other man when it comes to the meeting. It is dangerous to neglect a god, even when not knowing. Punishment can arrive before knowledge."

He spoke carefully, knowing the other for an enemy who would destroy him if he had the power. He *had* been given a sign as to who would be the victor, but it would have been unwise to talk to Chasimenos about this, as it had been of an unusual kind and he had mentioned it to no one. The outcome of the fight was of course the only thing Chasimenos couldn't organize. He was a gifted and devoted administrator, meticulous to the point of obsession, which was why he held his senior position in the palace hierarchy. He had been busy with this fight from the moment Agamemnon had given his approval of it, working out in close detail the order of assembly, the precise positions to be occupied by the allied forces when they lined up for the spectacle. A real headache that, Calchas thought, to remember all the quarrels, some of them ancient, keep feuding tribes at a safe distance from one another. But the outcome he couldn't fix. No one is bribed to lose in a fight to the death . . . "This wind that plagues us is an example," he said. "The punishment has come before the knowledge of the fault."

As if in support of him, the wind rose again now in a long gust that scattered the smoke and rattled the canvas of the tents throughout the camp like a fury of drums. One of the guards clutched at his helmet.

Disappointed at not getting the tip he had obviously been hoping for, Chasimenos reverted to his former aloof and slightly sneering manner. "Croton wouldn't agree with you. He maintains that Zeus cares what happens to every single one of us."

"Yes, I know Croton says that, he says we are the children of Zeus." Calchas paused, again conscious of the need for caution. Zeus was the father-god of the Greeks and Croton was the priest of Zeus, with a large following in the army. He and his two disciples paraded frequently through the camp proclaiming the power of their god. "Zeus is lord of all," he said. "But how can we be children of the gods when we are made of different stuff, when we are perishable and they are not? It isn't logical. We have one season only but the gods live forever. Of course, there is shelter in the thought of a father, and shelter is needed."

He was beginning to enlarge on this theme, which he had suddenly found interesting, the relation between the need and the thing needed, which thing existed at first only because of that need, but then, because of that need, took on true existence. "Perhaps it works the other way too," he said. "Perhaps we humans only exist because the gods need us."

But Chasimenos said nothing to this and did not stay to listen to more, turning abruptly on his heel and disappearing round the side of the tent. However, there was comedy in this that made up for the rudeness; the guards were taken quite by surprise and had to go lumbering after him, hoisting their spears awkwardly. Measured movement, a certain stateliness, were necessary for a person under escort; but Chasimenos, used to scuttling down palace corridors with no company but his own intriguing mind, had yet to learn this. A mistake in any case to talk much at all to him. Themes commonly discussed in Apasas, city of the diviner's birth, and the lands of the Hatti from Kadesh to Sardis, were too abstract for these gross Mycenaean minds. Even a scribe, he thought, a representative of their intellectual class. Chasimenos was hostile enough without having claims made on his intelligence which his intelligence was not able to meet.

He stayed where he was while the light strengthened. After a while Poimenos brought his drink and a wheat cake to go with it. They were in wheat country there, with fertile land to the south; and now, at the end of August, the harvest was in, though the troops had to go farther afield every day in search of full granaries—it was known now that the country people were hiding their grain. Unpatriotic scum, in the words of Menelaus. Since losing his beautiful Helen to Paris—that swine of an Asian, as he called him—Menelaus spoke often of patriotism and solidarity.

As Calchas ate and drank, the first darts of the sun struck through the canvas of the tent behind him, warming the odors of night still caught there in that narrow space, oxhide, crushed grass, the faint scent of bodies in the folds of the wool. Before his face was the radiant sky, a few bright curls of cloud low on the horizon, moving slowly, barely perceptibly—this wind did not change the sky, did not bring storms. He watched the clouds drift together, looked for a shape in them. A fleece, a swan's neck, the forepart of a chariot. He strove to empty his mind for the message, but he could read nothing there, they were random shapes; and he felt a constriction of the heart at this further failure, knowing that nothing in the world was random. There had been no sign for him in clouds or embers or the flight of birds, not one, in all these days at Aulis, when signs were so desperately needed, when Agamemnon waited for his words, when all the camp waited to know who was sending the wind that kept them huddled there along the shore, a thousand men, the greatest army ever assembled by the Greeks in alliance, trapped there while the useless ships rocked at anchor and the waves mocked them and slapped their hulls. In these sheltered waters, with the hills of Euboea making a barrier, the wind had a varying breath, sometimes deep-voiced, sometimes screaming, sometimes, as now, derisively gentle, hardly more than a breeze; but once round the promontories, when you were facing the open sea, the wind was a flail of terrible power, beating ships back, smashing them on the rocks.

He could see the masts from the rise where he was sitting. That August sky was so fiercely bright, they glowed as they swayed as if stirred in their own fire. Smoke was rising everywhere now, swirled by the wind, shot through with sunshine. There were voices and movements of men lower down towards the shore, where the main body of the army was encamped.

With the warmth, the pervasive smell of human excrement grew stronger. On the third day, Ajax of Salamis, called Ajax the Larger, who thought of himself as a practical fellow, had organized his people to dig a long trench for a latrine—a heavy job in the hard ground of the hillside. The whole force from Salamis had been employed on this, laboring in shifts. It kept them busy, an added advantage, as Ajax remarked to his small friend and namesake, Ajax the Locrian, called Ajax the Lesser. Mischief was bred by idleness; working together for a common purpose was good for morale. You form them into squads, appoint a few overseers, tell them you'll tan their hides if there is any slacking, and there you are. Unfortunately, however, in his enthusiasm for the project, Ajax had temporarily forgotten why they had all been obliged to wait there in the first place, and sited the latrine to windward of the camp. Being obstinate in the extreme, he would not admit his mistake, and now forced all the contingent from Salamis to continue using the latrine on pain of his severe displeasure—and all knew what that meant—if found defecating anywhere else. It was generally agreed that the people of Salamis had not been the luckiest contingent so far. Meanwhile the smell was getting worse. People grumbled, but in the general apathy that had fallen over the camp no one was ready yet to face the violent encounter with the enormous Ajax that any direct protest was certain to bring about.

Thinking of this brought back to Calchas's mind thoughts of the fight that was soon to take place. He believed he knew who would win it. He had been given a sign, not because the gods were interested in the outcome, but because their power pervaded human life, like this fire that glowed on the masts without consuming them.

On the first night of their stay there, when it was still thought the wind would be short-lived and spirits were high, he had walked alone along the shore, passing close to where the Locrians had their quarters. He had seen one of them dancing with wonderful grace in the firelight, to the music of pipe and drum. The man was naked but for a loincloth and his body shone with oil or sweat. The fire was veering and flaring in the wind and he brought these movements of the flames into the dance, stepping near to the fire with his arms raised and his head turning, now held in stern profile, now glancing down in serious pride. Such a dancer was he that Calchas had stayed to watch and seen him twice leap the fire, over and back, without faltering, without breaking the rhythm of the dance, so that those watching him shouted in exhilaration, their hearts leaping with him as he leapt. The firelight was cast upward and Calchas had seen the man's face clearly and the faces of those nearest. He had seen the Singer there too, a little apart, with his lyre laid across his knees, looking straight before him, and he had wondered what this scene might mean to the Singer, who was almost blind, what flickering, looming shapes of dancer and flame he might be seeing.

So he had watched for a while, then moved on; but the strong impression of the dancing stayed with him. Then there had been the brawl between groups of Locrians and Boeotians, and a serious wounding—a man stabbed in the right shoulder, disabled. Such incidents bred feuds when men had little else in mind; and feuds among the Greek tribes, once taking hold, spread like a virulent fever. Champions were elected in haste on either side to meet in single combat and settle the matter.

It was when he saw these champions brought forward to be presented to the assembled host that Calchas thought he knew which would be victorious. He had recognized the Locrian at once: it was the man who had danced in the firelight. The other was a half head taller, smooth-haired, narrow at the waist and powerful in the shoulders, an athlete. Moreover, a professional soldier who had fought for Thebes against the combined forces of Phocis and Megaris. They stood on either side of Odysseus, who along with Chasimenos had organized the business, while their names were shouted out: Stimon of Locris, Opilmenos of Boeotia. Both were acclaimed in equal measure for the promise of entertainment they offered, and the Boeotian smiled to hear the shouts but the Locrian remained as serious now as he had been among his own people.

As Calchas had watched and seen one man smile and the other not, it had come to him with luminous certainty that Stimon the dancer would be the one to die. He remembered how he had been drawn by the music and the shouting. And he knew now that he had been directed to turn his steps that way, so as to come upon the man in the pride of life, at the climax of his dancing, when he leapt the fire. The truth of things lay always in contradiction; as the cup brimmed, so it spilled. His own splendor had marked the dancer out for death. So Calchas had reasoned when the champions were brought forward; and so he reasoned still as the sun climbed in the sky and they waited for the event.

Poimenos was sitting on the other side of the dying fire,

keeping a distance in the absence of indications to do otherwise. Calchas noted that the boy had copied his own posture
with exact fidelity, sitting cross-legged with back held straight,
holding his bowl of tea with both hands. He would have dipped
his cake into the warm tea and eaten it so; Calchas knew this,
though he had been too much occupied with his thoughts to
notice. He knew it because it was what he did himself.
Poimenos watched him without seeming to and strove to imi-
tate his movements in the hope of being graced to read the
signs, and so take some part in the stories of the gods and in
their power. Perhaps then he would leave me, Calchas thought.
But there was no danger; the boy was devoted but he showed
no sign of a gift. There were those who were drawn to the
threshold never to enter the house; he was one of that number,
born to serve. At times Calchas detected the helpless knowledge of this already in him. He was beautiful to look at, slender of form and narrow-boned, with eyes black as jet, slanting
upward towards the temples, and a mouth with a full underlip,
giving him a slightly sulky expression as if needing kisses.
Poimenos had been a gift from the gods to him; he had found
the boy at Delphi when he had gone there from Mycenae, sent
by Agamemnon to consult the oracle of Ge, the Great Mother,
as to the outcome of the war which at that time was still at the
planning stage. The boy had been a server there at the sanctuary, the humblest of servers, sweeping the precincts, gathering
wood for the sacred fire, which was tended by others. He had
run away from home, a mountain village on the slopes of
Parnassos, and was living as he could on the leftovers from the
offerings. Poimenos had been at his side when he had half
fainted and almost fallen at the vision granted him by the ora-

cle, the river of blood and the warriors of Troy rolling over and over in the swift current, borne away on their own blood-tide. The boy had seen his power then and stayed by his side ever since. The vision he had recounted to Agamemnon and received gold beads and a silk vest . . .

More to get the boy to look openly at him than for any other reason, Calchas said, "They are wagering on the result of this fight, isn't it so?"

"They are laying bets, yes."

"But what kind of betting can that be? The mass of them have nothing but what they stand up in, apart from their weapons, and those they can't risk losing surely."

Poimenos hesitated a little before replying. He was easily abashed when it came to speaking and had difficulty in finding words. "The bets are what you say you will give, they are like promises."

"But that is always so with bets."

"No, master, the promises are for when we take Troy."

"Ah yes, I see. Then we will all be rich." From the fabled spoils of the city the debt would be paid. A girl, a gold seal, a bronze tripod, a certain weight of amber or silver. It was a form of dreaming. In that great tide of plunder there could be no losers. He thought of the other tide, the one he had seen as the scented smoke rose to his nostrils and the voice came from below the ground in broken words and snatches of song. A flood of red between the banks and the armed bodies rolling in it like the tumbling of debris in the swollen waters of the Maeander River in early spring, which he remembered from childhood. "The dead won't have to pay," he said. "But of course those making promises expect to kill, not to die, don't they?"

Poimenos might have found some answer to this, but

Calchas did not give him time. Prey to sudden curiosity, he said, "Who will be the winner today, in your opinion?"

This time there was no hesitation. "Opilmenos, master. Opilmenos will win."

Calchas looked at his acolyte for some time in smiling silence. The boy was particularly beautiful to him at this moment, touching too, his face radiant with the force of his opinion, not so much an opinion, the priest thought, as a view of the world. Poimenos had chosen the one who was better made, more handsome, more like the kind of hero he would have wished to be himself. These were the qualities that carried success, how could one live in a world in which things were otherwise? One day the boy would wake up in that world and never leave it again . . . With an intensity that brought the beginnings of tears to his eyes Calchas found himself hoping that this would not happen for a long time. In the candor and simplicity of the boy he had found solace and repose, a refuge from the tortuous purposes of the gods and his own tormented subtleties; and he never prayed to Pollein, whom the Greeks called Apollo, without remembering to give thanks for the gift.

Poimenos, emboldened by the kindness in the priest's regard, now gave way to curiosity in his turn. "Master, which do *you* think will win?"

But Calchas shook his head, still smiling. A diviner of status did not indulge in unofficial forecasts even to those he held dear. The question was the one Chasimenos had asked; and he gave now the same reply: "I have no ideas on the matter."

2.

The fire was out and he was already thinking of getting dressed when the army started to assemble. There was no need for him to make any immediate move. This was a military assembly, a marshaling of combatants. There was no place for him in these ranks, any more than for the priest of Zeus, or scribes like Chasimenos, or the bronzesmith and his slave assistants. He watched for a while, from this higher ground, as they formed up in rank upon rank on the shore under the direction of their officers and in accordance with the plans drawn up by Chasimenos, a naked host—in this hot weather they wore only loincloths and the improvised leggings essential for anyone moving about in the thorny scrub above the shore. The nakedness gave an impression of unity entirely misleading, Calchas thought, seeing how carefully the men were kept within their tribes, Molossians from the mountains of

Epirus, Aetolians from the northern shores of the Corinthian
Gulf, the seventy from Arcadia under their chief Inachus,
speaking a language that did not sound like Greek at all. Then
the combined force from the cities of the Argolis, headed by
Mycenae, four hundred men, the core of the army, then
Achaians and Messenians, then the Hellenes from Crete, under
their king Idomeneus.

On they came, mostly in bands of not more than a few
dozen, men of every physical type. They were silent and their
footsteps were noiseless in the soft sand of the upper shore
above the line of the dunes. There was only the loud sound
made by the wind as it moved over the water, something between a hiss and a whistle, as if escaping from some vast punc-
ture or breach in the sky. It was lower down, on the shingled
ground, that the two men would fight, and a space was left
there between the ranks.

They were still coming when he went back inside the tent
to prepare himself for the meeting which was immediately to
follow the fight. Agamemnon had not appeared yet, nor would
he until all other movement was over, and only he was moving.
Calchas felt a return of that earlier foreboding. Something
would be expected from him. It was important that he should
take care of his appearance.

It was hotter now inside the tent, with the sun striking
through the canvas. Poimenos mixed oil with a little lemon
juice in the shallow cup he always used and soothed it into his
master's skin where the skin was dry, as he had been taught to
do, at the nape and over the shoulders and back and over the
outer parts of the thighs. Under the pressure of the boy's fingers Calchas felt his body loosen and relax, the fear and worry
recede. Poimenos combed out the long dark hair, still tangled

from sleep, applied scented oil to the temples and scalp, dressed the fringe of hair back from the forehead with thin-toothed bronze combs. The loincloth was abandoned and Calchas struggled into the long, close-fitting skirt with its pattern of sacred circles. He kept his eyes patiently closed so that Poimenos could blacken the lids and outer corners with kohl, and his face held still for the makeup, the application of which required much concentration, as the white circles had to be perfect in shape and the chalk paste made lustrous by the careful addition of sheep grease, which Poimenos kept in a small terra-cotta pot.

When all this was done and he had donned his amulets and necklace of amber constellation signs, he emerged again to find that the chiefs had now joined their contingents. Achilles, wearing a bored look as usual, stood with his Phthians; the ancient Nestor, flanked by his two sons, was at the head of the force from Pylos; Odysseus of Ithaca was there with his stocky, fair-bearded compatriots from the Western Islands. The chiefs were clothed above the waist in order to mark the distinction — they wore the usual sleeveless tunic and short kilt.

There was some talking now among the waiting men. They stood there in their ranks between the sea and the hills in the hot, gritty wind — there was no chill in the wind, though it came from the north, another mystery that had exercised Calchas. He saw that the Boeotians and Locrians, whose representatives were to fight, had been placed as far apart as possible. A wise move. But it was more complicated than that. Even within the ranks of the Boeotians care had been taken to separate the people of Orchomenus from those of Thebes, ancient foes with a long history of mutual pillage and murder. The Ainians and Atticans, who were in feud because of a rape not yet reciprocated and who shouted insults and threats at the sight of each other, had also been sited at the greatest possible distance apart. If the gods were to glance down at this formation, it would serve them as a chart or plan of all the bloody discords that riddled the host assembled here, the expeditionary force, as Agamemnon liked to call it. The delay caused by the wind was envenoming these divisions day by day, loosening what loyalties there were, setting the King's authority more and more in doubt. It was why he had given his consent to this general assembly, this fight to the death. A spectacle would hold the men together, make them forget—at least for a while—their various discontents.

It would take more than this, Calchas privately thought, to keep such a rabble quiet for long. What did these people care about the pretext given out for the war, the honor of the house of Atreus, Helen's flight with the Trojan Paris, a boaster who put it about that he had seen Aphrodite naked, looked at her from every side, and that the sight had enhanced his libido to such a phenomenal degree that he now secreted semen as fast as he spent it? Who could take a man like that seriously? Even if it were true—a man might be favored, though undeserving— who but Menelaus would care about Helen's multiple pleasures and repeated cries of joy? Troy meant one thing only to the men gathered here, as it did to their commanders. Troy was a dream of wealth; and if the wind continued the dream would crumble, Agamemnon's authority would slip away and with it his command, that too like a dream gone wrong. Then it would be dangerous for those too close to him, people like Chasimenos. People like himself . . .

Now, as he watched, two guards brought out from the King's tent his great throne chair, straining with the weight of it, while a third followed behind with his footstool. These were set down in the space that had been allotted to them, at the exact midpoint between the two masses of waiting men, separated as these were by the combat area itself, a rough square of pebbled ground, twelve paces by twelve, sloping slightly down towards the sea. Thus chair and stool occupied the dead center of this universe of the duel, a calculated effect and a triumph of planning on the part of Chasimenos.

A certain silence descended as all gazed at these emblems of the wealth and power of Mycenae: the high-backed chair of African ebony, incised all over its surface in an elaborate pattern of gold wires, with panels of alabaster at the sides; the footstool inlaid with figures of men and lions in ivory and silver and amethyst. He had had them brought by ox train over the rough roads from Mycenae to the sea at Lerna, and embarked them at the place where for his second labor Heracles slew the fearsome Hydra in the time of long ago. Agamemnon understood the importance of symbols. It had been the one mission the hero had been not able to accomplish alone; he had been obliged to call on the help of his charioteer Iolaus, who had come with burning brands and as Heracles chopped off the monster's ravening heads had cauterized the wounds so the heads could not grow again. The vanquished Hydra was Troy, Iolaus represented the forces allied with Mycenae. All very well, so far as it went. But Calchas had not been happy with the choice of embarkation point. For one thing, there was the excessive pride, inviting rebuke or worse, of putting oneself on the same level as a demigod; and then there was the fact that the hero had taken the Hydra's venom to poison his arrows, and it was this same venom, after many enemies slain, that had later devoured his own flesh. This placed a dark question over the future, adding to the fears and anxieties Calchas was always prone to and which he nowadays felt were increasing. When it came to symbols it was all or nothing, you could not pick and choose. But he had been afraid to say this to Agamemnon, whose displeasure could take violent forms. Troy meant wealth to Agamemnon too, and it was easy to see why he was always so in need of it. Chair and stool together, made to order by Cretan craftsmen with ivory and alabaster and gold from Egypt, amethyst from Syria, silver from Thrace, would be roughly equal in value to a year's ration of grain and dried figs for a hundred of the slaves in the royal textile factories.

Now, after the calculated pause, he appeared at last, surrounded by six of his palace guard helmeted and armed with spears, who fell in around him as he emerged from the tent, men specially chosen for their height, which should exactly match his own — if they were taller, he feared it would enter the Songs that he was stunted of growth. The people of the Mycenaean League raised a shout at his appearance and their chiefs, Diomedes, Euryalus and Sthenelos, raised their arms to acclaim him. His brother Menelaus also shouted, as did the Spartan troops under his command. But many remained silent, so it was at best a ragged greeting he was given. Nonetheless, his darkly bearded face broke into a smile and he raised his right arm, palm outward, in acknowledgment. This smile showed the teeth, it was too broad for such scattered applause, or so it seemed to Calchas, and it was lasting too long. The guards held their spears upright, their faces without expression. The shafts of the spears shone in the sunlight, they formed the bars of a cage and Calchas felt his mind touched by gossamer wings. The King was waving and smiling inside a gilded cage. It was thus the mad were treated.

Agamemnon walked forward and seated himself and the guards fell into place around him. Still he made no signal for the proceedings to begin, but remained for some moments silent and motionless, sitting upright, his back not touching the chair. He had taken care with his appearance this morning, Calchas noted—just as he had himself. His dark, lustrous hair, thick and shaggy as the mane of an Argive pony, was combed out to his shoulders and he wore a gold circlet around the brows to keep the hair from his eyes in this wind. His robe was dark blue, color of royalty; it was belted and he wore a long dagger in a scabbard of polished leather at the belt.

There was a pause, filled by the sound of the wind and the cries of gulls circling above. Then the King raised his arm and brought it slowly down again. Shouts broke out and the two champions came forward from their places on opposite wings of the assembled army and walked down to the space marked out for them. Both wore the standard conical helmet with bronze cheekpieces and nose guards; and both carried the round oxhide shield and the heavy thrusting spear. But the Boeotian was more heavily armored, he wore a tunic of leather with bronze shoulder plates and he had chosen as his second weapon the short, broad-bladed stabbing sword. Stimon the Locrian had no sword, but he had a dagger slung low on his right side. For body armor he had nothing but a short coat of padded linen.

The two men came together and turned towards the King, standing side by side, waiting for his signal. When the nod came they moved quickly apart to the limits of the space. And now for a while it was as if they had decided to mock each other by imitation, circling with knees flexed, shoulders lowered in a crouch, spearpoints dipping slightly. For a space of time that was brief enough but seemed protracted to Calchas, watching with the fascination of the fearful, the two circled each other on the shingle. They were lost to everything, they had stepped into a private world from which only one would emerge to the life he had left, the waves, the painted hulls, the shit on the wind.

The movements were quicker now, from time to time the points of the spears snaked out in darting, feinting movements, caught by the sun in splinters of light. The Boeotian seemed stronger, twice his opponent took the shock of thrusts on his shield, heavy thrusts that briefly unsettled his balance. The sun of midmorning was still low enough to give a certain advantage to the one who had it behind him, and both men maneuvered for this position.

There comes always a moment, whether of fear, rage, confidence warranted or mistaken, when the first move is made, the definite one. Calchas knew this just as all those present knew it. Not a deliberate decision but a sort of gathering, depending on the god that prompts. It came now. Opilmenos made the drill movements he had learned when scarcely more than a child, raising and lowering his shield sharply, at the same time stamping the right foot, ploys to distract the other's attention for a split second from his spearpoint, which he thrust forward now with all the weight of his body behind it, a lunge that carried him forward three paces, the point raised as he advanced until it was aiming at a spot just above his opponent's collarbone.

Stimon could not block the thrust altogether, there was too much power in it, but he swayed to the right a second or two before the impact and thrust out his shield and so managed to deflect the spear across the right side of his body, not quite far enough, however: the point scored through the inner part of his arm, high up, below the shoulder. He took two staggering steps further to the right, exposing his flank. The padded linen of his tunic was suddenly red to the elbow on the right side. He had kept his grip on the spear but it seemed too heavy for him now, the point was hardly clear of the ground.

The sickness and exhilaration of prophecy fulfilled came to Calchas. This was the moment he had seen prefigured, watching the man dance in the firelight, the death contained in that fullness of life. It was what he had seen, what Pollein had guided him to see. As he waited now for Stimon to be killed he remembered that shaft of luminous conviction, felt some shivering return of it, the burden and tyranny of the god's favor.

The Boeotian's thrust had brought him too close to use his spear again without shortening his grip. This he now began to do, slamming his shield against his opponent's left flank to give himself time. The movement was well executed, in the same drilled and robust fashion as his first thrust. But the staggering movements of the Locrian were transformed now, by a miracle of balance and coordination, into the first steps of a dance, taking him round almost in a half circle, helped by the push from the other's shield, until he was sideways to the Boeotian, who had shortened his grip on the spear but had to make a half turn before he could deliver the killing stroke. It was the standard maneuver, the only possible one, but he was destined never to complete it. Stimon dropped his spear and sank to his knees. In a single movement he drew the dagger from his belt and made a wide, backhanded sweep with it. The blade flashed once and then dulled, as it sliced through the tendons behind the right knee. Opilmenos raised his face and opened his mouth wide and fell.

He was disabled, groaning and helpless there on the bloody shingle, crippled for life—with hamstrings severed he would never fight again. Whether he lived or died lay with Stimon the dancer, who had won the bout by dancing and was dancing still, on his feet once more and stepping carefully and delicately round the fallen man, holding the spear he had taken up again.

He kept out of range of the other's hands, which might still have sought for his throat or his eyes. He was waiting for the moment when he could get a thrust at the neck or abdomen, areas not protected by the cuirass. He was waiting, but he was not in haste; it soon became obvious to all watching that the moment of the kill was being deliberately delayed, that Stimon was playing up to the spectators, putting on a show. The Boeotian knew it too. As the hope of mercy left him he found the resolution to draw the short sword from his belt, the only defense remaining to him.

And now, amid the continuing hush, it became a dance for two persons, Stimon swaying his hips and raising his knees and setting his feet with exaggerated care while the wind scattered the drops of blood from his shoulder widely over the pebbles, Opilmenos twisting his body round to follow him, making attempts to rise, striving to keep his eyes always on the weapon in the other's hands, because to look away was to acquiesce in his death. Then Stimon quickened the step, the fallen man could not gyrate quickly enough, the thrust came, piercing the side of the neck, entering deeply into the throat. When the point was withdrawn, Opilmenos moved still, but it was the pumping of his blood that moved him. The Locrian turned away, not towards the King—he did not give a glance to

Agamemnon—but towards his own people. Calchas heard, or thought he heard, the metal shoulder pieces of the dying man scrape on the pebbles. Then all other sounds, even the lamentation of the wind, were engulfed by the great shout of triumph that came from the Locrians as they broke ranks, their leader, Ajax the Lesser, to the fore, and surged forward to raise the victor shoulder-high. Agamemnon rose to his feet, again smiling. The show was over.

3.

Calchas remained where he was while the army began to disperse, while the corpse of Opilmenos was carried away. Poimenos, who missed no change in his master's face, saw now that it was ashen below the caking of chalk. Without knowing the cause, he made to draw nearer, but Calchas waved him away and sat motionless, head declined, staring down at the ground before him. How could he have been so deceived? He was the more shaken as this had been—or seemed—a private message, not a matter for public pronouncement but an assurance that he was still held worthy of trust, still had the favor of Pollein.

The moving body, the moving flames, the Singer at the edge of the firelight—perhaps that sightless one had seen more than he? Fire and dance, the briefest of things and the most lovely. But not the same . . . Was that where he had gone wrong? He pondered it, eyes still fixed on the ground. The flame has no past and no future, it belongs only to now, it is born and leaps and dies, no other flame will exactly resemble it, though the number should be countless. Also the dance dies and cannot be reborn and no other dance will exactly resemble it, even though the dancer be the same. He had thought this consuming joy of life meant the death of the dancer along with the dance but Stimon the Locrian had killed while dancing and lived to dance again. Perhaps the god had wanted him to understand that the more intense the life the greater the power of death, and therein lay the divine contradiction. Or perhaps it had not been Pollein who had led him there, perhaps some other god altogether had directed his steps, visited him with that shaft of conviction, luminous and deceiving. Fear came with this thought, fear his familiar, the companion of his days, the nightmare fear of not knowing the sender, not knowing whom to placate. It was like the wind . . . he seemed to remember now that there had been laughter from somewhere in the crowd, or perhaps somewhere beyond. Laughter of men or gods? Had he simply been tricked, toyed with, or had his mistake somehow been necessary? And if so, necessary to whom and for what purpose? How could it be known? At least he had made no public forecast, he had merely hinted at knowledge, always a safe thing to do.

He was seeking to derive what comfort he could from this when he saw Ajax the Larger bearing down on them with his rolling gait, head and shoulders above everybody else, flanked by the usual group of sycophantic companions from Salamis, who were making a way through the crowd for him, jostling anyone who didn't move quickly enough. Calchas got to his feet as they approached and Poimenos followed suit.

"I wanted to have a word or two before we go in." Ajax made a motion of his huge head in the direction of Agamemnon's tent.

"Of course."

"I was against this fight from the start. These people will tell you. Speak up, was I or was I not against it from the start?"

"Yes, Ajax, you were, you were, right from the very start."

"I said as much, I told Agamemnon how I felt. Did I or did I not? *Speak up*."

"You did, Ajax, you did."

"Well, events have borne me out."

Calchas experienced the usual mixture of feelings Ajax of Salamis inspired in him, awe at his enormous strength and stupidity, fear of his erratic temper, a nervous, half-humorous sense of his dangerous absurdity. "How do you mean?" he asked.

"Well, it has ended in a death, hasn't it? I said that would happen."

"But it was a duel to the death, wasn't it? It was only to be expected that one of them . . ." He stopped short, becoming aware that the eyes of Ajax and those of the whole entourage were intently upon him. "Well, of course," he said, "it is undeniable that the Boeotian is dead."

Ajax continued to look down at him in silence for some moments. He had unusually wide-open eyes, very short-lashed, light greenish blue in color, eyes that looked somehow stunned, as if at some point in the past, perhaps long ago, they had registered a shock of surprise so enormous that it had never been possible to absorb it. He seemed out of temper now and Calchas wondered whether he had been backing Opilmenos to win. Like all exceedingly simple souls and some souls not so simple, he easily set down his disappointments to something that needed mending in the general state of things. More than once he had been heard to say that the smell of shit that lay over the camp was due to faults in the positioning of the army.

"The waste of a life," he said now. "This Opilmenos was a good soldier. Even the other chap, the Locrian, has a wound that will take time to put right. In his sword arm too. As a military man, I can't see any sense in it. It is not quarreling and threatening and bloodletting that we need. I've said it before and I'll say it again, what we need—"

"He has said it before and he'll—"

"Who is that fool interrupting me? I'll have your guts for garters if it happens again. What we need is something that will bring us together, something that will make us if not exactly friends . . ."

"Allies," a rash voice offered—despite the fear Ajax inspired, there was always someone among his followers who tried to curry favor by getting in early with the right word.

"Blockhead, we are allies already. Good grief, I am surrounded by cretins. We need something to take the men's minds off this wind and as a military man I know what it is."

"He knows what it is."

Ajax raised a hand, extending a forefinger that looked to Calchas the size and shape of the sausages they made in Pergamum from goat guts and corn. "Games," he said. "I intend to organize a Day of Games. Something never heard of before. It came to me in the form of a dream, which is why I have come to you with it, you being the chap best qualified in the dream department."

"Well, I am at your service," Calchas said.

But some shyness seemed to descend on Ajax now and he did not immediately relate his dream. "There's bound to be winners and losers, that's life," he said. "But we will come out of it, you know, not friends exactly . . ."

"Closer," Calchas said. "With mutual respect."

"That's it exactly, that's just the phrase I was looking for. Great gods, what it is to have a head on your shoulders." Ajax's eyes were as dazed-looking as ever but a glow had come over his face. "Mutual respect," he said, drawing out the syllables. "I like that, as a military man I like it a lot."

"We could have races," one of the followers said.

Ajax turned on him and half raised a fist that was roughly the size of Poimenos's head. "Numskull, there are races already. Everyone knows what a race is. I am talking about something completely new." He lowered his hand, it seemed reluctantly, and turned back to Calchas, shaking his head. "Thick as two planks," he said.

"What was your dream?"

"I was throwing a javelin across the sea. The sea was dead calm, not like this one, there wasn't a ripple on it. I stood on the shore and I hurled the javelin with all my strength. I was waiting, you know, to see the splash, so I could judge the distance. I mean, I knew it was a mighty throw, but I expected to see a splash sooner or later. But there was no splash, the javelin flew up into the sun and disappeared. There wasn't a mark on the sea at all. Then there was a great crowd all around me and everyone was shouting, 'Ajax! Ajax! Ajax has won the most points!' The shouts were still in my ears as I woke and it came to me that this was a message, that some god was telling me to organize a Games Day with different events, not just running,

I'm too heavy for running, javelin-throwing, for example, and give points to the winner and the one coming in second and so on."

"This is a most important dream," Calchas said. "We have to attend on Agamemnon shortly, but when I have had time for reflection I'd like to talk to you about it. I see nothing offensive to the gods in the idea. And they are clearly favorable to a javelin-throwing competition as one of the events."

A smile came slowly to Ajax's face. All expressions were slow with him and this seemed to be because of the great expanse of his features and the time it took for his moods to travel across them. "I'm glad you see it in that light," he said. "I would win easily. There is no one else in the world who can hurl a javelin as far as I can. We could have a weight-lifting event too. It is a pity that in my dream there was not more guidance about how to organize the points system. It must be groups, let's say the Spartans make one group, everybody tries to get points for himself and for his group, and then these groups . . ."

He paused and a frown spread over his face, replacing the smile. The fringe of ginger-colored hair that lay along his upper lip bristled slightly. "These groups, the people in these groups . . ." The frown deepened. "I am going to ask Ajax the Lesser to be my partner in the project," he said, "when I see him. He has a head for figures."

"Won't he be at the meeting?"

"No, he has had leave not to attend. He is with his Locrians, celebrating Stimon's victory. They'll be well on the way to getting drunk by now. He mixes with the rank and file too much, the officers should keep a distance, I've told him that before. I don't drink myself, it clouds a man's mind. Stand away from us."

This last was said to those clustered around him. He advanced and took Calchas by the arm in what was doubtless intended as a friendly grip. "I don't know whether you've noticed it, but there are deep divisions among us."

"Yes, I have, as a matter of fact."

"I want to change all that. I want to bring the allies together. When we get to Troy, that will be the war process. Here at Aulis what we need is a peace process. I'd like to feature in the Songs as Ajax the Unifier, the man who held the army together in the face of a hostile wind through the brilliant idea of a Games Day."

"And so you will. I'll make it my business to speak to the Singer about this at the earliest opportunity. He is a foreigner like me, we are both from over the water, and so I have some influence with him as to what he includes. And what he leaves out, of course, which is sometimes more important." In point of fact he had practically no influence with the Singer at all; between diviner and bard there was rivalry, both in their different ways being reciters, disseminators of stories; but Calchas lost no opportunity to encourage a belief to the contrary, as it added considerably to his status in the camp.

"You will do that?" Ajax's grip tightened. "I swear you'll not regret it."

Calchas saw the large face, radiant with gratitude, close above him. He was not himself a short man, but at this close range he had to crane his neck to meet the moist, emotional eyes below the unruly wisps and whorls of the brows.

"To approach him myself would be too lowering," Ajax said.

There was no intention of offense in this, as the diviner knew. Ajax was rarely aware enough of others to want to offend them, except when he got heated and then all he wanted to do was kill them. He had spoken openly and confidingly, like a child. Calchas's womanly dress and painted face were like the plumage of some strange bird to him, perhaps exciting. And then, he knew the diviner had access, not only to the Singer's ear but to the meaning of dreams and the signals of the gods. And, more immediately important, he enjoyed the favor of the Commander-in-Chief.

"The Singer will require a gift," Calchas said. His arm was beginning to feel numb.

"I'll give you a silver hair clip for him."

Calchas nodded. It sounded an unlikely thing for Ajax to have in his possession. It might be plunder of course. Whether this gift would ever materialize was a matter of doubt to him, as was also the question of whether, if it did materialize, he would ever pass it on to the Singer. To his intense relief he felt the grip removed from his arm. "He'll appreciate that," he said.

"You might speak to Agamemnon about this idea of mine for keeping up the morale of the army. Just mention it to him, he listens to you. I don't want to speak to him myself, it looks too much like toadying. Why should I ask him for permission just because he has the general vote for commander? Besides, we are related. My mother is Periboea of Athens and she is a granddaughter of Pelops and Pelops is Agamemnon's grandfather. That makes us cousins of a sort."

By now the crowd had thinned, there was nothing before them but the churned and bloodied patch of shingle, the swaying masts, the endless rearing and tumbling of the waves. It was time to present themselves at Agamemnon's tent. As they went, Calchas fell behind and loitered for a while, allowing Ajax to precede him. Not a good idea to enter together, he thought. All such things were noted and might sooner or later be used against one in ways not foreseeable. He was still wondering vaguely, as he entered, why the family connection with Agamemnon should be felt by Ajax an impediment to easy speech.

4.

The King was waiting, seated in his great chair. Calchas knelt before him and touched his forehead to the ground. He rose and was backing away to a respectful distance, but the King stopped him with a gesture and indicated a point close to his chair, a place of honor. Across from him but farther off were Croton and his two disciples, bearded like their god, their hair piled on top of their heads in the shape of beehives and thickly lacquered to keep it in place. They were dressed for the occasion in their white robes and white headbands, and they held their oak staffs grounded, like spears at the ready. All three looked at Calchas with hatred.

Most of the chiefs had already assembled. Glancing round quickly as he took his place, he saw Achilles and Palamedes standing together—natural allies, those two, he thought, alike in coldness of heart. Round-faced, red-haired Menelaus was there, whose cuckolding by Paris had provided the pretext for the war, and wily Odysseus and the aged and rambling Nestor, whose head trembled incessantly. Idomeneus, leader of the contingent from Crete, entered quickly, hailed the King and stood alone: he had no friends except among the people he had brought with him.

Calchas was still struggling to make sense of Ajax's words; it was his nature always to be tormented by what he couldn't understand. Was it because references to his grandfather were offensive to Agamemnon? Pelops after all had committed a string of notable murders, in Pisatis, in Arcadia, in Elis. A serial killer, basically—he had left a trail of blood wherever he went. On the other hand, the first of these killings had been for love, in order to gain Hippodameia for his wife. This should be a cause for family pride or at least fellow feeling in Agamemnon, whose first act as king had been to slaughter Tantalus, the husband of Clytemnestra, so he could take her for his own wife. He had gone one better. In his jealous desire to remove all traces of the man he had supplanted, he had ordered the child of the marriage, a baby still at the breast, to be smothered with a sheep fleece. So it was whispered at least. No, he was probably quite proud to be the grandson of Pelops . . . Then suddenly he understood. Nothing to do with family sensibilities at all. Even the impetuous and unreflective Ajax had been infected by the general distrust now gaining ground among the chiefs. It emanated from the King himself, who lay awake at night and listened to his enemies breeding in the wind. The nearer the claim, the closer the connection, the more suspicious Agamemnon would be about the motives. Better to say nothing about this Games Day himself either; Ajax would blunder on with it anyway. Only six days it had taken to bring them to this pass . . .

In accordance with his usual tactics, Agamemnon was waiting for movement among the chiefs to cease before he spoke. The constant billowing and collapsing of the canvas, like laboring lungs, was beyond his control, as were the flat, smacking sounds of the wind in it. He had put on the skullcap, black silk stitched with gold thread, which he used for audiences of state. Below this his eyes looked huge, dark-ringed and slow, eyes of the sleepless or the drugged. It was hot inside the tent, but he wore the same heavy blue gown, the same thick belt with its buckle of bronze and hanging dagger. When the people gathered there were still, he spoke, not loudly. "Let them be brought before us."

They filed in almost at once, four men, unarmed, accompanied by Chasimenos, still in his tunic of a palace official. They made their reverences, crouching with heads lowered and hands on knees. Then they straightened and stood together, side by side before the King. One of them Calchas recognized, a man named Phylakos, a captain in Agamemnon's guard. He was naked to the waist, dressed only in cotton kilt and leather wristbands and sandals, a powerful, deep-chested man, nearly bald, with pale scars on his body and a papyrus flower tattooed on his right thigh.

In the pause before the King spoke again, all heard, twining through the voices of the wind but distinct from them, the flailing of the bull-roarers down near the shore like the sound of many wings beating together. Every day the shamans of the Pelasgians, a people with their own gods and their own language, fronted the sea and whirled their long ropes, with flat pieces of wood attached, in great circles overhead, striving to outdo the wind with the whirling they made and so drive it back to its caves in the north. Perhaps stirred in his twilight by

this mighty wingbeat, old Nestor began some querulous complaint, hushed immediately by his two sons, who were in constant attendance upon him, one on either side. It was never
possible to tell whether these two were speaking separately or
together. In the years of trying to quieten their father, their
voices had become identical, like the cooing of doves. Calchas
felt again that shudder of warning within him. These things too
were exact, unrepeatable, as was the way they had chosen to
stand together, even though it might seem as random as the
stones in a streambed.

Agamemnon began to speak. His voice was slow, like the
voice of one who relates a dream immediately on waking and
strives to remember the order of things as they happened. He
spoke about the omen of the eagles, the two male eagles, one
black as night, one with a blaze of silver, seen about the palace
of Mycenae in the time before the expedition set out, seen several days in succession, haunting the walls, always on the right
hand, the spear side, auguring good fortune. Two full-grown
male eagles in company together, a thing never seen before.
"Those of Mycenae will remember this omen and the interpretation made at the time by our diviner Calchas?"

Nobody spoke but Menelaus nodded and after him several
others, as if they had needed the example. None of the four
who had been brought in made any sign. Agamemnon turned
his head slightly towards the diviner. "Calchas will remind us
of his words at that time."

Thus prompted, the priest began to speak in his careful,
slightly hesitant Greek, moving his body slowly and rhythmi-
cally forward and back in the way the priests of Caria did when
uttering prophecies—it was in Caria, as a youth, that he had
been admitted to the cult of the god whom he must always now

remember to call Apollo. A coldness gathered in his breast as he spoke, because his words at Mycenae had been uttered to please Agamemnon and establish his own position, he had not been properly mindful of the nature of his god, who was male and female in equal parts and so gave divided counsels, which then had to be reconciled. There was no choice now but to repeat the simple message.

"As the eagle is the king of birds, so Agamemnon and Menelaus are kings of men, the eagle brothers, sons of Atreus. The eagle is the bird of Zeus, and this has been so from the beginning of his rule, even before his rule was established. It was an eagle that flew towards him on the eve of his great battle with the Titans for supremacy in heaven, thus ensuring his victory. The eagles that came to haunt the battlements of Mycenae, and whose presence was remarked by many, were sent by Zeus in token that the quarrel with Troy is a just one."

He stopped here, the coldness still gathered around his heart. Croton was already raising his staff. He had known that the priest would intervene, would want, as he had wanted from the beginning, to make the augury his own, establish himself as sole interpreter of the god's will. But he had expected more ceremony. Now Croton broke into speech, scarcely waiting for the King's nod—mark of the power he had gained in these few days.

"The justice of Zeus demands that the outrage to hospitality committed by Paris in his abduction of Helen while a guest in the house of her husband Menelaus should be avenged. The justice of Zeus—"

He was interrupted by Menelaus, who said loudly, "Absolutely right, you've hit the nail on the head, Croton. A piece of shit like that, a beastly Asian who started life as a ragged-arsed goatherd, how could my Helen, who was always repelled by anything coarse, have allowed herself to be forcibly abducted like that if he had not used the wiles of the bitch goddess Hecate and all the demons of his filthy country against her?" He was fair-skinned and inclined to freckles and his nose had peeled, making it look strangely paler than the rest of his face, which had flushed with the force of his feelings. "Asians stink," he said, more mildly. "Their houses are like pigsties."

Croton's staff was still raised. He seemed not to have registered the interruption. "The justice of Zeus gives redress to the wronged, the justice of Zeus is vested in the eagle brothers Agamemnon and Menelaus."

His eyes were alight and his voice vibrated with passion. This was the new thing, this cry of justice, Calchas thought. It simply didn't make sense. Thoroughly unreasonable. It derived from the same error, that of regarding a god as a father. Naturally, the children will want a father to be just, especially since they can't achieve justice themselves. Zeus was cloud-gatherer, rain-giver, thunderer. Where did the justice come in? He glanced across at Menelaus's patched face. That reference to the uncleanness and evil habits of Asians, had it been a dig at him? On the whole, he thought not. The representative Asian was still Paris, who had seduced his wife while he was away at a funeral and then run off to Troy with her. All the same, these outbursts were getting more frequent all the time and more wide-ranging. Calchas thought of the houses of Tarsus, with their scrubbed steps and entranceways, the smell of wet dust in the courtyards of Hattusas when they scattered water to clean the paving stones. In Kadesh they employed street sweepers, a thing unheard of in the Greek lands. Menelaus had seen nothing of Asia, of course—except perhaps the slave markets of Miletus . . .

Croton seemed about to continue, but Agamemnon raised a hand to stay him. No one had yet mentioned the wind and it seemed unlikely to Calchas that anyone would, not here, not unbidden. It was too dangerous a subject. But the question must be there in all minds, as it was in his: If Zeus had sent the eagles as a blessing on the expedition, why was the army being held there in Aulis, why were they being prevented from sailing?

Agamemnon looked round at the faces as if he might see treason on the wing among them. "It was to Mycenae that the eagles were sent, not elsewhere," he said. "They were sent to me. By consent of my brother first, and then by consent of you all, the conduct of the war is given to me."

No one had questioned this, at least not otherwise than in private with those he could trust, or in the thoughts of his solitude. For Agamemnon to assert it publicly now was a mistake, a sign of weakness. Calchas sensed the knowledge of this twisting through the minds of all those in the tent. He saw Odysseus glance aside, but could not tell where his eyes were directed. Chasimenos, standing beside him, appeared lost in thoughts of his own. Achilles was turning his perfect profile upward, towards the roof of the tent, with his usual air of bored indifference. No particular expression showed on any face; but Calchas could sense the twisting course of the knowledge of weakness as it went from mind to mind, a serpent of thought, moving like the snakes of light that coiled and loosened on the walls of the tent as the wind ruffled the flaps of canvas at the entrance. The snake, sign of the Mother . . .

"There is something we did not know before," Agamemnon said. "My captain, Phylakos, has words for us."

Phylakos took a step forward from the other three and

stood in a position of attention, arms at his sides. "These men saw something more. They were at the lookout post on the northern side of the citadel on the third day of the eagles, early in the morning, soon after dawn." He paused to look briefly round at the others in the tent. "The light is good at this time," he said. "That I can vouch for. I sometimes inspected the guard posts then. It is the time you find men sleeping, before sunrise, before the guard is changed."

His face was impassive but it was immediately apparent to Calchas that he was trying to secure belief beforehand for what they were going to hear; or at least to anticipate objections. But this, after all, was no more than anyone would do when there was a story to tell, a story he believed and wanted others to believe.

"This man will tell you what they saw," he said now, indicating one of the three. "He is called Leucides."

Leucides stepped forward in his turn and braced his shoulders preparatory to speech. He was a bony man with a conspicuous rib cage and a long, sad face. "There was a hare," he said. "We saw the eagles stoop at this hare. They killed it and tore it to pieces."

In the startled silence that followed on this, the plaintive muttering of Nestor became audible, rising above the shushing of his sons. His concentration span was short, and he had lost interest in the proceedings at an early stage, embarking yet again on the interminable narrative of his own past deeds. He was talking now, Calchas realized after some moments, about a cattle raid into Elis that he had made in his distant youth.

". . . show these Trojan dogs a thing or two, I'd be over there in two shakes of a duck's tail if I was young again, in those days I could outdistance the wind, I would race ahead of it, as I did when we went rustling cattle in Elis, they couldn't stop us, they tried to stop us but they couldn't stop us, nobody could stop us, Achilles is a runner but he isn't a patch on what I was, I tell you I could outrun the wind, bounding and bounding over the land and the wind falling short behind me, I heard the wind behind me, wailing because it couldn't keep up . . ."

"That is a striking image, father, but running is no good now, there is water before us."

"Father, that wind was behind you, whereas this one . . ."

"They couldn't stop me, they tried to stop me, nobody could stop me, we got away with fifty cows, Itymoneus tried to stop me, or was his name Iphitomenos, he was the son of Hypeirochus or Hypernochus, I'm sure of that, they were his father's cattle, he came against me, he fancied his chances, but I took my sword, it wasn't a javelin, the singers have said it was a javelin but it was a sword, who would carry javelins on a cattle raid, you need to make a quick getaway on a cattle raid, it was a sword, I went down on one knee and quick as a flash I gave him an upward thrust with it, straight up the crotch, ha, ha, he wasn't expecting that, the blades were longer in those days . . ."

The old man raised his head and a brief light blazed in his eyes. "I split him open," he said in a stronger voice, "the point went in at the crotch and I pushed up with it, I got both hands to it, got it in up to the hilt, they knew how to make swords in those days, he couldn't fall, he wanted to fall but he couldn't fall, I was holding him up on the sword, he was skewered from his balls to his belly like a stuck pig, then I twisted the blade and his guts came spilling out, there, you bastard, I said to him, now you know the stuff Nestor is made of and he said, what did he say, no, he didn't say anything, he just —"

"Those were happy days, father, you were young then, but now we must listen."

"Now we must be quiet, now we must listen."

Their voices were like the notes of doves, yes, Calchas thought, but contented doves, doves in the sun, clucking together, the sounds overlapping. Blotted in these cooing remonstrances, the old man's voice faltered away into its habitual muttering, half querulous, half plaintive, and then trailed off into silence.

"I think Nestor needs to take a good long rest," Odysseus said. "I propose that he be escorted back to his own quarters."

There was a quality of anger in his voice, something that seemed to Calchas more than mere impatience at the delay. Was it because Nestor's reminiscences had lowered the level of attention, reduced the impact of this strangely belated news about the hare? If so, there must have been some prior knowledge on Odysseus's part, on that of others too. He felt a gathering of suspicion.

"No, no," Agamemnon said. "Absolutely out of the question. Nestor must stay. No council is complete without Nestor. He has attended more councils than any man alive." He looked again at Leucides. "We are listening."

"We were on the wall, on the side that looks towards the sea. We saw the eagles rise together into the sky and wheel in a wide circle. Just below us a hare was feeding. There *are* hares, they come in the first light, anyone who has been on guard duty on that side can tell you. We shoot at them sometimes, the ground is open there, you can recover the arrows."

He paused and swallowed, still in the same rigid posture. Calchas studied him with quickened attention. Constraint was to be expected, even awe: he was in the tent of the

Commander-in-Chief, among the heroes of the army, men who featured often in the verses of the Singer. Awe yes, but Leucides looked frightened. He spoke in the manner of someone who had rehearsed his words—or been rehearsed in them. But this was natural enough, he was without practice. His speech was rough, half bitten back in the way of the country people of Argos. In some remote village, herding his goats, tending his strip of vines, turning over the stony ground, he had been fired by thoughts of Trojan gold, a life of ease.

"The eagles swooped down on the hare both together and killed it and devoured it, sharing together."

As these words were uttered Calchas's gaze fell on the face of the man standing next to the speaker, on his right. A febrile face, the yolk of the eye too much visible, something too excitable and tremulous in the mouth. Prone himself to the tremors and fevers of strained nerves, the priest recognized the signs. This did not look like a reliable witness. But of course they had not been able to choose, it had to be these three, the three on guard on the northern wall in the hour before sunrise, when few people were about . . .

The silence was broken by Chasimenos, who raised his narrow, pale-eyed face and spoke directly to the King: "This is news indeed."

"Why do we know it only now?" The question came from Achilles, who looked at nobody as he spoke and moved his smoothly tanned and perfectly proportioned shoulders in the usual narcissistic shrug. "Why was it not reported at the time?"

"They did not think it important," Phylakos said.

"Not important?" Calchas looked directly at the captain, raising his eyebrows in an attitude of surprise he was conscious of assuming. Commander of a hundred, a professional soldier from the mountainous country around Larisa, in middle age though strong still. Not many campaigns left, not many chances, this perhaps the last one, the big one, an occasion for plunder he could retire on. Yes, it was easy to see that Phylakos would want to strengthen belief in victory at a time of trial like this when the army's resolve was wavering in the wind. "I find it strange that they should not think it important," the diviner said.

Phylakos looked at him without expression. "They are simple men."

"Those simple men should be hanged for not thinking it important," Achilles said. "I've a good mind to string them up myself." He moved his beautiful shoulders again in the same shrug, lithe, luxuriant, deeply self-loving. "Or drown them in Ajax's latrine," he said.

"It's not my latrine." The booming voice of Ajax filled the tent. He was staring at Achilles with furious hostility. "Good grief," he said. "Do you think I use it myself? It's for the men, not the officers."

Achilles showed no sign of having heard this. "By Zeus," he said, "it's hot in here. I fancy a dip. Not in Ajax's latrine, though."

Calchas watched his movements and listened to his words with the usual mingling of dislike and fear. Achilles was a natural killer. These Mycenaeans were all warlike and brutal, but Achilles was a special case, he enjoyed homicide as a leisure activity. These last words of his had been a deliberate provocation. Nothing ever led anywhere, with Achilles, except back to his own pride and perfection, to the gestures with which he endlessly celebrated his own marvelous existence. He was dressed this morning in one of the outfits he had had made for him at home before leaving, a short-skirted, sleeveless linen tunic with gold-tasseled epaulettes and a matching cap. His splendid legs were enhanced by shin guards of polished bronze. Conscious of the eyes upon him, he took out an ivory and papyrus fan from a tuck at his waist, flicked it open and began to fan himself, very slowly.

"There's a man there with faulty hearing," Ajax shouted. His huge face had flushed to a shade of dark crimson.

Achilles continued with his fanning. "Better deaf than daft."

The wind at Aulis, continuing so long, had sensitized men's hearing in some ways, as if it was necessary, to avoid going crazy, to distinguish sounds not caused by it, or even to invent such sounds, there were those who swore afterwards that they had heard Ajax's teeth grinding in the massive jaws. But his mind worked slowly, even when not clouded by rage, and Croton took the opportunity to intervene.

"The justice of Zeus—" he began loudly, but Agamemnon silenced him with a slight movement of the arm.

"Calchas will give us the meaning."

"My lord, fountain of benefits, I will do my poor best." The meaning was obvious of course—suspiciously so to Calchas's mind: the hare was Troy, by its death and devouring victory was established in advance for the Greek alliance. Not only was the cause approved and the favor of Zeus confirmed, but the total destruction of the enemy was guaranteed. However, no diviner worth his salt would blurt out the obvious, there had always to be the ceremony of interrogation, the spending of words.

"How often did the birds wheel in the sky?" he asked Leucides. "Once only or more than once?"

"Once only."

"Did they cry out?"

"No, they were silent."

"The eagles came in the days just after the full moon, when the face of the moon was crumbling. At the hour you saw the hare the moon would still be clearly visible in the sky?"

"Yes, the moon was still to be seen."

"The eagles, in their flight, did they cross the face of the moon?"

For the first time Leucides hesitated, but not, it seemed to Calchas, in the way of one striving to remember. "No," he said, "no, they flew lower."

"Did they fall on the hare with folded wings or wings extended?"

Leucides was hesitating again, but it was a question destined never to be answered. The man whose excitable face Calchas had noticed earlier now broke into stumbling speech:

"The hare was fat with young, the eagles swooped on her and ripped her open, the young ones came spilling out, they were fully formed . . ."

The voice seemed not his own, it was thick, with a strange bubbling in it, as if struggling up from somewhere lower in the body. Calchas felt fear at the voice, at the staring face, at the convulsive movements at the throat.

"And then?"

"Mother and young were torn to pieces and devoured."

The silence inside the tent was so loud now that it smothered the crying of the wind. Yet they heard the sound of the man's swallowing, the click of his tongue in the dry mouth. His eyes had opened wide as if he could still see the ravenous descent, the ripped flesh, the gorging. Calchas felt the clutch of fear grow tighter. The man was possessed, a god was speaking through him, pronouncing the one and only truth to be found in this whole account, though it did not belong to that dawn at Mycenae, it was happening now, here in the tent, he knew it from the stillness of the man's companions as they stood there, stillness of shock, knew it even as he saw Phylakos, readier than the others, raise his chin as at a call to battle, and heard him say, "Yes, this killing of the young was also in the report they gave me, the hare was pregnant, the eagles ate the mother and the young."

But it came too late and the knowledge of this was on the face of Phylakos as he spoke. The hush was broken now. As if a quilt had been lifted they heard again the clamor of the wind in the world outside the tent. The brain-soft Nestor, again growing restive—and perhaps jogged by these details of the gutted hare—raised his lamenting voice again, sought to return to that ancient disemboweling of Itymoneus or Iphitomenos, only to be silenced again by the pigeon notes of his dutiful sons on either side.

Taking advantage of this diversion and the breathing space it brought with it, Calchas moved forward and turned to the King and bowed low. On behalf of all, he asked for time to interpret the meaning of what they had heard, a day and a night for reflection. He heard the request granted and uttered thanks, struggling to control his voice, to betray nothing of the trembling he felt within him at his first dim perception of who it might be that had spoken to them through the belly and throat of this staring man.

5.

Poimenos was waiting for him outside and supported him back to his own tent. Once there, however, he could not rest. He sent the boy away and covered his face and head with a dark cloth and sat in the close heat of his body, seeking through this warmth and enclosure to find again a time before he knew a difference between his body and the space surrounding it. He felt the run of the sweat on his brow and chest. In the darkness under the head cloth the tranced face of the man took form again, uttering the words that had been forced from his mouth, the lie that had changed from lie to truth as it was uttered, truth for everyone present in that tent, but most of all for him, servant of the Divine Companion, who united male and female in one being and blended them like water and the light on water. It could only be she, the Lady, whom the Greeks knew as Artemis, one of her many names, protectress of the young, mistress of wild things, goddess of child-birth. Always alert for opportunity, she had found the slack mind and the slack mouth, and used them to warn of a price to be paid. The eagles were from Zeus, yes, but the pregnant hare was hers.

In a day and a night he would have to announce this to the King. The reader of omens takes the omen for himself, takes it over, makes it his own, together with the danger of it. Calchas felt fear in the darkness, felt it in all the pulses of his body, customary fever, companion of all his travels. With it came the need for a time apart, in which to consider. He would have to get away from the camp for a while and for that he would require the King's permission—there was no leaving without it. Agamemnon needed, demanded, to know where he was at all times of the day and night; in the hours of his insomnia he would send a summons, or at the moment of waking, the sweat of his dreams still on him. And he was sudden now and terrible in his rages. Poimenos had brought back from the gossip of the camp the story of the slave boy who for spilling water had been struck so heavily by the King that he had lain lost to the world for most of a day and now did not put words together in a connected way. Even when Agamemnon was not enraged, Calchas sensed a malignancy that was new, felt it in the glances he received, even when his understanding was being asked for. It was as if the King, hating his own misery, had begun also to hate those who were witness to it.

There was a cave shrine to Potnia, the Lady, on the island, just across the narrow water. Calchas had heard the priests of Zeus inveigh against it in their regular processions through the camp, denouncing the presence of an ancient pollution, this nearness of unclean earth cults, pointing to it as one of the causes of their troubles. It was there he would ask leave to go.

The wind had strengthened, he heard it loud in the scrub of the hillsides and felt it push against his face as he walked the short distance to Agamemnon's tent. He spoke to the armed guards at the entrance, was checked for hidden weapons, as everyone now must be who sought audience with the King. One of the guards went inside, returning moments later to admit him. Agamemnon was sitting in the same place, on his chair of state, staring somberly before him. Two dark-skinned male slaves were fanning him with squares of woven rush attached to long canes. The displaced air lapped in warm waves against the priest's face as he approached to make his obeisance. Bowing low, he smelled again the sweetish odor of hemp that hung about the King's person.

Agamemnon kept his face averted as he listened; but Calchas was not discouraged by this, knowing it for the habit of kingship among the Mycenaeans. There was a haggardness, a look of nightmare, in the face thus presented in profile. As he made his request, Calchas felt some sorrow mingling with his fear; and while he waited through the long silence for the answer he tried to conquer the fear with the sorrow. Ruler of the most powerful kingdom in all the Greek lands. A sacral king by virtue of his forefathers in the House of Atreus. By common consent and election of his peers, commander of a great invasion force. Troy waiting over the water, a city famous for her gold and her horses. The eagles of Zeus, blessing his quarrel. The prayers all uttered, the libations all made. And now this raging wind from the north, prolonged in a way never before heard of in this season, implacable, keeping the fleet penned there. And he wonders, Has the god turned against me? What mistake have I made, how have I offended? And no word or sign. And not far away there are those ready to blame him for the wind, for the vicious fault which he cannot discover, ready to proclaim themselves to the army as more fortunate, more favored. People with a following already, Palamedes, Idomeneus . . .

Agamemnon raised his right hand in the gesture of consent. "By sunset tomorrow you will return. You will tell us the meaning as you have understood it. I will call an assembly of the chiefs. We will also hear Croton and any others who have a mind to speak."

Calchas was beginning to back away, but the King spoke again, in a different, sharper tone. "This morning, before the meeting, you were seen talking to Ajax the Larger. The two of you, faces close together, he gripping your arm."

"Yes, we spoke together."

"What was the subject of this talk?"

"Lord Ajax spoke to me about his idea for a Day of Games."

"And what may that be?"

Calchas did his best to explain Ajax's idea, no easy matter, as he had been so muddled about it himself. There would be competition in various things, running, jumping, weight lifting, throwing the javelin. Those who did well would gain points and these points would also belong to the places they came from. In the end, one person and one place would have more points than any other person or place, but the person with the most points would not necessarily be from the place with the most points . . .

Agamemnon stirred in his chair with a restless motion. A

look of frowning incredulity had appeared on his face. He could not believe, in the midst of the troubles that plagued him, that he should find himself listening to such stuff. Calchas said, "He sees it as a way of bringing the men together in friendly competition, keeping their minds off the wind and putting an end to all this quarreling and bloodshed."

"Why did Ajax not come to me himself with this?"

"Lord, I do not know."

In the silence that followed he felt the King's eyes upon him and kept his own gaze fixed on the ground. Since this affliction of the wind Agamemnon saw conspiracy everywhere and he was dangerous in his suspicions because any trifle might be taken to confirm them.

"Well," he said at last, "it sounds a dubious enterprise to me but I don't see anything against it, it will keep him busy at least." A sudden contempt lightened the misery of his face, restored for a moment or two its normal expression of tight-lipped, watchful pride. "He'll need help with the adding-up," he said. "That much is certain."

"He spoke of bringing the other Ajax into it, Ajax the Lesser."

"Did he so?" A faint smile came to the King's face. "Two likely peacemakers there, they do nothing but quarrel whenever they are together. You have our leave to go. See that you are here again by sunset tomorrow. And see that you come with the right words."

He smiled again, saying this, and the smile was terrible to Calchas, as was the threat contained in the quickened tone. They were still present to his mind as he left the tent. Hatred there, not for him only. Again it came to him that the King was mad. A man who had scented in his soul the disfavor of the gods and still demanded the right words rather than the true ones . . .

Poimenos had returned and together they made ready. The diviner abandoned his long-skirted robe and girdle for a sleeveless vest and short kilt such as the Greeks used. Poimenos wore cotton drawers, tied at the waist with a strip of crocodile skin which Calchas had given him and of which he was very proud.

Calchas watched him as he moved about, passing inside the tent and out again, getting together the provisions for their journey. And again his heart was wrung by the boy's beauty, which was without knowledge of itself in this bustle of preparation, the slight but well-defined muscles of the shoulders and thighs, the warm olive tone of the skin, no flaw or fleck in it, lustrous—it was as if the hot sun oiled him, spread him with unguents. By what mystery, what casual gift, had a goatherd, a descendant of goatherds, been endowed with such unconscious grace of movement and form? In the crisis that had come upon him, in the danger that he felt, Calchas was swept by longing for negation, freedom from the torment of alternatives, he wanted the boy's body next to his, in a light so pure and strong that it contained no faintest hue and so was indistinguishable from darkness. No conflicting voices could live in such a light, only peace of the senses and vacancy of the mind.

It was not possible now, as it had never been before, to know whether Poimenos understood the refuge he gave, the sheltered place where the light and the dark were one. Almost certainly not, the priest thought; it was outside the range of the boy's conceptions, though he was sensitive and quick when it came to the messages of the body. He recognized the need in the eyes, but thought it only for the pleasure he knew how to supply. Now, it seemed, he saw something of his master's fore-boding too, for he paused in his preparations to touch the priest's shoulder and smile and say, "The goddess will reveal the truth to you, and you will reveal that truth to Agamemnon, tamer of horses, the great oak that shelters us."

He had not understood—it was the truth itself that Calchas feared most. But as the priest made up his mixture of hemp seed and dried bay leaf, as they put their bread and cheese, and the wine for the libation, into a cloth bag, as they set out along the shore together, away from the camp, to look for a local fisherman who might take them across, all the while he held to the simplicity of the words. For Poimenos truth was triumph over uncertainty, peace after struggle, complete and unmixed. It was why he would remain always a server, always in the anteroom of the temple, never knowing the terrible obscurity of the god's purposes. Like looking at a great tree, Calchas thought. At a distance, one single shape, a dome, a spire. Approaching, one saw the articulation of the limbs, the separate masses of the foliage. But what mortal man, drawing nearer yet, looking up through the canopy of the branches, could keep the whole marvelous structure present to his mind? And if, nevertheless, there was still the terror of failing to see the vein in the leaf . . . Suddenly, unexpectedly, Calchas felt envy for the boy at his side, who would never stand in that place and look up. The envy was new, born of his fear; and contained in it was the first impulse of a fatal desire to share, to instruct. "Tamer of horses?" he said. "Great oak? These are the Singer's phrases. You must not pay too much attention to the Singer, he does not deal in truth."

THE

Heavy Burden

OF

Command

1.

"What went wrong?" Odysseus took care to keep his tone casual. The last thing he wanted to do was antagonize the man before him, who might then decide to change sides. Unlikely, he was too deeply implicated. But Phylakos was corrupt, and so more easily offended in his dignity than an honest person. "I mean to say, it was a simple enough matter, wasn't it? All you had to do was coach the men in the story so they didn't contradict each other."

He had thought at one point that Calchas would take it into his head to interrogate the three separately, in which case discrepancies would certainly have been revealed. But he had seen almost at once that there was nothing to worry about. Behind his professional manner the priest was terrified of discrediting a symbol so potent; to do so would have been to cast doubt on the success of the expedition in the presence of the man who was leading it. A braver man than Calchas would quail at that. "Just a device, really, wasn't it?" he said. "The hare, I mean. A proof of our loyalty and devotion, strengthening belief in victory, holding things together through these difficult days. Agamemnon was ready to believe it, so was everyone else. Almost everyone." He thought of the priest again. Something would have to be done about Calchas. Too much play of mind. He glanced at the dogged face before him, weathered by a score of campaigns. Not much play of mind there. "How did this pregnancy business get into it?"

Phylakos stared unwaveringly before him, habit of an old soldier who felt himself under reprimand. He had been summoned to Odysseus's tent early for this private talk. Chasimenos, who had also been party to the story, was due later. "We couldn't have known he would come out with that," he said. His voice was scraped, painful-sounding, as if always proceeding from a parched throat.

"But you must have known he was a hysteric. Those with him must have known."

"Hysteric?"

Odysseus sighed. "They must have known he had a screw loose. You only have to look at his face."

"They said he screamed in his sleep sometimes, and sometimes laughed for no reason, but they were used to him. They thought nothing of it and neither did I. All the fool had to do was keep his trap shut."

"Well, he didn't." Odysseus paused for a moment or two, then said in a tone of wonder rather than of reproach, "And you backed him up."

There was no reply to this and Odysseus expected none. It had been a bad mistake, but he knew that Phylakos had not been

THE SONGS OF THE KINGS

able to help himself, it had been in the nature of a reflex action. The backup, the closing of ranks, the solidarity to the group, this was the conditioning of military life. It counted for morality with many, even in support of a lie. Only very rare beings were free of such limiting factors, such blindness to their own interest: clear-sighted men, who saw things steadily and saw them whole. Men like himself. "Well," he said, "it's too late to do anything about it now. I trust this blabbermouth will be rendered harmless, made incapable of further damage, what's the word I'm looking for?" He liked this fishing for words, casting, seeing the float bob, pulling up a plump one. But Phylakos, still staring doggedly before him, was not the right sort for it. This time he was obliged to answer his own question. "Neutralized," he said.

"Snuffed out, you mean? Already taken care of. That's one motherfucker won't talk out of turn again, I can promise you that."

"Your patriotism will be remembered and rewarded," Odysseus said. "Liberally rewarded. You know, when we get across the water."

In the reflective silence that followed these words, one of his Ithacan guards came in to announce that Chasimenos was outside, asking to be admitted. Odysseus went himself to the entrance to accompany the scribe inside — it was essential that Chasimenos should feel valued.

"What went wrong?" Chasimenos said to Phylakos as soon as he was inside the tent. He took less care than Odysseus had taken to keep his tone free of annoyance. "All the planning that went into it and you people couldn't even stick to the story."

But Phylakos was not prepared, in a military camp, to take rebukes from a civilian, however high-ranking. "It wasn't me telling the story," he said, in a voice like the dragging of gravel.

"It wasn't my story at all, it was yours. You schooled them in it, you should have seen the bastard was off his chump."

"Good heavens, do you think I have time for character analysis? Have you any idea of the administrative difficulties involved in organizing a meeting like that, making sure that the chiefs are notified well in advance, so no one is drunk or out hunting or pillaging some local farm or busy raping someone? No good sending out memoranda, none of them can read." This clodhopper, he thought, all he can do is swing a sword. "And you backed him up," he said. "You supported that nonsense about the eagles eating the young of the hare. It's the official version now."

"No good crying over spilt milk," Odysseus said. "The harm is done now, recriminations won't help." How ridiculous, he thought, these two standing glaring at each other, the soldier and the civil servant, each feeling he belonged to a superior race, when in reality they were as alike as two peas, both hirelings. Phylakos had physical courage but he would sign up with anyone he thought likely to win; he took orders and hoped for promotion if he did well. Chasimenos was devoted to the King's interest, as he saw it, but he was a natural subordinate, dreaming of a Greater Mycenae across the water, where his services would be rewarded and his power and influence increased. One in steady employment, one up for grabs, that was really the only difference. "We must look forward, not back," he said. "The past has less substance than a shadow, it can hardly be said to exist at all. Besides, it isn't such a disaster. The omen has become more ambiguous than we intended, that's all. Phylakos, can I ask you to do me a service?"

Phylakos raised his chin and squared his shoulders. "Yours to command."

"Either go yourself or send one of your people, find Croton the priest and bring him here to my tent as soon as possible."

"I will go myself." With this, he raised his hand in salute and strode out, without a glance at Chasimenos, who said, as soon as he was out of the tent, "That man is an oaf, he has no manners at all, he really gets my back up."

"Well," Odysseus said, "you are two very different kinds of person after all. But we'll have to forget our differences and forge ahead if we want what is best for Agamemnon and the Greek cause."

"That is true."

"Before Croton comes, there are one or two things I thought we could talk over. As you and I both know, the ex-peditionary force is far from united at present. Less than half of the people here are from regions anywhere close to Agamemnon's power base in the Argolis. My own Ithacans are a case in point. Of course, I'm bound by oath to the Mycenaean cause, through thick and thin, but the same can't be said for everybody. There are plenty here who think only of their own interest. The alliance was always shaky and it's getting shakier day by day. People are homesick — home being the place where there is no wind, no sense of being under sentence of doom. Before very long, if we don't find a way of holding things to-gether, the army will start melting away. I've seen it happen be-fore. Desertion is contagious. It starts here and there, in ones and twos, then before you know where you are it has devel-oped into a mass movement. By then it's too late to do anything about it, much too late."

Chasimenos nodded, lips compressed. He had a habit, when pondering deeply, of switching his eyes from one side to the other, as if following the flight of some small, erratic insect, and this lent a look of slight alarm to his narrow face. "What we need," he said, "is some way of guaranteeing the end of the wind, some promise of an end to it that they will believe in."

"Brilliant." Odysseus felt the customary throb of pleasure at subjecting another's intelligence to purposes of his own. It was hardly necessary in this case, their interests more or less coincided; but deceit was more than an inveterate habit, it was power, it quickened the blood in his veins. "I never thought of it in quite that way, but it's true," he said. "Duels won't do it. Omens won't do it. That is all spectacle, it is all part of the entertainment business. What we need is something more, something definite." He paused a moment, brow furrowed. "Something that will reconcile them to waiting."

"We need an event, a significant future event."

"A significant future event, bravo, that's it exactly." He looked with smiling wonder at Chasimenos, who was still tracing the flight paths of the insect. "Absolutely brilliant," he said. A delicate moment had arrived. Chasimenos was loyal to Agamemnon, and even loved the King in his way, or at least regarded himself as the King's creature. That could be put to use, but it needed a light touch. "Of course," he said, "whatever this future significant event turns out to be, and I am confident of further ideas from you on that score, we must take care that Agamemnon is kept informed."

Chasimenos's look of concentration disappeared and he stared at Odysseus with surprise and the beginning of indignation. "Kept informed? It must proceed directly from the King, it must be seen as his will, his intention, his idea. It must be he that guarantees an end to the waiting, no one else. Surely you see the importance of that."

"Well, now that you put it like that . . . Of course, whoever guarantees an end to the waiting will be hailed as leader, and as we know only too well, there are those among us ready to seize any occasion to take over the command. No, I see it now, we daren't allow Agamemnon to be set aside, relegated, what's the word I'm looking for?"

"Marginalized."

"Marginalized, brilliant. No, we can't allow Agamemnon to be marginalized, whatever happens we can't allow that. But the thing is, if he is not to be marginalized, if he is to act as guarantor, he will have to accept responsibility, wouldn't you agree?"

"Certainly. Responsibility is the essence of command."

"Essence of command, there you go. But responsibility for what?"

"Why, the conduct of the war, of course."

"I couldn't agree more, but we are still here at Aulis, still waiting to embark. How to deal with this waiting also belongs to the conduct of the war, wouldn't you say?"

Chasimenos was looking less certain now. "I suppose so, yes," he said.

"So Agamemnon, if he is to be responsible for the conduct of the war, must make himself responsible for the waiting, which means that he will also be held responsible for the cause of it, the wind. If he is not to be marginalized, I mean. We can't allow him to be marginalized, can we?"

"Certainly not. But no one knows the cause of the wind."

"Exactly, you've hit the nail on the head, no one knows the cause, that's why it's so demoralizing. But if they *believe* they know the cause, if they believe it lies in him, in the King, if they believe he has it in his power to end it, not now, not immediately, but through some significant future event, to use your excellent phrase, something only he can do, what then?"

The two men looked closely at each other for some moments. Then Chasimenos said, "We could hope to discover the sender and make sacrifices of atonement. In that case, the curse would be lifted before the future significant event needed to take place. Then there would be no problem. But the King will suffer in the meantime."

"He will, he will," Odysseus said, infusing his tone with compassion. Agamemnon was already being blamed for the wind, they both knew that. It surprised him slightly that Chasimenos, for all his undoubted intelligence, understood so little of future significant events and relative probabilities and the nature of public promises. Or perhaps he wished to seem ingenuous. Either way, it didn't matter.

The scribe was nodding slowly. "I can't see any way round it," he said. "No one will believe that Agamemnon can put an end to the wind without also believing that he is the cause of it. It's inescapable."

"Inescapable, brilliant, that's just—"

At this moment, Phylakos reentered the tent, the tall and lantern-jawed Croton beside him. Odysseus briefly debated within himself whether the captain should stay. As a general principle, the less the trust, the less the risk, but Phylakos could be useful, he had influence with certain sections of the army, especially those from Mycenae; and his own interest could be expected to keep him faithful.

"I am glad Phylakos found you," he said to Croton. "Can I offer you a cup of wine?"

THE SONGS OF THE KINGS

The priest's long hair, which he wore piled in the shape of an inverted bowl on top of his head and waxed to keep it in place, had been disordered by the wind and hung round his face in glistening strands. His lips were very pale and sometimes had a writhing motion when he spoke. "I am under a vow," he said. "I take nothing to eat or drink during the hours of the sun."

"I see. Is there some special reason?"

"Until this uncleanness ends and the will of Zeus is clear to all."

"Let us hope it will be soon, for your health's sake." Odysseus glanced away from the priest's face, which was disturbing in its contrast between the fixed gaze and the convulsive movements of the mouth. Croton inspired a strong distaste in him, but one could not always choose one's instruments. And the priest would go to any lengths to spread the power of Zeus and his own. "I am told you have a theory, let us call it that, regarding the sender of this wind and the reason it is sent?"

2.

The Singer was in the place he usually occupied in the middle hours of the day, sheltered from the wind and protected from the sun by an overhang of rock. He had been silent for some time, leaning back against the rock, between sleep and waking, his lyre resting over his knees. The dazzle of reflected sunlight from the white surfaces of granite on the hillside, the shivering of light from the scrub as it was endlessly agitated by the wind, the vague gleams of human forms as they moved before him, these were splinters that could still hurt what was left of his eyes. He kept them closed now as he took up the lyre again, feeling the thin, bitter tears beneath the closed lids.

It had been a day like all the others since they came there, the wind contending with his voice. Earlier, the boy had come again, bringing bread and figs. He had sat close as he always did, not speaking or moving, listening intently—the Singer could sense the intensity of this listening. He did not know the boy's name and had never heard his voice. He came every day, though not at the same time, and generally brought some gift of food. Today he had not stayed long. Then, sometime later, there had been the face of Ajax the Larger hovering above him like a reddish, cratered moon. From one of the craters came a request for a song of praise dedicated to Ajax the Unifier and celebrating the brilliant idea of a Games Day. Ajax had asked if Calchas the diviner had already approached him with this, but the Singer never gave information about his sources. He had forgotten, he said, his sight was poor, there were so many requests, so very many. Ajax had promised him a silver hair clip and he had promised in return that he would compose the song in his mind and then, on receiving the hair clip, sing it.

A lie, of course. He never composed verses beforehand. He possessed a vast stock of epithets and phrases inherited from his father, who had also been a Singer. For the rest, for what was new in the Song, he relied on the prompting of the gods, which came to him more strongly and urgently at some times than at others but never entirely failed him. He sighed as he struck the preliminary run of notes, his usual way of attracting attention. How many dusty roads he had traveled. It was shameful that people should try and take advantage of a blind old man. He would give his services free when he chose; but not for a skinflint like that one.

He began with a Song completely familiar to all in the camp, the one he had been requested—politely but very firmly—to recite at least once a day so as to keep the just cause of the war well to the forefront of men's minds. This was the story of Paris, prince of Troy, the handsomest man in the world, who had gone on a visit to Sparta, stayed in the palace of Menelaus and, while his host was away, seduced his queen, the fabulously beautiful Helen, who in addition to this beauty had the unusual distinction of having been hatched from a swan's egg after her mother, Leda, had yielded to the embraces of Zeus, who visited her in the form of a swan. Paris had taken Helen back to Troy with him, an outrage to Greek honor that could not be taken lying down. Hence this great army, united in their patriotic duty to avenge the insult and recover the queen.

He did not linger on the story, being himself thoroughly bored with it by this time, but passed quickly on to the epic battle between Stimon the Locrian and Opilmenos the Boeotian, their bronze helmets and breastplates glittering in the sun, their speeches of defiance one to the other, the marvels of valor and dexterity both had displayed. The wretched end of Opilmenos, butchered at leisure as he scrabbled on the pebbles of the shore, came over the more graphically, he felt, for the contrast with the physical splendor that had gone before. Such a downfall gave a sense of doom, a note of tragedy. He liked this version of the duel and intended to repeat it several times before any of Opilmenos's friends or relatives could get at him with requests to dignify the hero's manner of dying. But of course no story was ever final and requests came sometimes in a form one couldn't refuse . . .

Next he sang of the wind that held them there. Day by day this wind was heaping up the fabled wealth of Troy, making her towers and walls more wondrous, more lovely to destroy. As the embers of their campfires glowed and flamed in the endless wind, so the heaped gems took fire, so the gold flamed in the fanning wind of their desires.

It was no more really than a sustained simile, but he liked it. He was coming to the end when he was again aware of someone drawing near. It was a shape of face and quality of voice he recognized. Face and voice came very close. "I am Chasimenos of Mycenae, chief scribe to Agamemnon. You know me, don't you?"

"Yes, I know you," the Singer said.

"We want you to make it known to the people of the army that this wind is sent by Zeus because of an offense."

"Whose is the offense?"

"No need to go into specifics. You can say it's somebody high up."

3.

On the edge of the camp they found men who had come with fish to sell, and one agreed to ferry them over. Even here, in this narrow, sheltered strait, the wind chopped at the water, breaking the surface into shallow ridges that reared and flashed. Hoping for a good reward, the man made a show of the labor involved in taking them across in such weather. This he did by gesture and expression of face — he spoke a language they did not understand, it had no words of Helladic in it. As they set off, in pursuance of his new intention to instruct, offspring of kindness and envy, Calchas tried to explain to Poimenos that the people of these shores had kept their own tongue, which was not related to Greek and so must have been theirs already in that far distant time before the Greeks came. But this was too abstract, it soon became clear to him that Poimenos had no concept at all of such a time, or of one system of sounds that could be older than another.

It was that time of day in summer when the sea and sky seem more definite in color and more substantial than the land. When they looked towards the island it seemed that water below and air above were clasping the land, keeping it in place. This too Calchas pointed out to the boy. "Like the hands of a Titan," he said. "See, he keeps his hands flat, one above and one below, so the island cannot slip away, cannot escape." He saw the quickened interest in the boy's face as his imagination caught at these giant hands; it was always stories that held him.

The man rowed from the prow with a single oar, standing upright, grunting with each forward lunge of his body. The wind was all around them now, ruffling the sea, stirring scents from the land they were approaching. Poimenos's eyes were shining and he uttered some laughing exclamation. He was glad to be on the move, in this rocking boat, away from the tedium and oppression of the camp. Some tincture of this gladness came to the priest and he experienced, as sometimes before, a feeling of gratitude for the boy's vivid, quick responses to all things of sense, an eagerness that helped for a while to allay his own doubts and fears.

He had it in mind to speak of this to Poimenos, something he had never done before. But at this moment he saw two crows flying towards the sun. They came from the direction of Thrace, the homeland of Boreas, god of the north wind. Calchas followed them with his eyes as they flew towards the sun, followed them as far as he could, till they were lost in the fire and his eyes were blinded. When he could see again, the sky was empty, there was no smallest speck of a bird in it.

On the evidence of sight—the main evidence the gods gave to men whether awake or dreaming—the birds had flown into the sun and been consumed.

As they approached the calmer water on the lee shore of the island, he strove to understand the meaning of this immolation. The crow was the bird of hope, the messenger bird of Polunas, a god of the Hittites. She had once been a white bird, pure white, but one day Polunas, furious at some unwelcome news she brought him, pronounced a malediction on her, and she turned black as night. Afterwards he repented, but the color of a creature cannot be restored; further changes there can be, but there is no reverting to the original. Not even Zeus could do that, he thought. Though Croton would doubtless say otherwise. Croton preached that the power of Zeus had no limits, an obvious absurdity. No god known to man could undo the effects of his own power, no god could take back his words, no god could restore to mortal life a creature destroyed by his breath.

The reason for that anger of Polunas was that a girl he desired had fled from him, and it was the crow that brought this news. Calchas remembered Agamemnon's face and his smile. *The right words*. The crow had not brought them. Was it only this then, a warning? But hope could not be extinguished or consumed, even in the furnace of the sun . . . Zeus had launched them with the eagles, Artemis was detaining them with the wind. As patron of guests and hosts, Zeus was offended by the behavior of Paris, cuckolding Menelaus while staying in his house, then escaping with his prize, getting off scot-free. As protectress of childbirth and the young, Artemis was offended by the slaughter of the innocents that the war would entail. Male justice, female compassion. One looking back, one looking forward. Were they in conflict or blended in a harmony as yet too obscure to see?

These thoughts and the return of dread they brought with them so occupied him that he was hardly aware of nearing the shore. Only when they were out of the boat and wading, with Poimenos holding his arm, did his mind clear. They agreed with the boatman by signs that he should return next day when the sun was overhead, and in order to be sure he came Calchas promised payment only then.

They could see from below the place of the goddess; it was marked by the presence of water, a cluster of close-growing plane trees, the glint through leaves of a thin cascade. They began to climb, following the rocky path, passing through straggling bushes of broom, brown with seedpods. After this, where the water came closer to the surface, there were ferns and two walnut trees, the nuts still green. Bees were busy among the thyme and origan, rifling the tiny flowers, releasing their scent, performing miracles of balance and tenacity as they clambered and clung, endlessly jostled by the wind, which brought scents of the sea and pine resin and summer dust.

Higher up the spring bubbled out over the flat, mossy stone, rippling the trails of moss like hair in the wind. Below it a pool had formed, clear water under the trees, with cress at the edges. Dragonflies hovered here and gnats rose and fell. Beyond was the dark mouth of the cave. It was a small, separate world of water they were in, set apart from the dry scrub of the hillside, the loud concert of the cicadas and the myriad brittle creatures of drought.

Close to the entrance was a formation of rock in the shape of a belly and a navel, and as they paused here an old woman came towards them, walking upright but slowly. From the absence of greeting they knew her for the guardian of the shrine, the keeper of the fire. She stood before them and bowed her head but did not speak. They gave her the woven shawl they had brought with them as a gift to the goddess and she took it and stood aside. They entered the mouth of the cave and stood together at the edge of the low wall of stones built round a raised slab for offerings. There was the smell of woodsmoke and they felt a faint heat against their faces from the hearth below the table, where a fire of charcoal was kept alive under its quilt of white ash. The ground at their feet was scattered with cold ash and the bones of animals.

The old woman lit the lamp that stood on the earth floor inside the entrance. They were able now to see the dark stains of blood on the table, and the votive offerings that lay over the stains: bronze knife blades, the simulacrum of a double-headed ax, a wide-mouthed jar. Beyond this, in the center of the cave, rose the shrouded figure of the goddess, in the shape of a column, streaked with eternal dew.

The priest felt Poimenos draw closer to him, press against his side, felt the fear transmitted through the boy's body, helping him to control his own fear, relieving the constriction of his heart. In these moments of silence they heard the slow drip of water from the darkness deep inside the cave, a sound strangely distinct. Calchas prayed in his native Luvian to the goddess, mistress of animals, Mountain Mother, asking her pardon for this intrusion of strangers, her blessing for Poimenos and himself, her help in lighting up his mind with the meaning of the message she had sent them through the man's throat. Touching the stone of the wall with his forehead, he thought he heard a hiss of breath from deeper inside the cave, sign that he had been heard. They poured libations of wine, using the bronze beaker they had brought with them, and they left this as an offering and came away to the clear space outside.

From here, from a point just above the pool, they could see through the trees and look back across the water, see the way they had come, see the tilting masts of the ships and the wind-driven smoke of the fires. It was this view of the tormented camp that made Calchas understand. The distinctness of the water drops, the hiss of the goddess's breath . . . There was no wind in this enclave, the leaves were still, the flight of the gnats untroubled. He should have known: the author of the wind could not be touched by it—the calm was a proof.

The light was fading, the summer dark would fall quickly. He sent Poimenos to gather dry sticks. When the boy returned with an armful of kindling, he went and took some fire from the hearth, a small ember from under the ash, holding it between two twigs. He built a small pyramid of twigs around it and blew till the twigs took fire. Poimenos went again for thicker pieces. When he returned the priest told him to sit farther off and he obeyed, though Calchas knew he was afraid and would have liked the comfort of nearness.

He waited till the fire had a red heart, then raked it over. When the flames had died he took his bag of hemp seed and crushed bay leaf and cast a handful over the embers and sat with his face close above, covering his head with a piece of silk woven with gold stars, which accompanied all his travels, a gift to him from a merchant of Byblos whose future wealth he had foretold, though without staying long enough to see how things turned out. The heavy folds of the cloth hung down on either side, closing off the air. Eyes fixed on the pattern of the embers, he breathed in the scented fumes, striving to empty his mind of all that might obstruct.

Three handfuls he gave to the embers, feeling the sweat run on his face from the heat of the fire and the deep breathing in that hunched position. Then there was heat no more, he was on the banks of the Maeander, in the land of his birth. The water was clear, he saw the pale shapes of the stones in the streambed as he had seen them in childhood, and the swirls and eddies where the current fretted, and it was autumn because the surface was suddenly covered with bronze-colored leaves and these were borne away swiftly and they trembled and quivered with light, they were not leaves but the bodies of men in armor, it was the river of blood he had glimpsed at Delphi before his mind clouded, but now the water and the drowned warriors were all one color of bronze, Greeks and Trojans mingled together in it, drained of blood, limbs and weapons tumbled helplessly together in the tide of metal that was bearing them away into the far distance, where the stream ran silver and was quite empty.

It was this emptiness that brought fear. He cried out and flung the cloth from his head and tried to move back from the fire, but his limbs would not obey, they shone like bronze, like silver. He felt hands at his back and spoke some words without knowing what they were. Then nausea rose in his throat and he turned away from the hands and choked up the drained soldiers and the bronze blood; and in the coldness and loneliness after the vomiting no slightest sign or mark of favor came to him from anywhere in this enclave devoted to the Mother.

4.

The departure of Calchas and
Poimenos was witnessed by one of
Chasimenos's people and reported back to
him at once. Little went unnoticed now in
this camp, where rumors were rife and
spies multiplied by the hour. It was impossible to meet and talk without this becoming known to the chiefs, especially the
more powerful among them. However, it
was one of the several advantages of asso-
ciation with Chasimenos—and all were
well known to the wily Odysseus—that
the scribe enjoyed Agamemnon's trust,
was in fact Agamemnon's chief informer,
the one on whom the King most relied. It
was Chasimenos who had told him of that
intimate talk between Calchas and Ajax
of Salamis before the meeting. In this
Chasimenos did no more than continue
one of his main duties at Mycenae, which
was to keep tabs on everything that went
on in the palace. Thus, whatever he did

now, and wherever he went, it was assumed to be in the King's interest; and indeed it was in this light that the scribe himself regarded it. No one reported on Chasimenos—not to Agamemnon at least. The suspicions of others did not matter. The camp was a hive of suspicions anyway, as Odysseus pointed out later that day, when the two were discussing Calchas and the reasons he might have for going across the water.

"No need to worry about Calchas," Odysseus said. The other *was* worried, he knew that. "Calchas is a damp squib."

"But he must have some purpose, some plan, in going over there. Otherwise, he wouldn't absent himself at such a crucial time." Chasimenos was a dedicated planner himself, and long years in the palace bureaucracy had refined this talent.

"He doesn't think like that." Odysseus glanced at the other's face, which was unpleasing with its indoor pallor and unsteady eyes—he was tracking insect flight paths again. Chasimenos saw everything in his own terms, he had no insight into honest minds. It was a limitation. "He doesn't think politically. He's an intellectual, he spends his time trying to establish what things mean, whereas you and I know that meaning jumps this way and that according to circumstances. Calchas is one who will always be surprised by events." It was neat, it was pleasurable, to be prophesying the doom of a prophet. "First surprised, then overwhelmed," he said.

Chasimenos shook his head slightly, as if the fly had come too close. "I have been making inquiries," he said. "There is a cave shrine to the Mountain Mother there, on the other side. She whom we know as Artemis. They say it has always been there. The boatman was sent back, so it seems likely Calchas intends to stay overnight."

"He will have gone to consult the goddess. Let's hope she will have words for him."

Chasimenos stared. "Why should that be a thing to hope for?"

"My dear Chasimenos, because it will confuse him further. And the more confused he is, the more he will complicate the matter, and the more he complicates the matter, the less dangerous he will be as counselor. Agamemnon is in deep trouble, he will need simple words, he will not welcome subtleties."

"Calchas is close to the King, he has established himself as an authority, his words are believed."

"That is true of course, he has had some lucky hits. That is why he constitutes a threat. Normally, what should we do in such a case? We would try to discredit him, sow doubts about him in the King's mind, reduce his influence, kill his voice, deaden his tongue, what's the word I'm looking for?"

"Delegitimize."

"Delegitimize him, brilliant. You have a first-rate vocabulary, Chasimenos, you are seldom at a loss for a word. But you should spend more time on the study of character. You don't mind me saying that, do you? We are both past our first youth and we can speak frankly together, pooling our experience in a spirit of friendship and trust. We don't need to delegitimize Calchas, because Calchas will delegitimize himself."

"How?"

"Imagine his situation. He is a foreigner, an outsider, totally dependent on the King's favor. He is not very brave. I saw his face when that madman was gulping out the stuff about the

young of the hare. He took it seriously, in some sense he believed it. Now he goes to the shrine of Artemis. His god as worshiped in the lands of the Hatti is a hermaphrodite god. Did
you know that?"

"Yes, the slaves we buy in the markets of Miletus sometimes have knowledge of this god." Chasimenos's mouth, normally thin enough, had drawn even thinner. "We have called
him Apollo," he said.

"I very much doubt whether Calchas does. Now, in the
schools of Karkemish or Hattusas no doubt he could debate the
matter brilliantly, the blending of the male and the female natures, balance and harmony, but this is not a debating chamber,
it is a military camp with a leader at a crisis in his fortunes.
Calchas will be driven to complicate things, and at the same
time he will be afraid of losing his privileged position. As I say,
he is an intellectual, and the fate of the intellectual awaits him,
powerless to act, unable to make himself understood, lost in
useless speculation, what's the word I'm looking for?"

"Paralysis."

"Paralysis, brilliant."

Chasimenos's face, relieved for the moment from anxiety,
was smooth, with only the faintest of lines in it, the face of a
worn child who had never known childhood. "Good thing we
have Croton on our side," he said. "No danger of paralysis
there."

5.

ater, when Chasimenos had left, it occurred to Odysseus to go and check up on the Singer, in whom he had small trust. His way led him past the Ajaxes, Larger and Lesser, who were standing side by side shouting at a small group of men that had gathered and at each other.

Odysseus paused—to watch rather than to listen. He did not expect to hear much of interest but the pair made an amazing spectacle standing there together, the one red-faced and gigantic, always on the brink of violent wrath, the other dwarflike, bowlegged, sad-looking and more or less permanently randy—there was generally a tumescent bulge discernible below the stuff of his kilt.

"Suppose you are the winner of the footrace," Ajax the Larger was bellowing. "That is to say, one of the footraces . . ." He floundered here, staring furiously before him, confounded by the bothersome intrusion of detail.

Ajax the Lesser came to the rescue. "There are three footraces of different distances. The hundred paces, the five hundred paces and the thousand paces. My friend here is asking you to imagine that you have won one of them."

"No, first there are the heats." Ajax the Larger glared at his partner. "Good grief," he shouted, "you are forgetting the heats. Each of these three footraces will have a certain number of heats, and each heat . . . The winner of each heat goes on to the next heat . . ."

"No he fucking doesn't. Everyone is in just one heat and the winners of the heats—"

"I've told him before about this bad language. The winners of the heats get five points for winning the heat and the winner of the final will get a total of fifteen points, no, wait a minute . . ."

"You are getting it all fucked up again." Ajax the Lesser stamped a small foot in exasperation. "The overall winner will get twenty points. Ten for getting to the final and ten for winning it."

"That's what I was going to say," shouted Ajax the Larger at the top of his voice. "Step forward, anyone who is interested in training for these events. There will also be wrestling, jumping, throwing the javelin, weight lifting. Any of you men listening now could be a winner. Think of the credit you will bring to your town, returning after the war is over with twenty points notched up."

"Or thirty, or fifty. Think of the success you will have with the ladies. Your fame will go before you. They will line the streets to give you a hero's welcome."

Here the little man, thinking to liven up the audience a bit, did some steps of a jig and made obscene thrusting motions with his pelvis. He was quick on his feet and though lacking in stature very strong in the arms — he always received mention in the Songs when the list of notable rapists was recited. "The man with the fifty-point power pack," he shouted.

Ajax the Larger had gone a deeper shade of red. "I've told him I don't like that dirty talk," he yelled. "I was brought up to respect women. Step forward, men, don't be shy."

No one in the audience made any move in the forward direction, though several, seeing that the entertainment was drawing to a close and some contribution from them expected, began to drift away. Odysseus was about to move on too when he saw a staring fixity descend on Ajax the Larger's face, and knew that the huge fellow was in the painful grip of an idea.

"Wait! Don't go away! Ye gods, I've got it!"

He held up a mighty arm. "Prizes!" he shouted. "Not points, prizes. Points *and* prizes. I and my small friend here will offer prizes to the winners, handsome prizes."

Before turning away, Odysseus had time to notice from the little man's expression that this joint offer had not been welcome to him. Dissimilar as the two were in every other way, they were alike in their extreme stinginess. All the same, as he proceeded on his way, he wondered what the prizes might be. Both the Ajaxes had come back from raiding in Mysia loaded with booty. He was chronically hard up himself and the crew of his one ship were in arrears of pay. In fact, they had not been paid at all. This poverty was galling to him, aware as he was of outstanding abilities. Few could match him in fluency of speech and readiness of wit, in the subtle stratagems of deceit. He loved falsehood for its own sake, saw beauty in it. But these gifts had not resulted so far in the amassing of wealth or the acquisition of power. And he was approaching middle age, with a wife and son at home.

This Trojan campaign would change everything of course. From lordship of a few barren acres to an empire in the lands of gold, the fertile East. For the moment his only possession of value was the great bow that his friend Iphitus of Oechalia had given him when he was only eighteen. It had belonged to Iphitus's father, the famous archer Eurytus, and Odysseus valued it so highly that he had not wanted to risk its loss by bringing it with him, but had left it at home in a safe place. While still a very young man and eager to get the best product available on the market, he had traveled all the way to the mountains of Thesprotia, braving many dangers, to get arrow poison from Ilus, grandson of the noted poison maker Medea, heir to all her expertise. Anyone who was anyone got his arrow poison from Ilus, it was quite simply the best. It came in elegant bags with silk strings at the neck and Ilus's trademark woven on the side, instantly recognizable everywhere. But by the time he got there Ilus had gone mad and spent his days muttering in a corner, possessed by dread of the gods' disapproval. He had refused to sell any poison, on the grounds that the gods might disapprove. Odysseus had had to be content with an inferior poison from the nearby island of Taphos. Yet another failure, he thought, remembering how he had minded at the time. But Troy would change all that. Troy would make up for everything . . . He thought he could probably win the wrestling, if they were planning to have that as one of the events. He was broad at the shoulder and well knit, a good build for wrestling. It suited his temperament too. There were stronger men in the camp, but he knew how to use the strength and weight of an

opponent to defeat and disable him. And a man well oiled, who
knew the holds, could slip out of any grasp.

He was drawing near now to the place where the Singer
was generally to be found, where there was an outcrop of rock
to provide some shelter from the wind, in the open space between the Cretan, Locrian and Achaian encampments. That he
so regularly chose this place had led all three of these to claim
him as a fellow countryman; but there were others who said he
came from Lydia or from Ephesus or from the island of Chios.
It was not possible to find certain proof in his accent; and when
asked where he came from, he merely gestured, sometimes towards the mountains, sometimes towards the sea.

As Odysseus approached, he heard the high clear voice
with its usual note of lament, and the sound of the lyre, at the
same time swooning and vibrant. However, he was annoyed to
find that the Singer, far from following instructions and pro-
mulgating the message of an offended Zeus as the sender of the
wind, was singing about the early life of the hero Perseus, how
he had been born in a brazen cell where his mother Danae was
imprisoned, and where she became mysteriously pregnant, the
very thing she had been imprisoned to prevent.

None of this had anything to do with the wind, though it
had much to do with Zeus; but there was a considerable crowd
there, people were listening, he could not simply barge in and
interrupt. All the same, it was infuriating. Early evening, when
people were gathering, when it was cooler and more comfort-
able and minds were receptive. Prime time, in other words, and
it was being wasted.

His rank precluded sitting among the others. He waited
standing, at some distance apart. Despite his annoyance — and
the fact that, in common with many people there, he had heard

the story before—he soon found himself drawn in. It was one of the greats, and the Singer was telling it well. She had been locked up there by her own father, Acristius, king of Argos, who had been told by an oracle that a son of Danae would one day kill him. She claimed that Zeus was the father of the child, that he had visited her in a shower of gold, but Acristius preferred to believe that some lecherous and burglarious human had picked the lock. "Where is the gold then?" he asked. "Why is there none on the floor? Why is not even the slightest trace left?" Questions to which there was no answer. "A likely story," Acristius said, and he set both mother and child adrift in a chest. However, with his own hands Zeus guided the chest across the sea to the island of Seriphos, where it was beached up and found by Dictys, younger brother of the king of the island, whose name was Polydectes. The kindly Dictys looked after the castaways and it was here the Perseus grew to manhood. But then one day Polydectes happened to see Danae and he was smitten immediately and wanted to possess her, but she didn't fancy him at all, she refused and Perseus backed her up. "My mother's decision must be respected," Perseus said.

There were exclamations of approval at this from various parts of the audience, and the Singer observed a pause here, the customary pause for dangerous situations. He resumed with a rhetorical question. How did Polydectes react?

By a cunning falsehood. He announced that he intended to ask for the hand of Hippodameia, daughter of the Pisan king, Oenomaus, and he asked for a gift of horses as part of the bride price. Knowing all the while that Perseus possessed no horses.

This Polydectes was a shrewd fellow, Odysseus reflected. Part of the bride price, brilliant. The lustful king had always been his favorite character in the story, even though things had ended badly for him. He knew what he wanted and he worked things round. He had calculated on the hero's pride and rashness; rather than lose face, Perseus would make any sort of wild vow. And so it had happened. He had undertaken to bring anything that the king might ask, even to the head of the Gorgon Medusa, who had snakes for hair, a glimpse of whose hideous face turned men instantly to stone. No one had ever survived an encounter with the Gorgon. Naturally, the king at once accepted the offer. "Well, since you mention it," he said, "the head of the Medusa is just what I would like."

The Singer proceeded now to describe the appalling difficulty of this self-imposed task. The Medusa had two sisters and all three Gorgons were equipped with wings of gold. On foot, how could he get near her? And then, how could he kill her and cut off her head without once glimpsing her face? Even if by some miracle he brought it off, how could he escape the sisters' vengeful pursuit? But Perseus had one trump card, unknown to everyone, even to himself: he had the support of Athena, who hated Medusa for reasons that belonged in another story, one that the Singer, digressing a little, professed himself well able to relate if there was popular demand for it. Athena appeared to the hero in all her splendor and told him how he could get the better of the Gorgon. She gave him exact instructions . . .

The Singer paused here, at least his silence was at first taken by the audience as simply another dramatic pause. But nothing followed, the silence lengthened and they became aware again of the plucking and clawing of the wind and its voice on the hillside like the shuddering indrawn breath of some creature inconceivably huge. There was a restless stirring among the people, and several called out, demanding that the story should continue. But the Singer laid his lyre aside. He had been reciting for many hours, he was tired, it was time for his meager evening meal. Besides, the appearance of Athena was an excellent point at which to break off, an exciting moment in the story. He would continue next morning. The morning audiences tended to be sparse, they needed beefing up. Having heard the first episode, people were likely to return; and every return increased the possibility of gifts. He heard the rustle of the crowd's disappointment, the faces glimmered before him like soft, very pale flames. He turned his head towards where he knew the sea to lie. "Tomorrow morning," he said, "when the sun is still low enough to make a bar on the water, I will give you the words of Athena, you will have the sequel — there are two episodes in the story of Perseus and the Gorgon." This evening the boy had not come with his gift of food. He had not come even for the shortest time, to sit close by and listen to the Songs. Perhaps he would not come again.

The crowd began to move away, quietly enough now — they were after all accustomed to sequels and installments and adventures told in series. It was the wind that had made them feel lonely and unprotected, once the voice of the Singer had ceased. Odysseus waited until the last had gone, then went up to the Singer, who was eating bread and small black grapes. "I am Odysseus," he said, close to the Singer's ear.

The movement of the jaws did not cease at this announcement, nor was there any change in the angle of the cropped and bony head, always tilted upward, as if to catch some distant sound.

Odysseus hesitated for some moments. The Singer was not an easy proposition. He was an entertainer, he had power. The audience had been gripped by the Song, spellbound, for a while they had forgotten the wind. One who could distract the people in this way, turn them from discontent and the breeding of revolt, was a very valuable instrument, especially at a time like this. But instruments had to be controlled.

"I don't want to tell you your job, of course," he said, speaking close to the whorl of the Singer's left ear, "but it might have been a good idea to insert a reference to the wind that detains us here in that Song you have just been reciting. There was a good occasion when you brought Zeus into it. You know, the god takes his pleasure in a shower of gold, shows his displeasure in this wind that is so bitter to us, sent to punish our offense, an offense, you might have hinted, that involves someone high up in the chain of command."

The Singer chewed for some moments more on his grapes and bread. He enjoyed the blended taste when he put both into his mouth together. Chewing took time because a number of his teeth had gone. He did not like this voice. "The wind doesn't belong in the Song of Perseus," he said.

"Doesn't belong? I am astonished to hear you say that. Have you never heard of flexibility? You of all people should know that anything can go into a Song, it just depends on the way you deliver it."

The Singer wanted the rest of his bread and grapes, but he could not eat them while a conversation was going on; and this, combined with his dislike and fear of the voice, frayed his temper, took the guard from his tongue. "Do you think a Song is like a political speech or a funny story?" he said. "Do you think you can shovel anything into it to suit the purposes of the moment? A Song has the form that belongs to it and that is also the soul of the Song. Anything that touches the soul of the Song must depend on the Singer and the gods that speak through him."

"Is that so? Well, now, I'll tell *you* something," Odysseus said, still aiming at the Singer's ear. "I didn't come here to talk about art and soul and all that stuff. As far as that's concerned, I may be a philistine, but I know what I like. I'm going to have someone in that audience tomorrow morning and he's going to report back to me. I don't care whether you wrap it up in something else or tell it as a separate story, but if you know what is good for you, you'd better make sure this message about the wind goes over loud and clear, with briefer repetitions in subsequent sessions to reinforce the point. It must be noised abroad, made common knowledge, disseminated on a large scale, what's the word I'm looking for?"

"I haven't the faintest idea," the Singer said with sudden weariness. "I have enough to do to find my own words." And with this he lifted a compound wodge of bread and grapes to his mouth.

6.

Calchas slept heavily by the dead fire and woke to the warmth of the sun on his face and the sighing sound of the wind. The sea below was covered with low ridges, white along the crests. The hills beyond the camp were half lost in the morning haze. He felt no sensation but hunger. He shared with Poimenos the bread and cheese they had brought, leaving some aside for the keeper. They did not speak much but he felt the boy's eyes on him; and when he returned this gaze he did not see inquiry or curiosity on the other's face but an expression brooding and grave, which he could not remember seeing before. It was as if years had been added to the boy in the course of this one night. He had slept badly, he said. Perhaps it was only this. Or perhaps my eyes wither what they look on, the priest thought.

The keeper held out thin brown arms for the food and bowed in thanks, but she

did not eat before them and it was clear that she was waiting
for them to be gone. They descended by the same path and
waited near the shore, in the thin shade of a pine tree, for the
boatman to come for them. Sure enough, as the sun rose overhead, they saw him plying across. As they waded through the
surf and climbed into the boat, he made the same gestures of
exaggerated toil. And Calchas felt a blankness in his mind, as
if some power moved the man's limbs in exact repetition, so as
to cancel all the time that had elapsed since he left them there,
the presence of the Mother, the scented fire, the vision of the
drained warriors and all the interval of night. In payment he
gave the man the bronze belt buckle marked with a wave pattern along the edges which he had brought with him for the
purpose; and the man was pleased with this, and even smiled.

The walk back took longer than the apparent distance
seemed to warrant, generally the case by the sea, when there is
no obstruction to the view; and Calchas was tired and walked
slowly. So there was no time for rest when they returned, and
not a great deal for preparation. Poimenos brought water and
helped his master to wash away the traces of vomit and the
heavy, sweetish smell of hemp that still hung about him, afterwards rubbing oil scented with jasmine into the priest's shoulders where they felt painful and cramped. Calchas put on his
amethyst necklace and the white silk vest that had been the gift
of Agamemnon, and a long skirt of dark blue cotton with gold-
stitched hems. His long black hair was wetted and combed out
and gathered at the nape with a piece of white ribbon. The
chalk circles and the tiny crimson sunbursts within them were
deftly applied to his cheeks. Then Poimenos was sent to ask
when his master might approach and returned to say that the
King required him immediately. But after all this haste

Agamemnon was alone with his guards when he arrived, the chiefs had not yet begun to assemble.

"I wanted to speak to you alone," Agamemnon said. "I sent for you in the night but you were not there."

"My lord, I had your leave to be absent for the night, to go to the shrine of Artemis."

"Yes, I know that, but I needed you." He spoke as if the need alone should have brought his diviner back across the water. "I had a dream in the first part of the night and I needed you to tell the meaning."

Calchas felt a premonition that restricted his breathing, like the drawing of strings within his chest. He too, by that fire, in the first part of the night, had been dreaming. "Does my lord remember the dream still?"

"Yes, I remember it perfectly." Agamemnon's dark face, with its straight mouth and prominently curved beak of a nose, was suddenly younger, innocent-looking. "It was dark," he said, "thick darkness, there was no light at all. I was in a forest, I had to feel my way among trees. There was a nightingale singing somewhere not far away. I knew it for a nightingale because I have heard them singing at home, on the slopes below the citadel. This song was beautiful and loud. I moved towards the song through the trees, reaching out with my hands because I could see nothing. As I drew nearer the bird sang more loudly, always more loudly with every step, until the darkness was full of this song and it seemed that the bird was very close, almost within the reach of my hands, but as I reached to take it, the song ceased and I was standing alone in the dark and I woke and heard the wind in the canvas and sent for you, not remembering, in the toils of the dream, that I had given you leave to go."

Calchas had felt the blood drain from his face as the King spoke. It was immediately clear to him that Agamemnon had dreamed his own death, a death on the threshold of triumph, when the trumpets were sounding. That music of death came from the battlements of Troy. Dark and light held the same message, and it was the message of Pollein, god that blended two natures, water and the light on water. The silver of the river in the distance, empty of bodies, the darkness when the song ceases. Turning away from the song was the only salvation; but Agamemnon would not turn away from the promise of conquest. And Calchas knew he would kill the one who advised it.

"You can come closer," Agamemnon said. "Speak to me closely, the guards need not hear."

"My lord and king," Calchas said, striving to control his voice, "I have made a study of the natures of the different birds. The nightingale is a special case. He is condemned to sing in the dark and yet he feels fear of the dark. The beauty of his song is caused by fear. When he senses a presence, this fear increases and he sings more and more loudly as the danger draws near. The bird felt your power in the darkness, and sang the more loudly till you reached to grasp him and then his heart burst with fear and with the effort of his song. There is also the story of Philomela, which the King will remember, of how she was seduced by Tereus, who was married to her sister, and of how he cut out her tongue to prevent her from speaking of this, and of how, at a moment of extreme fear, she was changed by the gods into a nightingale and given the tongue and throat of marvelous song. But Philomela remembers her fear, and when danger comes close she again becomes tongueless. Beyond any doubt, the bird in your dream represents Priam, king of Troy, who fears your greatness and puffs himself up and boasts the more loudly as the fear grows."

He stopped short of saying what he knew the King wanted to hear, must already be assuming, that a burst heart was the fate that awaited Troy. The fewer words, the better; it might be possible yet to leave the bird to its song. "Your power goes before you," he said.

"In that case," Agamemnon said, "why was I left alone in total darkness?"

The exercise of his profession had taught Calchas that the memory of dreams and portents was generally subject to the embroidery of hope, and always the more so when it concerned the ambitious. "Great king," he said, "pardon me, but are you certain there was no lessening of the dark after the bird fell silent? Think carefully. Was there not a faint light that grew among the trees?"

It had worked with others and he saw from the King's face that it would work now with him. "Well, now I come to think of it," Agamemnon said after some moments, "I believe there *was* a change in the light. I seem to remember that I could just begin to make out the shapes of the trees."

"The dawn of the new day," Calchas said. "Extremely auspicious, a fortunate dream indeed."

Luckily he was not required to say more, because Menelaus entered at this moment, the first to arrive. "Ye gods, what next?" he said. "It's all over the camp that Zeus has visited this wind on us because of some offense in the high command. I don't think it's me. We all make mistakes of course, but I can't think of anything I've left out, and in any case Zeus is squarely on my side because I'm the one whose hospitality was violated. No, the only thing I can accuse myself of, and even then it's the result of my generous and trusting nature, is letting that shitty Asian get anywhere near my Helen. I'm pretty certain now that he slipped something into her drink, otherwise how can you explain it? I have it on good authority that all Asian males hang weights on their pricks from early childhood to make them bigger, not that my Helen would have been interested in that. She rises above it."

Absorbed as usual in his wrongs, he had not immediately registered the presence of Calchas. "Present company excepted," he said now, with false joviality. "No evidence of weight-hanging there. Besides, you are an honorary Mycenaean by now." Calchas was still trying to express his appreciation of this compliment when Odysseus and Chasimenos entered together, followed shortly afterwards by Achilles and his lover Patroclus. Then the aged Nestor came shambling in, flanked by his cooing sons.

When all were present, the King turned to his diviner. "Let Calchas speak first," he said. "Calchas will give us his interpretation of the omen of the eagles and the hare and the hare's young."

"Lord of men, it is not a simple matter." His throat had gone dry. Fear, from which he had been briefly rescued, returned now in full force. He had no plan, no policy, only what his cowardice prompted: to delay, to seek the refuge of a few more hours, the cover of another night. "There are things still not quite clear to me," he said. "I need to speak again to the man who first told us that the hare was pregnant. I have some further questions for him."

He saw the King frown. Croton raised his staff as if claiming the right to speak, but Phylakos forestalled him, stepping forward and coming to attention before the seated Agamemnon exactly as he had done on the previous day, when he had made himself spokesman for the men on watch. Again Calchas had the feeling that time was circling back on itself, that intervals were being canceled.

"It's not possible to produce this man for questioning," Phylakos said. "He does not answer the call."

"He must be somewhere," the priest said.

Across the short space that separated them Phylakos regarded him without expression. "He cannot be found," he said. "It is thought that he has deserted."

There was a brief pause, then Calchas saw the King turn his head and knew he could delay no longer. As he spoke, he kept his eyes on the face of Odysseus, whom he knew for his greatest enemy. And Odysseus returned the gaze steadily, with an expression that seemed close to a smile.

"Zeus sent the eagles to bless our expedition. So much we know to be true. But our mistake has been to believe that this blessing was binding on us or that it was a guarantee of victory." The dangerous words, once uttered, brought a sense of release almost reckless, he felt an easing of the heart, saliva gathered again in his mouth. "It was neither," he said.

There came voices at this from different parts of the tent, but they were silenced by Odysseus, who had the gift of gaining attention without raising his voice. "Calchas is right," he said, "as far as concerns the eagles. By the eagles we know we have a just cause, but cause and outcome are separate things. However, there is also the hare. The hare is the outcome, the hare is Troy devoured. That is our guarantee." The suggestion of a smile disappeared from his face as he glanced at those around him, enlisting support. "As to what is binding," he said, "the oaths of loyalty that unite us are binding, our national honor is binding, but perhaps a Hittite priest would not appreciate that."

"Excuse me, I am not Hittite, I am Carian, we were there before they came, as were our gods." He was tasting already the bitterness of defeat. He was too alone and too afraid. He knew that in argument it was fatal to have the premises of the adversary placed beyond question; but he could not question the story of the hare, could not say it was a fabrication, that the only truth in it was the word of Artemis gulped from that chosen throat, because the King clung to the story as he would cling to that dawn of promise in his dream. "The eagles fall on the hare and devour her," he said. "But they also devour her young, ripping them from the womb. These are the innocent, this is the blood of the innocent, it must reflect on the justice of the cause, I mean in the sense that it obliges us to inquire into the true will of the gods in this matter."

Chasimenos now stepped forward to speak, casting his usual quick glances from side to side. "I'd like to make one simple point," he said, "and ask one simple question. If the cause of the war is just, nothing that happens in the pursuit of the war can make the war less just. The slaughter of the innocent cannot detract from the justice of the cause, though we may possibly call it an unjust effect of a just cause. If this were not so, there would be no such thing as a just war, only a necessary war, which is clearly absurd. Can Calchas be saying that Lord Zeus, in embarking us on a just cause whose inherent nature was that it could subsequently become less just, was in fact embarking us on an unjust cause from the very beginning? Let him answer that one."

The scribe paused here and smiled in the manner of one who knows he has made a devastating point. Calchas was saved from the need to answer by Ajax the Larger, who now raised a voice hoarse from much shouting. "An end to this riddling," he said. "Good grief, how can a fellow make head or tail of all this bullshit?" He glared at Chasimenos, whose smile disappeared abruptly. "Some people are too clever by half, they don't get enough fresh air, they need to do a few press-ups. A bit of healthy competition on the sports field wouldn't come amiss either. How about enrolling in one of the more light-hearted events which my small friend here has been organizing, the egg-and-shield race, for example?"

How Chasimenos might have responded to this invitation was never to be known, because it was at this moment that the senile Nestor, who had been preternaturally silent until now, raised the wavering song of his voice. "Who would carry javelins on a cattle raid? You need to make a quick getaway on a cattle raid, it was a sword, they knew how to make swords in those days, we crossed over into Elis in the dead of night, we rounded up their cattle, we got away with fifty cows. Iphiclomenos tried to stop me, I think that was the name, they were his father's cows. I went down on one knee, I stuck him in the belly, he wasn't expecting that, no . . ."

"There, there, father, that raid is a classic, it is in all the Songs."

"Father, your exploits will astonish future generations, but now we must be quiet, we must listen . . ."

As the old man trailed off into querulous mutterings, Agamemnon spoke for the first time since opening the council. And he spoke with a face of anguish, addressing all those present. "Who sends the wind against us? *How have I offended?*"

It was the question Calchas had most dreaded; but it was one he knew he had to be the first to answer or be thrust aside and silenced, his influence with the King lost beyond recovery. He said, "It is Artemis who speaks to us through the wind. She is offended by the slaughter of the hare's young, the innocent young of Troy. She is Mother, mistress of animals, goddess of childbirth. The offense is threefold."

Agamemnon leaned forward in his chair, turning so as to look full at the diviner—a bad sign. "Speak more clearly, priest," he said. "Are you saying the wind is sent for an offense not yet committed?"

With this half-incredulous question, Calchas knew he was finally in the open, driven out of hiding, with no comfort but knowing where the hunters' darts would come from. Fear always made the same approaches, catching at his breath, constricting his chest, as if bands were being drawn and tightened. He opened his mouth a little, so as to breathe more freely. Never in his life had he chosen truth before safety. He said, "We are between male and female, sky and earth, the justice of Zeus and the compassion of Artemis."

As he again hesitated, the people his eye fell on seemed more intensely and completely themselves. Chasimenos peering round as if casting for a scent, Odysseus bearing a look of cruel and serene relish, Phylakos staring before him with wooden fixity, Menelaus sun-blistered, fuming with his wrongs. There was no one in this tent that wished him well. He saw Achilles flick with his fingers at some speck on his beautiful tunic, in a gesture like that of a preening bird. He noticed now that Croton, standing in his usual place on the King's left, was in the grip of some strong emotion; his face, his whole body, rigid with tension. It looked like fear, but why should the priest of Zeus be afraid?

"A balance must be found," he said. "If the conflict has been created for us in order to tell us something, the reconciliation must be contained in it. The wind must be within the god's will, as it is within the will of the goddess. So it must be within the scope of their joint will that the young of the hare are restored to her womb."

He checked on this, but it was too late. He had gone too far, he knew it as he finished speaking, knew it as he waited and saw the darkness gather on the King's face. But Agamemnon made no immediate reply. Instead it was Diomedes the Argive who spoke, a man who was sung about often for the part he had played in the wars with Thebes, a strong ally of Mycenae, he had come with eight ships. "The gods have their provinces whether of earth or sky," he said, "no one will deny that. And they have to collaborate, otherwise we would end in fire or flood. But we don't know the arrangements they make and no one can tell us. This priest of Apollo talks about reconciliation and so on, but it's obvious that he hasn't a clue how this can be achieved. And if he thinks you can fight a war without collateral damage, he's totally mistaken. There will always be accidents. You can try to keep them to the minimum but you'll never avoid them altogether. Reconciliation is a long-term project anyway. It may suit priests, basically all they need to do is show their hearts are in the right place, they don't need to deliver the goods. But we are here in this camp and the wind is killing our hopes from day to day."

Now Croton raised his peeled staff with its blue ribbons of the Sky God. His arm was unsteady and the staff shook a little and the currents of wind that moved through the tent sported with the ribbons and made them flutter. "Lord Zeus sends the wind," he said, and he looked fiercely round him. "It is Zeus who keeps us here. We have killed two goats and scanned the entrails, we have cast the stones, the message is always the same. Artemis, the subordinate one, how could she question his will, who has already blessed our expedition? How could she go against the eagles? She is the female, the daughter, how could she have the power?"

His voice had risen and there were flecks of foam on his lips. He was working himself into a passion — perhaps, Calchas thought, his way of overcoming fear. But the impression of fear remained. It was nonsense, of course, this claim that Zeus was the goddess's father, though it was one his priests now commonly made. He was briefly tempted to intervene, to point out that she they called Artemis had been worshiped in his homeland by generations of people who had no knowledge of Zeus. But such words would not be received well. His stock was low enough already . . .

"Who is the weather god?" Croton said, and he shuddered with the effort to control the passion of conviction which threatened to distort his voice. "Is it Artemis who gathers the clouds? Is it Artemis who cages the winds?"

"Why should Zeus contradict his own messages?" It was a despairing attempt at logic and Calchas knew it for useless even as he spoke. The feeling was against him, they preferred this madness of Croton's.

"There is no contradiction in the messages. The eagles were sent to bring us here, the wind is sent to keep us here. This is the place Lord Zeus has chosen."

"For what purpose?" The question came from Agamemnon, who spoke in his usual tone but had braced himself back in his chair.

"As the place of choice," Croton said. "We are away from our homes here." He was calmer now, having arrived at the authority his soul aspired to. There was no doubt that everyone there was hanging on his words. Even Achilles looked interested—he had forgotten to put on the supercilious, preoccupied look he generally wore at these meetings, as if his mind was elsewhere.

Croton remained silent for some moments, staring before him with eyes that seemed too wide open, unnaturally prominent in his face. He had grounded his staff now and held to it with both hands, as if otherwise he might be dislodged, swept away. "Zeus has me in his care," he said. "Who does hurt to me incurs the anger of the god. It is because of Agamemnon that we are kept here. His eldest daughter Iphigeneia is a priestess of Artemis, this duty was handed down to her by her mother, Clytemnestra, when the girl reached the age of fourteen."

"This is common knowledge," Chasimenos said. "It is customary, there is no blame in it."

"Not so commonly known is that the cult of Artemis is exalted above that of Zeus in Mycenae, the daughter is raised above the father, as Calchas tries to do here."

"How do you know this? You are not of Mycenae."

It was again Chasimenos who spoke, and again apparently in defense of his master. The question had followed quickly, immediately, giving Calchas no time to respond to the reflection on himself; but he saw now that the intention was not to defend Agamemnon at all. Croton was being encouraged, given the stage, possible objections were being anticipated. With this realization came the sickening knowledge of conspiracy: this was a scene that had been rehearsed.

"We have had reports," Croton said. "There are plenty here

in the camp that know of it. She makes offerings to Artemis as universal mother and as moon goddess, aspects of her cult displeasing to Zeus. Moreover, we know for a fact that the image of the male god, who holds the scepter of power, is relegated to a lower platform in the palace shrine at Mycenae. The image of the goddess they call Potnia, the Lady, rises higher by a head. And the King knew of this and did nothing, thus offending Lord Zeus. And the wind will not be lifted until the King makes amends."

"What amends?" Chasimenos said, still playing his part as questioner. "What steps should the King take to recover the god's favor?"

The question hung in the air for some moments, heavily, oppressively. The King's face was expressionless; but his left hand was pressed against the ribs on that side, as if to contain the violence of his heart. "I have neglected nothing," he said. "I have always honored the god."

"Amends must be made through the two persons who have offended. When was a bull last sacrificed on the altar of Zeus at Mycenae? It is only the goat whose blood they offer, the animal sacred to Artemis. The girl has offended by her practices and the father by permitting them."

A sudden, fearful intimation came to Calchas of where this might be tending. If they had rehearsed the questions they must have rehearsed the answers . . . "It has no sense, it is madness," he said. "Are we to judge on doubtful reports and unreliable memories, idle talk about the position of the images on one shelf or another? The wind is something that touches us all. How can the fault lie only in one when the wind affects a thousand? Where is the justice of Zeus in that?"

But no murmur came to support him. They had found the

offense that was needed. Croton's strength lay in the narrowness of his vision, the simplicity of his message. Simplicity, when it was passionate, would always win, something Calchas had known and forgotten a thousand times and would forget again, helpless to avoid the anguish of doubt, forever adrift among divided counsels. It was no comfort to him to know that the simplicity came from darkness, that Croton confused the justice of Zeus with the power of the priesthood, and his own personal need to suppress the fecund female divinities, worshiped of old, who disgusted and frightened him as did women uncontrolled by men. Knowledge which another enemy might have known how to turn to account. Useless to him now, in any case, as he stood there and saw the King's face turned away from him.

"What amends?" Chasimenos said again, and there was an eagerness in this repeating of the question.

Croton drew himself up with a visible effort. "Iphigeneia must be brought here and sacrificed on the altar of Zeus before the people. Only when that is done will—"

At a bound the King was out of his chair. A hoarse, panting breath came from him, strangely like an echo of the wind, a sound within a sound. He took two steps towards Croton and the knife was in his hand. Then Odysseus and Diomedes were on either side of him, speaking low. He stood still for a moment between them, then raised his face and gave a single cry, deep in his throat. There were some seconds of irresolution as the wind rattled the canvas as if in answer, and the chiefs looked at each other's faces, not knowing what to say or do. Then Odysseus said, "We must all leave, our Commander-in-Chief will want to be alone in order to consider what he has been told."

As they filed out in silence, too occupied with what had happened to quarrel over precedence, it came to Calchas in the midst of his shock that even at that terrible moment, with the scream of the King still seeming to sound in the tent, Odysseus had made a point of giving Agamemnon his military title.

He found Poimenos waiting for him, but seeing his face, the boy asked no questions, remaining silent with the tact that seemed part of his innocence, while he saw to the fire and cooked the barley porridge and the fish for their evening meal. After they had eaten, Calchas motioned the boy to come and sit beside him. "The chiefs are persuaded that this wind is sent by Zeus because of the King's offense," he said.

"This is what everyone thinks. It's all over the camp."

Calchas glanced sideways at the boy's calm face. "Is it so?"

"While you were there, at the meeting, I went round. They talk of nothing else. While we were away on the island, Croton and his people were going among the men with pipe and drum and the banners of Zeus."

"I see, yes."

"Even the Singer . . ."

"You have been listening to the Singer?"

Poimenos lowered his eyes, in what seemed some confusion. "I was passing by," he said.

"They want the King to turn away the wrath of the god by offering his daughter as a sacrifice."

The boy's eyes widened. "Will he do it?"

Such immediate faith in his judgment would normally have touched and amused Calchas, but now it served only to intensify the pain of his defeat. "No one can know yet," he said. "Much depends on how it is presented to him. There will be people ready to present it in certain ways."

"Not you?"

"No, not me. The King will not listen to me now." He at once regretted this admission of lost ground, which might diminish his importance in the boy's eyes. "He can listen to no one for the moment," he said.

"Did you tell him about the sign the goddess gave you, the river of metal and all the Greeks and Trojans carried away in it?"

It was clear Poimenos knew the answer to this in advance. "They would have listened," he said. "They would have listened to a story like that." His face wore a look that Calchas could not remember seeing there before, hurt and disappointed. "And the river empty in the distance, all silver," he said.

"How do you know what sign I had from the goddess? We do not speak together about such things."

The boy looked at him in silence for some moments with a deliberateness of regard unusual with him. "No," he said, "it is true you do not tell me things. But you said things as you drew back from the fire, before the vomiting came. And then again, during the night."

"It was not the moment to speak of it." A lie, as he knew in the cold depths of his heart, a lie to join the many he had told to this boy and others to disguise his faintness of purpose. The moment had been then, he had drawn back from it and it had gone. And he had lost favor even so. Self-contempt brought a wave of anger with it, anger against the boy before him, who showed his disappointment too obviously, too childishly. And with the anger there came again the desire to instruct, which is also the desire to destroy.

"A story," he said. "Do you think we have been telling stories back there?" He paused on this, however, his anger disappearing as abruptly as it had come. A kind of story it had been, not a contest of priests, nor even of gods, but a struggle for possession of the King's mind. Who had the King's mind would have the conduct of the war.

Poimenos had cast his eyes down in awareness of being rebuked, but he made no answer. Calchas felt nothing now but weariness and the premonition of loss. "Will you leave me to myself for a while?" he said. "Go about the camp a little, try to learn the feelings of the people."

The boy obeyed, still in silence. Alone in the tent, Calchas strove to close his mind against the bitterness of defeat and the fear he felt for the future. He prayed in whispers to Pollein, god of blended natures, to act as peacemaker in this quarrel, reconcile the goddess and the god and restore the King's favor to his diviner. For answer there was only the beat of his heart and the grieving of the wind as it searched among the scrub of the hillsides. And he was visited with an anguish worse than all his fear. In that voice of the wind there was no urgent will, no intention, no message of god or goddess, only a desolation as old as the hills themselves.

7.

This would be the moment," Odysseus said. "Croton has done his stuff and come out with a whole skin—only just. Agamemnon has had time to absorb the shock and start thinking about the consequences of refusing. The consequences to him personally I mean." He paused here, smiling a little. "That's always the first thought, isn't it?"

"A great man like Agamemnon cannot think only in personal terms," Chasimenos said. "He has to consider the people who depend on him."

"The people who depend on him, brilliant. Be sure to bring that in when we go over there."

The daylight was waning now, it would soon be dark. They were in Odysseus's tent and kept their voices low in case of eavesdroppers. "People like you and me," Odysseus said, still smiling. He was looking forward to the visit, it should offer a good field to his talents. "Strike while the bronze is hot. He won't have had time to hit on an alternative, not with any firmness anyway. I know Agamemnon. He wants to decide for others but he needs advice on how to decide for himself."

"Timing is important, certainly," Chasimenos said stiffly. He had sometimes noticed before a lack of due respect for Agamemnon in the other man's words; and now that they were associates in this enterprise, Odysseus took less trouble to conceal it. This distressed him, but he tried not to show it, knowing that Odysseus, whose cruelty he had early recognized, enjoyed his distress and found it laughable in someone busily engaged in exploiting Agamemnon's weaknesses. But to Chasimenos this was a cynical view, it was not what he was doing at all: he was working to bring out all that was best in Agamemnon, that quality of lordship which he lacked himself and knew to be there in his master, and which, with him aiding, could conquer the world. He had been in the palace service since the age of twelve, when he had been taken on as a page boy; he had worked his way up to a position of power and trust and he was devoted to the King's person and his interests. With this great campaign, there was an opportunity for Mycenae, already the strongest kingdom in Greece, to control the approaches to the Euxine Sea, to found not just a string of trading posts but a vast maritime empire. He was stirred by this thought even now; and when he was stirred his speech became elevated. He said: "In view of the importance of the matters under consideration, it is hardly surprising that the King should take time to review all his options on the information currently available."

"Quite so, well said, this is a difficult moment for him, that's what makes it a good time for us to go to work. For the common good, of course, always for the common good." His smile came again, an engaging smile, slightly lopsided as it grew broader, wreathing his face in lines of good humor, though the eyes remained the same, at once watchful and calm. I'll know the eyes of a twister from now on, Chasimenos thought. He knew he was on higher moral ground than the other, he was acting out of loyalty. Anyone who looked into his eyes would see the eyes of a faithful public servant.

"Well, I am glad we see eye to eye in this business," Odysseus said. He still could not quite believe his luck in having found such an ally, a man besotted with military power who had never worn a sword in his life, whose highest aim was to live in the light of another's glory, who saw in this rabble of hostile factions and predatory chiefs the makings of a nation, the founders of an empire. Chasimenos would play his part, probably without fully knowing it, in the two-pronged assault Odysseus had in mind; he would soften the King's defenses by defending him. Really neat. "We must take Nestor with us," he said.

Chasimenos frowned. "Is that really necessary? Nestor lost his marbles long ago. He'll only keep interrupting us with this interminable saga of his exploits as a rustler."

"It's not for the sake of anything he says, only to have him there. He's an accustomed figure at all councils. Haven't you noticed how he is brought out whenever there is an assembly of any kind? He puts a sort of stamp on the proceedings, an official endorsement. The Atreid brothers never change their view of things once it is formed, they are quite impervious to physical realities. Surely you must have seen that? Look at Menelaus, who goes on asserting that Helen was taken from him by force, as if only by force she could have been made to leave his side, when he is fat and short-legged and short-winded and Paris is like a god in looks and moreover Helen was what you might call easily led even before Paris came along. But Menelaus sticks to his story. It's useful of course, it provides a pretext for the war. But he didn't persuade himself to believe it, he believed it from the beginning. Questions of how Paris, alone and unaided, got an able-bodied woman—and Helen has an able body, we all know that—out of the palace and onto a ship against her will simply don't come into it. And Agamemnon is just the same. Nestor is wise in council, he has to be present, the fact that he is in his second childhood is neither here nor there."

Odysseus paused and his smile faded. He had felt the touch of caution, like cold fingers laid on his mouth. He was talking too much and too fast and taking too much pleasure in it. His own fluency betrayed him sometimes, when he felt the sort of excitement that possessed him now, the prospect, through words alone, of prevailing over another mind, using the fears and desires of that mind to disarm and control it. "It's peculiar, all the same," he said, "that we should depend for legality on a doddering old cattle raider."

"And Nestor's sons? They accompany him everywhere."

"No reason why they shouldn't be present. Pylos is a close ally of Mycenae, they have the same need for cheap metals, the same need to expand their markets. They are strongly in favor of the war. Besides, we will need witnesses when the King, you know, undertakes to do what we urge on him, agrees to embark on the required course of action, what's the word I'm looking for?"

"Commits himself."

"Commits himself, brilliant. Menelaus should be there too,

I think. He is stupid but he has some influence with his brother. Can you see that these people are sent for?"

So it was decided. In the gathering darkness of the summer night, by the light of torches guarded from the wind, these several people began to make their way towards Agamemnon's tent; while Calchas prayed for reconciliation and heard only sorrow; while Croton and his acolytes went about the camp with the standard of the Armed God, proclaiming Iphigeneia a witch; while Poimenos sat by a different fire, close to the Singer, listening to the second episode of Perseus and the Gorgon repeated by popular request.

He had missed it in the morning, much to his disappointment, getting back too late from the island. As soon as his master had gone into the meeting, he had hurried across to the outcrop of rock where the Singer was almost always to be found, but by then the morning stories were over, there was only a news item to the effect that Zeus was now believed to be the sender of the wind and that according to informed sources Agamemnon was in some way involved. This evening, however, left to his own devices at an ideal moment, just the time people were gathering to listen, he had been able to get in at the beginning. He had listened spellbound to the story of the bronze giant Talus, guardian of Crete, who was kept alive by a single vein closed at the ankle by a bronze nail. And now he was absorbed in the continuing adventures of Perseus, who was on his way to do battle with the hideous Medusa. In his usual place, just behind the Singer, facing the audience, he was close to the heart of the Songs.

The Singer, unusually, had permitted this closeness from the start. He was glad now that the boy was back. For one thing, he was obviously a good forager, though this time he had brought nothing with him; and such listening as his gave power to the Song, though this one, of course, was a winner anyway. The Singer felt in full command of his material, both form and content, as he related the visit of Athena to Perseus and how she told him of certain weapons he would need for the encounter with the Gorgon. There were those who held that the goddess actually described these weapons and told the hero where they were. There were others who believed that Athena did not possess this information. Both views were equally mistaken. She knew but she did not tell him. Why not? The answer was simple: a hero cannot take shortcuts. All Athena told him was where he could go to find out.

Following her instructions, Perseus made his way to the Libyan mountains. Here, in the depths of a cave, he found the Graeae. These were two hags who had been born with gray hair and had only a single eye and a single tooth between them. Naturally, they quarreled all the time over these. Perseus acted casual, waited for the right moment, then, quick as a flash, he snatched the eye as one of the crones was passing it to the other. They went groping round the cave to get at him with their nails, but he avoided them easily. "Now," he said, "enough of this fooling around. If you want your eye back, you'd better tell me what I want to know, otherwise I'll throw it into Lake Tritonis. Don't think I'm joking. I mean what I say." So they were obliged to tell him where the nymphs were who kept the weapons Athena had spoken of. These were river nymphs, they lived in the waters of the Styx, so Perseus had to make a trip into the Underworld in order to visit them, but they readily gave him the things he asked for.

And what were these? Most people in the audience could have answered this question, but there would have been general outrage at any attempt to take this knowledge for granted and cut the story short. It was familiarity that cast the spell, everything was savored in advance. The Singer knew this well, knew he couldn't take shortcuts any more than Perseus. A pouch to sling over the shoulder; a pair of sandals fitted with wings which enabled him to fly; the cap of darkness which rendered him totally invisible as soon as he put it on his head. Then Hermes appeared and gave him the assault weapon, a sickle made of adamant, razor-edged, unbreakable. He kept his own shield, which was of bronze and highly polished. Fitted out from head to foot, he flew off to find the Gorgons.

There in his privileged position, at the source of the words, Poimenos felt his soul expand with wonder. Often it was the lesser details that absorbed him, filling his mind long after the song was over, things that the Singer did not mention or passed over quickly. Those two gray-haired babies, lying side by side, who had been the guardian of the eye and tooth? What was adamant? Why did Hermes give Perseus a sickle rather than a sword? What was the pouch for?

Now, as the Singer observed the customary dramatic pause, striking slow notes on his lyre, Poimenos observed the angle of the head, the set of the shoulders. Slowly, almost stealthily, he adjusted his own body to an exact imitation. And it was in this posture, carefully maintained, that he listened to the rest of the wonderful story. The lair of the Gorgons was set in a strange forest of petrified forms, men and animals turned to stone by the glances of the terrible sisters. Perseus avoided this fate by keeping his eyes on the polished surface of his shield, which reflected the scene like a mirror. No one had told him to do this, it was his own idea. Wearing the cap of darkness, he soon tracked down the hideous sisterhood, with their hands of brass and wings of gold, their huge lolling tongues between swine's tusks, their heads permanently writhing with snakes. He waited till they were asleep, then crept up on Medusa. The other two were immortal, so he didn't bother with them. He had to move fast. Keeping her in view by means of the shield, he severed her head with a single stroke of the sickle, stuffed it into his pouch and took off. The other two rose up, but how could they pursue an enemy they couldn't see? All they could do was return to the corpse and fly screaming round it.

Poimenos sat on, still in the same posture, while the Singer fell silent and the wind raised its voice again, echoing the lamentation of the Gorgons. His mind was flooded by the story. So that was what the pouch was for. And the sickle, perfect for close quarters, it would almost encircle the neck, one sweep, bam. Everything had been thought of. It hadn't been a contest at all really. She would never have known what hit her. Careful planning, backed up by the most advanced equipment available, a tale of triumph. However, it was not the homeward-speeding hero that engaged the boy's mind, but the two grieving monsters, flapping round the headless corpse and screaming, screaming. The more deadly and ugly they were, the more he felt their sorrow.

And so, that evening, without fully realizing it, Poimenos joined the addicts, passed for the first time into the true, un-governed realm of story, where the imagination is paramount, taking us to places not intended, often not foreseen, by the framers of the words and the makers of the music.

8.

Menelaus was already there when the self-appointed delegation arrived. Nestor, accompanied by his two sons, came in soon afterwards. Agamemnon had left his chair of state and was half reclining on a couch of cushions, an oil lamp with a fretwork guard close beside him on a low stand, as if he wanted to keep near to the source of light. There were no soldiers inside the tent, only two attendants, neither of them armed; a good sign, Odysseus immediately thought: if Agamemnon did not feel in danger of human harm, it must be because he believed himself to be in the hands of Zeus.

The attendant brought cushions and the King motioned his visitors to be seated. There followed a brief period of waiting, the silence of respect, while they listened to the rippling detonations made by the canvas, sounds that would swell and fall as the night wind breathed and paused and breathed again. The flame swayed inside the delicate grid of the guard and bolts of light flickered like lizards over the walls.

Chasimenos began. This had been agreed beforehand; he was the one most trusted. He spoke of the danger of mutiny among the troops, the growing popularity of Palamedes, the Carian, son of Nauplius. "A fellow countryman of Calchas," he said, infusing his tone with significance—it never came amiss to hint at conspiracy. "I have sent people out through the camp. Whatever the fireside, the talk is always the same. Croton's messages are repeated. You are blamed for the wind because of the malpractices of Iphigeneia. They say that if Palamedes were leader, we would be free of the wind."

They had chosen Palamedes from among several possible contenders because he was generally liked, and known to be ambitious. Also he was clever. In the Songs he was credited with having while still a youth invented the game of dice, which had become very popular of late years. Odysseus detested him because of a malicious story he had put about, one which still found its way into the Songs, that the Ithacan had tried to dodge the war by feigning madness, yoking a horse to an ox and attempting to plow with them. For this slander, he had sworn to kill Palamedes one day. For the moment, however, he kept these feelings to himself.

"Palamedes," Agamemnon said. "A slack-wristed fellow if ever I saw one." His insomniac eyes moved slowly from one face to another. "I could split him down the middle," he said. "If the people blame me for this misfortune of the wind, that is only natural, I am the leader, my shoulders are broad enough to bear the blame of a thousand men." He had become enraged as he spoke. He ground his teeth and his eyes flashed. "Who says I have not shoulders broad enough to bear the blame of a thousand men?"

"No one would dare to say that, my brother, not about either of us," Menelaus said. "We were born to command, we are the eagle kings." He was shorter than his brother and inclining to fat and sometimes his words came accompanied by a wheezing sound, as if there were some clogging in his lungs. "Eagle kings," he said, "swooping down on Troy on strong pinions to revenge the rape of my Helen and teach these snotty-nosed Asians a lesson they'll never forget."

"My lord," Chasimenos said, "greatest of men, excuse me, shoulders are not the issue here. Atlas had broad shoulders and look where it got him. It's not so much a question of enduring the blame as atoning for the guilt. You have incurred pollution through Iphigeneia, whereas Palamedes has respected the altars of Zeus. Moreover, his father was one of that band of heroes who sailed with Jason on the *Argo* in the quest for the Golden Fleece. That's the sort of thing that is bound to look impressive on a person's CV." He stopped short at this; but everyone there knew that Atreus, the father of Agamemnon and Menelaus, had a record far from heroic, having murdered the children of his own brother, even though they had taken refuge in the temple of Zeus, and afterwards served them up in a stew to their unsuspecting father.

"His father lived by wrecking ships and taking off the cargoes," Agamemnon said. "Everyone knows that. He and his gang lit beacons on the headlands of Caphareus to lure ships onto the rocks. If they found any sailors still alive, they—"

"Palamedes is free of blame, that's the point." Odysseus spoke brusquely. He saw now that Agamemnon, though fully aware of why they had come, was playing for time, trying to wriggle off the hook by slithering into irrelevancies. Despicable. "He is and you're not," he said. "It's got nothing to do with anybody's father."

"I will have him killed."

"Far from easy. He is well guarded. And then, as we have said, he is popular, the consequences might be dangerous, unpredictable in any case. No, the remedy lies elsewhere, it was pronounced in your hearing not long ago in this very—"

"You can't kill them all."

No one knew for a while who had spoken, where this clear and deliberate voice could have come from. It was as if the wind had suddenly found human language. Then, from the look of dismay on his sons' faces, they realized it was old Nestor, until then silent except for occasional low mutters and chuckling sounds. "When there is division among the people," he continued in the same clear tones, "there will never be any shortage of leaders. You put one out of the way, others come forward. It is analogous to the problem encountered by Heracles when he was trying to kill the monster with the hundred heads. But in this present case the monster is not rival leaders but our own discord, the conflicts that divide us. This began, as we all know, with the ill-considered gift of the golden apple by Paris to the goddess of love."

There were some moments of stunned silence while all regarded the ancient counselor, who now was dribbling a little. His sons wore a look of total consternation, as if their worst fears were being realized. Even Odysseus gulped and swallowed. The old fool had found his voice again—and quite the wrong message. The only one not to seem surprised was Agamemnon, who nodded and said, "Wise words, we thank you for them. What is this story you refer to? Refresh our memories."

"Story?"

"Yes, this apple that—"

"Apple? They tried to stop us, they couldn't stop us, no one could stop us, we were unstoppable, it wasn't a javelin, it was a sword, we got away with a hundred cows . . ."

"There, there, father, shush, shush," the sons said, speaking together in visible relief.

"Agamemnon," Odysseus said, "I won't mince words with you. My kingdom is Ithaca, as you know. You probably haven't been there but I can tell you it's very rocky. I love the place, I wouldn't dream of living anywhere else, but there is no denying that it is rocky. People who grow up there, they come to resemble the rock. A bit on the rigid side perhaps, possibly lacking in finesse, but absolutely incorruptible. You can't corrupt rock, can you? We are people that speak our minds."

He paused here, savoring the moment. The King was suffering, it was in his face. Odysseus had seen that look before, in his courtroom at home, on the faces of convicted malefactors awaiting his sentence while he deliberately delayed. Agamemnon knew he was being played with, but he could do nothing, he was helpless. Seeing the King's stricken face, Odysseus felt pleasure gather in his mouth, so that his next words came more thickly. "We do not make pretty speeches or go in for poetic figures or false comparisons. The leaves of the trees change color and fall, the flowers of spring deceive us with their promise and sadden us when they wither and die, but the face of the rock endures forever." He paused briefly to swallow down the excess saliva. "I am the king of these people, I *am* Ithaca, I am rock personified. So do not expect anything from me but plain speaking and the blunt truth." Slow down, he told himself, take care, you're enjoying this too much.

He had a mannerism, a way of inclining his heavily muscled shoulders forward as he spoke, as though putting his physical weight behind the point he was making, then drawing his head back sharply to look his interlocutor in the eye, with a great effect of openness and sincerity. Chasimenos's style was quite different; pale-faced and peering, still in his narrow-fitting tunic of a palace bureaucrat, he was continuously shifting his behind on the cushion and shuffling his feet, as if the honesty of his thoughts and words were making things too hot for comfort. Together these two, while still remaining seated, performed a sort of dance before the reclining Agamemnon, a pattern of movements that seemed to keep time with the flapping of the canvas, the wavering shadows cast on the wall behind them by the thin bars of the lamp guard.

"If it hurts you, I can't help it, that's the way I'm made," Odysseus said. "This concerns your daughter, as you know."

Chasimenos gave him a straight look. "No one will harm my king while I am standing on my own two feet and able to prevent it."

"My faithful Chasimenos, you will be rewarded," Agamemnon said, and the words came with just the hint of a sob.

"I ask for no reward but to be there by your side at the conquest of Troy, making a detailed inventory of the booty that falls to Mycenae."

"This is all very well," Odysseus said, "but it isn't getting us anywhere. It certainly isn't getting us any nearer to Troy. Agamemnon, you heard the words of the priest of Zeus. We all did. Those words are all over the camp, on everybody's lips.

Croton is widely respected for his upright character and he is known to have the favor of the god."

"He was contradicted by Calchas."

Chasimenos squirmed on his cushion."My lord king, what is Calchas? He is a foreigner, an outsider, priest of a god unknown to the Greeks. He has no loyalty to our great cause, he has no idea of patriotism or honor or—"

"Worst of all, he is effeminate," Menelaus said. "I noticed that from the start."

"The facts are not in dispute," Odysseus said. "Croton has firsthand testimony, eyewitness accounts. Iphigeneia exalts the mother over the father, she dances with her attendants at the time of full moon, she denies that Artemis is the daughter of Zeus, or any younger than he, she pours libations of milk. In short, she has been possessed by Hecate and has become a witch."

Chasimenos practiced his straight look again. "Odysseus, take care, a little respect, you are talking about a princess of the royal house of Mycenae, you are talking about a daughter of great Agamemnon."

"Faithful servant, I will give you five measures of lapis lazuli. Write it down somewhere."

"I am talking about what the army believes, rightly or wrongly. That's the only thing that matters. The army has accepted this as the explanation for the wind. If you don't do something about it, or promise to do something about it, the command of this great enterprise will slip from your grasp."

"The promise would be enough," Chasimenos said softly. "A significant future event. Something dear to your heart, offered up for the common good."

Odysseus gathered himself. The moment had come.

Agamemnon knew, it was written on his face, but the words still needed to be said. "It is not only Croton now. Why should I be the one to bring your anger down upon us only because I am honest and speak as a friend?"

A brief silence followed upon this. The wind had dropped for the moment to little more than a harsh sigh, the sound that a man might make with open mouth in relief from pain, or endurance of it; and this quietness seemed strange, and was remembered, coming at such a moment.

The King rose and his shadow loomed on the canvas behind him, blotting into one dark shape the wavering shadows cast by the lamp guard. Then he moved to his chair and seated himself and raised a haggard face. "Let me hear," he said.

He had addressed Odysseus, but it was Chasimenos who spoke now, shuffling forward and coming to his knees before the seated figure of his master. He said, "O King, I would give my life for you at any time it was required." A lump came to his throat at the trueness of this. "Take my life now if you need it, kill me as I kneel here. I have only your good at heart. The conquest of Troy will give Mycenae, as the most powerful member of the alliance, rule over the shores of western Asia and all the Green Water. It will secure for us the trade in amber from the Baltic, in copper and tin from northern Anatolia and in the gold that comes down through Thrace. Control of the straits will fall into our hands, we will be able to levy dues on all the shipping that passes through into the Euxine Sea."

He kept his eyes to the ground as he spoke, not venturing to look up. He felt the presence of anguish above him, near and far, in the King and beyond the King, an anguish that rose into the night sky, where the wind had again become clamorous. "Iphigeneia must be sent for," he said. "She must be brought here. You must announce your intention to have her sacrificed on the altar of Zeus before the assembled army. Only in this way can the expedition be saved."

The voice of Odysseus came from behind him. "An immediate announcement is necessary. They will believe it. Instead of waiting for an end to the wind, which is maddeningly uncertain, they will be waiting for the arrival of Iphigeneia, a definite event. It will do wonders for their morale."

Raising his eyes at last, Chasimenos could discern no particular change of expression in his master's face. "It will save us," he said. He got up awkwardly from his kneeling position and bowed and went back to his cushion.

"Why not Menelaus?" the King said. "He has a daughter. It was his wife that was seduced. It was for his sake that I embarked on this expedition, not my own, to redeem the honor of the house of Atreus, to show the people of Troy and the whole world that when a blow is struck against us we will strike back with double force. We have the men, we have the ships, we have the gold. We did not seek this war, but by all the gods . . ." He broke off and a sound like a groan came from him. "Menelaus has a daughter," he said again.

"I must say, brother, I did not expect this from you," Menelaus said. "Haven't I got trouble enough? Must I remind you that my Helen is currently in a Trojan dungeon, being violated on an hourly basis? And I've told you before, she wasn't seduced, she was kidnapped."

A terrible sneer distorted Agamemnon's face. "Paris bound and gagged her, did he?"

Chasimenos said, "Menelaus has a daughter, Lord King, but in the first place he is not the Supreme Commander, and so, secondly, he does not bear the responsibility. Thirdly,

Hermione is only nine years old and so a bit on the young side. Fourthly, she is not a priestess of Artemis, and so, fifthly, she has not incurred the wrath of Zeus."

"Bravo, Chasimenos, well said." Odysseus gazed admiringly at his fellow advocate. "You are always very good on the detail." It was all going much better than could have been expected. Agamemnon was making speeches already, easing his soul with rhetoric, a very good sign. The more speeches the better. Words were what was needed now, words and more words. Words would take the life of Iphigeneia before ever she set out from Mycenae, long before the knife touched her throat; and the words that would kill the daughter, the same words, would swaddle the father, make a warm wrapping for him. He said, "Whether Helen went willingly or not, it is the same just cause that inspires our arms, the same concern for honor and justice that has brought this great army together, united in the sense of what it means to be Greek, yes, Greek. Our ancestors came from the north under the guidance of Zeus to occupy this land. A common origin, a common language, that is what makes a nation. But this nation does not yet know itself, it turns upon itself in division and strife. This is a nation waiting to be born, and Zeus has chosen you to be the one to give it birth. On the plains of Troy we shall fight under one banner. But before that, before we set out from here, we shall be a united force, confident in your leadership, your care for the common good, because you will have given us full proof of it at the altar of Zeus."

"It is a high destiny," Chasimenos said, "and a heavy burden, but my king is fitted for it, he carries the burden for us all."

"Burden, there you go, brilliant. The heavy burden of command." Odysseus felt again that gathering of saliva, threatening to obscure his speech. "The knowledge that others depend on us, the sense of obligation that comes with high office, what's the word I'm looking for?"

"Responsibility."

"Responsibility, absolutely brilliant. That is the heavy weight that those who are born to high command have to suffer, have to endure."

"Yes, yes, to endure," the King said, speaking so low that the others could hardly hear him. "Responsibility, the burden of command, yes."

"And you are responsible several times over, which makes the burden even heavier," Odysseus said.

Agamemnon's head had slumped forward and down, as if under a physical weight. He raised it now to give Odysseus a look in which ferocity mingled with bewilderment. "How is that?"

"Chasimenos will explain, he is always very good on the detail."

"Pardon me, Lord King, but you are firstly responsible for Iphigeneia's offense, and secondly responsible for accepting the responsibility for the conduct of the war when you were already responsible for the aforesaid offense, thereby becoming, thirdly, responsible for the wrath of Zeus, and following upon this, fourthly, for this hostile wind which is destroying the morale of the army."

"More responsible than that, it is hard to see how any mortal man could be," Odysseus said. "Think of the consequences of refusing. You could not serve under another leader, it's probably too late for that anyway. The army would break up, the expedition would be abandoned, you would return to Mycenae with all credibility gone for good, together with the chance to get your hands on all that Trojan gold. As the strongest power, Mycenae would be entitled to the biggest cut. Think of it, the lion's share passing through the Lion Gate. Think of the people who have gathered here, who have put their faith in you. From the Pindus and Pelion they have come, from Aetolia and Locris, from Achaea and Arcadia, from the islands of the Aegean to the shores of Messenia, from the Saronic Gulf to the farthest headlands of the Peloponnese, from the wheatlands of Thessaly to the rugged slopes of Epirus. Greeks, yes, Greeks, our fellow countrymen."

"Odysseus, do you really think my king is going to let these faithful people down?" demanded Chasimenos.

"By the gods, no." Agamemnon raised his head again and glared about him. "I will not betray that trust. I have a sacred duty. This is a nation waiting to be born, I am the one chosen by Zeus to bring it forth into the light."

Thinking the issue decided, Chasimenos sank to his knees once more and lowered his head. "What god-given wisdom my lord speaks," he said.

However, from above there came a deep groan and from behind the sudden voice of Nestor, whom the groan must have startled. "Is Agamemnon in pain? All this sitting around is bad for the digestion, we should organize a boar hunt, I remember one boar hunt I went on, in Laconia, a huge boar, it stood higher than a man, it had already killed half a dozen dogs, I remember it had the giblets of one of them hanging from its right tusk, no, it was the left, no, wait a minute . . ."

Chasimenos remained kneeling while the aged counselor was shushed into silence by his sons. Then Agamemnon groaned again, less loudly. "She is only fourteen," he said. "She was always my favorite. And in public too. If it were in private, for some stain on my honor, in that case, yes, tragedies like that can occur in the best of families. But to have her lifted up in the gown of the victim, through which her limbs can be seen, to make a public display of her before the dregs of humanity we have got here, this bare-arsed scum from Locris and Aetolia, this beastly rabble from Boeotia and Attica, these rapists and butter-eaters from Epirus, these turds from Thessaly who come to take part in a military expedition armed only with hay-forks, is it for this I raised her?"

"These Thessalians are degenerate, into the bargain," Menelaus said. "They fuck their own goats, it's a habit they have picked up from the Asians."

Chasimenos got slowly to his feet again. He was visited by a sense of discouragement. He was getting old, his joints felt stiff. "This is your raw material," he said. "This is the clay that awaits the potter's hand. It is in the nature of raw material to be, initially at least, raw. That is the challenge."

"Challenge, that's it, you have hit the nail on the head there, Chasimenos." Odysseus was scenting victory now. A little fellow feeling, a suggestion of intolerable shame . . . "Think of it this way," he said. "For you as a father there is a certain point of view, no one would deny it. But a father is only one individual. As Commander-in-Chief you are responsible for a thousand individuals. What about the massive collective pain that would follow from the collapse of this expedition, the frustration of all our hopes? Have you the right to be so selfish? I know you are a family man, with a belief in traditional values. I am like that myself, but there are times when we need to be

alive to changing circumstances, responsive to the require-
ments of the moment, ready to yield a little so as to achieve our
goals, what's the word I'm looking for?"

"Adaptable."

"Adaptable, brilliant, there are times when we need to be
adaptable. Do you want to go down to posterity as a man who
was so hidebound that he passed up on his patriotic duty and
neglected the opportunity to forge a nation? I can just see what
the Singer will make of it, I can hear those verses rolling out
through generation after generation. Once things get into the
Song you will never entirely succeed in getting them out again.
Think of the shame. I wouldn't care for it myself, that's all I can
say."

"What will they sing about me?"

"They will sing that you lacked resolution, honesty,
courage, patriotism, ambition."

"Lord Agamemnon has never lacked ambition," Chasimenos
said, practicing his straight look again.

"No, I mean what will they sing about me if I . . . accept
this heavy burden?"

"They will sing that here was a hero who was ready to
shoulder his responsibilities, ready to set his private feelings
aside for the sake of his country. They will call him the con-
queror of Troy, they will call him the founder of Greater
Mycenae. They will celebrate his return from the war,
Agamemnon, Sacker of Cities, loaded with slaves and plunder,
a five-star general, clasped in the welcoming arms of his queen,
Clytemnestra." He paused for a moment and there was no
sound but the fretting of the wind and the distant howling of
wolves. "We know what you are going through," he said. "Our

hearts are with you. But what choice has a man when the gods have singled him out for greatness?"

It was the *coup de grâce*, he knew it as he spoke, the timing was perfect. Agamemnon's eyes filled with tears. "It is true," he said. "We who are destined for greatness must bear the burden for all. It is a heavy thing that is laid upon me. My own child, who I dandled on my knee, whose first steps I witnessed, who sang to honor me at the banquet table, among the guests, before the third cup was offered to the god. She always had a good singing voice. But I must go forward in spite of the pain, I must shoulder my responsibilities. The army depends on me. Chasimenos, I make you responsible for conveying my decision to the Singer. Make sure he understands the nature of this sacrifice. Promise him a fur-lined cloak for the winter. Singers work best on promises."

The intense relief at having won the King over, coming as it did after feelings of discouragement, caused Chasimenos to lose track of things for a moment. "The nature of it? No need for him to sing of that, the men will be familiar with the nature of it, they will have seen it before, not with a royal princess, I grant you, but the procedure doesn't vary much. The victim undergoes ritual purification, the hair is cut short so as not to—"

"No, you fool, I was speaking of the sacrifice of a father for the sake of the army, for the sake of the war, so that Zeus will lift this curse of a wind from us. You can forget about that lapis lazuli."

Chasimenos recovered himself and bowed low. "Pardon me, Lord King. I will go at once and give him a full account of it, making sure that your noble motives are present to his mind.

He will be somewhere out there." He made a gesture towards the night outside the tent. "He never seems to sleep," he said.

Odysseus hesitated a moment; but there was nothing more to say now; Agamemnon must be left for the night to the voice of Zeus, which would come to him on the wind, and to the knowledge that the Singer's voice would soon—and irrevocably—follow. "I'll go with you," he said to Chasimenos. "We must make sure no detail is overlooked that could add to Agamemnon's glory and his reputation for statesmanship."

AT

Mycenae

1.

The morning of the day the delegation arrived from Aulis was remembered by Sisipyla as being her last happy one at Mycenae. It was the day before the full moon and for a part of the morning she was alone with Iphigeneia, just the two of them together.

They had gone to the foothills below the citadel, as they did every month at this time, to hang the effigies in the grove of plane trees sacred to Artemis, leaving the women attendants and the guards of the escort and the grooms below, ascending the last part of the way alone, on foot, carrying the straw figures.

She had loved the place, though never the grove, ever since first seeing it years before. They had come here as children sometimes, in the care of Iphigeneia's nurse, before the princess had assumed the duties of priestess. It was a fold among the hills with a narrow stream that sprang from the rocks high above and fell through a steep ravine in a series of cascades. You could see the course of it as you approached. At first the water was a mist, a soft dazzle in the morning sun, then it gleamed and shivered, half concealed among foliage, then it was sheer and smooth like silk or oiled hair when it is combed out. This last was a sort of beautiful swelling of the water, as it seemed to Sisipyla, a mood of the goddess whose place this was, who had many moods, who was present in the voice of the water and the dazzle of the mist and the shine on the rock face where the water skimmed and the seething where it met with obstacles. She was still there when you saw no water, only movement. Like a breath, like a snake.

She had said nothing to Iphigeneia about this feeling of hers, this sense of the goddess's presence in the light and the water and the stirring of the leaves, being afraid that her mistress would not share the feeling or even approve much of it, that she might think it sloppy—a term she used often and for a variety of things. She thought it more than likely that for Iphigeneia the goddess was only to be found in definite places, before her altars, in her shrines, in this grove of plane trees. The princess knew far more than she did and was more firm-minded; she knew a great many facts and could put her ideas into words without hesitating, and find answers to remarks that were made to her on difficult subjects, things beyond the range of a slave girl from Lydia, who knew only how to attend on her mistress.

The sacred grove oppressed her and she was ashamed of this feeling but unable to overcome it. Near the foot of the falls where the water broadened into a pool among the rocks, the tall trees grew in a straggling circle round an inner group of

four, marking the quarters of the moon, where the effigies of
the Divine Child, Hyacinthos, nursling of Artemis, were hung
at the time of the full moon. The children of past moons were
never taken down and the trees were cluttered and lumpy with
forms of straw. Birds had raided these to build their nests, and
time and weather had taken much of the human likeness from
them. Much, but not quite all; and this it was that disturbed
Sisipyla and made her always glad to quit the place, the likeness still in the dangling, ruinous dolls. She struggled with the
thought that she might somehow be left to hang among them.
In the end they slipped through their traces and fell, leaving
tassels of rope on the branches, covering the ground at the base
of the trees with a whispering quilt.

First Iphigeneia, then Sisipyla hung up the offerings by
their rope loops. Then Iphigeneia raised her arms and cried out
the invocation to the goddess, praying for favor, vowing the
next day's sacrifice of a goat in her honor. And it seemed to
Sisipyla, standing as usual a little to the left and two paces behind, that there came an answer to this high, clear voice, a stirring in the foliage of the planes, among the leaves that had
always seemed to her like the fingers of a hand held out in
warning.

The sun was hot when they emerged and she felt the usual
relief at being out in the open. Released by the performance of
her duty, which she took with utmost seriousness, Iphigeneia
smiled for the first time since they had left the others below.
"We could bathe," she said, and Sisipyla inclined her head in a
gesture that was both agreement and submission. The bathing
was an established practice between them in the summer
months, begun years before when they were hardly more than

children; but the suggestion had always to come from Iphigeneia, had always to seem a motion of her will for the one occasion only.

On the side nearer to them the eddies of the water had made a shore of smooth pebble. Here, as always, they laid their ceremonial dresses, garments the same in every respect, identical in size, woven in the same undyed linen. This day of the effigies was the only time they dressed in the same way. Below the dresses they wore nothing but underskirts of the same material, quickly stepped out of.

Naked they stepped together into the water and flickering shoals of the minnows that lived in the warm edges fled at their approach. The pool was shallow and the sun had taken the chill from the water but it was cold still, they gasped and laughed as they waded deeper. Sisipyla waited till her mistress crouched and immersed herself before following suit; she was trained to attend, never to initiate. Neither of the girls could swim; they fought the cold by jumping up and down, striking at the water with flat hands, splashing their own faces, sending up bright arcs of drops across the surface all around. They laughed together, seeing each other's wet faces through this glittering spray of their own making. Then came some moments of quiet, a pause for breath. The water was still and Sisipyla was aware again of the sameness of their faces and bodies; the same dark hair and eyes and the same deep brows, the same straight shoulders and sharp breasts and long, slender thighs. It was herself she was looking at, and yet a being utterly distinct from her and beyond her. With characteristic abruptness Iphigeneia turned towards the shore. At the last moment, before moving to follow, Sisipyla saw her own reflection lying on the surface of the water where it ran shallow over a bed of dark rock; and it was as though their two bodies had fused into this single perfect image, shivered at once into fragments as she moved forward.

Afterwards they lay for a short while on the warm pebbles,
waiting for the sun to dry them. Sisipyla felt the heat gather
and dwell on her eyelids and breasts and abdomen. She
thought in a drowsy way of her next day's duties, the preparations for the sacrifice. She would be bearing the basket and the
knife. She would have to make sure the musicians were assembled beforehand, that the goat was properly decked out . . .

Her eyes were still closed, but she heard Iphigeneia shift on
the pebbles nearby and then get to her feet. She waited a moment or two longer, allowing time for her mistress to take the
first steps. Then she rose and followed. They dressed quickly,
not speaking. But when they were ready, when Sisipyla had
brushed out the princess's damp hair and clasped it at the nape
with an ivory comb, when she had restored some sort of order
to her own hair, they still lingered a while longer at the edge of
the pool; and once again Sisipyla's mind became crowded with
the signs of the goddess's presence, signs hidden and revealed,
in the water when it was still and when it was flowing, in the
loitering flight of dragonflies over the surface. Her eyes felt
pressed upon, besieged by detail. It was like trying to see the
pattern in the wall hangings and the woven rugs that covered
the floors of the royal rooms in the palace, the flowers and the
leaves and the birds, trying to take it all in at the same time, at
one single moment . . .

"What a long way you can see today." Iphigeneia's voice
came from above. Unnoticed by Sisipyla, she had moved onto
the track above the pool. Sisipyla went up to join her and they
stood together looking across the broad valley towards the flat-

lands of the south and the distant girdle of mountains. In this pellucid light perspectives were canceled, the mountains seemed depthless, as if they stood on a single plane.

"That's the river Cephinthos we are looking at," Iphigeneia said. "It flows into the Gulf of Argos. I've told you that before, haven't I? Do you remember?"

"Yes."

Iphigeneia shook her head. "You never remember the things I tell you. It goes in at one ear and out at the other. You should repeat things to yourself, over and over until you have got them fixed in your mind, that's what I do."

"You said it is where the sea begins."

"Good, so you do remember. It flows into the sea just below Tiryns. If you set out from there in a ship you would get to Asia." Her face wore its teacher's look. From their childhood days she had enjoyed instructing her slave-companion, passing on stories, snippets of information, sometimes in garbled form, things she had had from her own teachers. It was she who had taught Sisipyla her first songs, her first words of Greek. "It is good that you remembered," she said gravely.

Sisipyla felt happy to be commended, but she knew that the sea did not begin at any one definite place, though it might seem so to Iphigeneia because she had never seen the sea. But Sisipyla had seen it, at the age of seven she had been brought with her mother and a shipload of other slaves from Miletus to the port of Tiryns, which she knew that her mistress had not seen either. She remembered the exposure, the terrible openness of the sea, after the narrow wooded valleys of home. They had passed through scattered islands and she had seen how these were nothing compared to the sea, which stretched all around them and was still there when they had vanished from sight. It was as if the sea had swallowed them up.

The memory had remained vivid, kept fresh by the misery of her condition then, and the fear on the face of her mother. It was not possible to speak of it to Iphigeneia, to seem to know more than her mistress about the sea or anything else; but she had guarded it as something of her own. That fear, that lack of shelter, was a kind of possession, and she had very few. Not that much guarding had been needed: Iphigeneia had never shown any curiosity about her previous life. A barbarian child, chosen for her prettiness, she had been a gift for the princess's sixth birthday. A gift has no history, its life begins with the first glance, the first touch of the one to whom it is given.

This talk of the sea, in conjunction with the immense sweep of land that stretched before them, brought back, quite suddenly and unexpectedly, the lonely anguish of those days. She wanted to retreat from this great gulf of space, to go back to the play of water and light, the loitering dragonflies, the shape of pebbles, the shelter of detail. But she could not move until Iphigeneia moved. "It's like the sea," she said, gesturing before her, the words coming almost before she was aware of uttering them. "You could fall into it and drown."

"Like the sea? What in the world do you mean by that? You say the strangest things, Sisipyla. It doesn't look in the least like the sea, there is nothing watery about it. People are living and working down there, they have huts, they have families. I mean, it's not even the right color, is it? You really should try to be more focused."

"Yes, I will try." She had again been guilty of sloppiness. However, it did not seem to her that Iphigeneia herself was always so very focused, not as Sisipyla understood the word. Her eyes looked often as they looked now, clear and unfaltering but somehow enthralled, as if she had been sustaining a light too strong. Our eyes are different, Sisipyla thought, they are set a little differently, mine are more on a slant, but the real difference is in the way of looking. I can only look at single things, one leaf, one shape of stars.

While she was still in the midst of this thought, Iphigeneia raised an arm and held it out, fingers extended, saluting, as it seemed, the whole shape of things, the river valley, the wide plain, the distant tawny mountains. She made a slow, sweeping gesture, as if unveiling a monument or drawing aside a curtain. "All this is Mycenae," she said. "As far as you can see on every side, beyond what you can see. They told me that on the day we first came here, to make me understand the greatness of my father's power. We were standing just here. You were here too, do you remember?"

Sisipyla had no smallest recollection of this. She would not have understood it in any case, having no knowledge of Greek at the time, a fact that Iphigeneia was overlooking. "Yes," she said, "I remember. Princess, will you let me shade your face against the sun?"

The suggestion was met by silence, a mark of consent. She took the short veil from the basket and arranged it over the head and around the face. It was white silk lace, embroidered with a pattern of saffron-colored butterflies, fine Cretan work, a gift from her mother, Clytemnestra. When she had made sure that the veil was falling properly, she put on her own cotton scarf, tying it round the head in the manner prescribed for palace domestics, so that the ends hung down at the sides of her face.

As they turned to descend the path, she caught a last glimpse of the river in its furthest reach to the north, where it flashed in the sun as it came down through the high pass. Sometimes she forgot the names of places that Iphigeneia told her, not seeing reason to remember them so long as they were only names. A river or a mountain was as real to her without a name, perhaps more so. But she remembered stories; she knew that Nemea lay beyond the pass, because it was there that the hero Heracles had slain the lion and taken its skin.

They began to descend the narrow track, Iphigeneia in front. As Sisipyla followed, watching her own feet in their sandals going one before the other, she thought about the terrible lion, and its even more terrible mother Echidna, daughter of Ge and Tartarus, half nymph, half speckled snake, who had lived in a cave in Arcadia, from which she rushed hissing out to seize and devour passersby. She would hear the scrape of a footfall, a faint scrunch on the loose stones of the path—a path like this one, sounds like those they were making—and she would gather herself into a coil in the darkness of her cave and wait for the moment to come rushing out. The passerby would draw near, thinking his thoughts, suspecting nothing . . . However, it was not the attack itself that was so frightening to Sisipyla, it was the thought of the ravenous creature, coiled in the dark cave, listening. And then there was the monstrous brood Echidna had produced. It wasn't only the lion. All her offspring were the stuff of nightmare, without one single exception, the fire-breathing Chimaera, the Hydra that could sprout its own heads, the monstrous hound Cerberus, watchdog of the Underworld, who licked the hands of those entering and ate those trying to leave.

Of course it was comforting to think that neither the lion

nor his mother were in the world any longer, the first having been killed by Heracles, the second by Argus the All-seeing, who had crept into the cave when she was gorged with feasting and severed her head at a stroke. Argus possessed four eyes and was therefore well able to find his way about in the dark. But the comfort to be found in this was only partial, because the stories always came later than the events. Echidna had made her home in the cave and started devouring people long before these things came to be related. There might be a monster anywhere, just installed, just at the beginning of its career, before any stories were going about. There might be one somewhere nearby. Sisipyla raised her face to the hot sky. That would be worse than ever, if it was too soon for a story or if you hadn't heard the story yet. If you knew the story, at least you could avoid the place . . .

The path broadened as they descended, following the curve of the hillside. Where it met the road that led up from the valley to the citadel, the people were waiting in the thin shade of wild olive trees. The two girls mounted their stocky, short-legged black horses, sitting sideways in the wooden saddles. They rode ahead, followed by the mounted guards, the women making up the rear in a four-wheeled cart drawn by two mules. The road was good, cut deep and level and laid with stone cobbles squared off and fitted together. It had been built by Agamemnon's father, Atreus, a notable builder of roads—the great trade route to Mycenae from the north had been built in his day. These were things that Sisipyla had learned from her mistress.

Now, quite suddenly, as the road continued to follow the flank of the hill, they came within sight of the citadel above them, with its inward-curving, horn-shaped peaks on either side, rising above the valley. She had seen it thus often enough before; but at the sight, even with mind prepared, she experienced always the same involuntary intake of the breath, as at some pause of life within her. She had first seen it soon after being taken from her mother, sitting in a cart like the one that was following behind them now, on her way to becoming a birthday gift for Iphigeneia, though she had not known at the time that this was intended. Her mother had been put to work in one of the royal textile factories at Lacinthos, three days' journey away. Sisipyla had not been able at first to make that journey, and later, when she might have had permission, she had lost the desire. She had become a new person with a new language and a new home. She belonged in the palace, where she was sheltered and fed, where she had the love and protection of her mistress. She had no idea where her mother was now, whether she was in the same place, whether she was still alive.

These things did not come so much to her mind now; but there was still this clutch of memory when she looked up at the citadel. Something of dread too: the peaks were like the horns of a bull, so it was commonly said, the animal favored by Zeus, signifying male strength and fertilizing power; but to Sisipyla Mycenae seen from below had always looked like a gigantic spider, with the peaks for its legs, extended on the web of the sky.

They passed below the massive bastion on the left and approached the narrow entrance to the Lion Gate under the gaze of the two rampant stone beasts above the lintel, a gaze as unfriendly as that of any lion could possibly be, Sisipyla thought. This morning the sun, by now well clear of the peaks, caught the bronze lumps of their eyes and made them glitter fiercely.

The party waited while the wooden gates were opened

from within, then rode through onto the long stone ramp, passing the storehouses built against the wall and drawing level with the ancestors' grave circle. From just beyond here the road to the palace rose steeply. Iphigeneia dismissed the guards and the women got down from the cart and began to disperse on foot.

At this moment, when Iphigeneia, with Sisipyla behind her, was about to turn her horse onto the road upward, the entrance gate was again opened and a light chariot with two men in it, followed by a small party of mounted men and panting dogs, passed onto the ramp and advanced towards them. The man driving the chariot was Macris, an officer of the garrison and a kinsman of Iphigeneia, some six years older. He jumped lightly down from the still-moving vehicle when he saw them, throwing the reins to his companion and ordering the men behind to ride on to the stables below the palace. He bowed as he drew near, rather hastily, and greeted the princess with an impetuosity of tone clearly habitual to him. "Nothing but a couple of hares," he said. "The ground is so well hunted round about, you have to travel half a day to get anything." He checked at this and smiled and bowed again, very slightly. "Excuse me, princess," he said, "I blurt out news of my doings before it is asked for, one of several habits I am trying to get rid of."

"Well," Iphigeneia said, "if the others are no worse than that . . . I suppose it exercises the horses."

The young man's smile broadened. "Certainly it does that," he said. "Us too."

He was tall; even standing thus he was not much below eye level with the two girls on their small horses. It was immediately clear to the jealous eye of Sisipyla, to whom he paid small attention, that despite his smile and his casual words, this unexpected morning encounter, outside the usual round of the palace, had thrown him into some confusion. He bore himself with the confidence of the privileged class to which he belonged; but his face expressed his feelings more than perhaps he knew, a face rather broad at the temples for a Greek, deeply tanned, with prominent cheekbones and brown eyes generally careless in their regard, but not so now, Sisipyla noted—there was no mistaking the admiration in them. Neither he nor the princess had eyes for her, she was at leisure to take him in, and she was compelled to admit that he made a handsome figure as he stood there, with his tallness and ardent looks, his hair the color of dark straw, his legs shapely and strong without heaviness below the short kilt, the breast of his sleeveless tunic stitched in gold thread with his clan sign of the dolphin. The princess's feelings were less easy to read. Her gaze was always open and direct, not easily deflected; but now she glanced away, as if unwilling to return such close looks.

"You will have been to deck the trees," he said, in the tone of one who has glimpsed an important truth. And this at last made Iphigeneia smile. Her smiles came rarely, but they were captivating when they came, warming her face with joy. "That was not such a difficult deduction, cousin," she said, "seeing the day it is and the robes we are wearing." The smile faded and her face returned to its usual expression of serene gravity. "Is there news from Aulis?"

Macris shook his head. "Nobody knows anything. My father says they have made a chain of beacons, and the last one will be visible across the water at Megara. They have people waiting there to ride down with the news that the wind has changed and the ships have set sail."

His father was in command of the garrison left behind at

Mycenae and a second cousin of Agamemnon. Both the father and now the son—since his recent twentieth birthday—belonged to the Followers, an officer corps of charioteers who alone had the privilege of riding into battle, the bulk of the army always fighting on foot. When the Mycenaean force had set out for Troy he had been away in the Cyclades with an uncle, trading for obsidian. Since returning he had spent his time checking the guard posts overlooking the approaches from the north, making sure the sally ports and posterns in the walls were properly maintained, badgering his father for permission to join the expedition and—increasingly—thinking about Iphigeneia. Aware now that he should be moving aside to let the princess pass, he cast round in his mind for a topic that might delay this a little. But he had not much play of mind when it came to topics. All he could hit on was his own situation. "My father still hesitates to give me leave to join the army," he said. "Though I hope to weary him out in the end."

It was Sisipyla's suspicion, which naturally she kept to herself, that the young man had not been quite so persistent of late in these attempts to persuade his father. She was beginning to wonder how long they were to be detained here. Macris was standing in the middle of the road, they could not proceed until he moved—which at present he showed no sign of doing.

"Well, you are the only son," Iphigeneia said, "and some must stay, we cannot be left undefended. But of course you must be sorry to be left behind here, when your friends have gone. Then there is the fame for those who do well in the fighting and have a good war, and all the spoils when Troy is taken." Her eyes shone, saying this. The just cause of the war, the avenging of the insult to her uncle Menelaus, the heroism that she was sure would be displayed on the field of battle, the wealth and prestige that victory would bring to Mycenae and her father and the whole family, herself of course included, all this made a single shining shape in her mind.

Macris looked at the glowing face a little above him, framed by the folds of the veil. It entered his mind to say a very bold and felicitous thing, that he wouldn't change places with anyone, that Troy was all very well, but those there didn't have the prospect of seeing Iphigeneia every day. But these were things too large for him to say; moreover they did not correspond to the truth of his situation. Without making a name for himself, he hadn't a chance; and he would never make a name for himself as an officer of the garrison at Mycenae, however well he performed his duties. Iphigeneia was said to be her father's favorite, he would be seeking a brilliant match for her. Macris was ambitious and well aware of his personal advantages, but his own father had no great name and the family was not rich. With all this in mind, he said nothing, simply gazed mutely and intently.

"Then there are the ancestors." Glancing away again from this sustained regard, Iphigeneia's eyes had lighted on the ring of upright stones marking the grave circle where the rulers of Mycenae lay entombed in their narrow shafts, the kings and their consorts, with their rings and weapons and gold face masks and favorite hunting dogs. "They will be honored in the war," she said.

"Indeed, yes." Not able to frame his lips to praise the daughter, Macris felt all the more eager to speak well of the father. "It was a noble work on Agamemnon's part to bring the sacred site within the walls. He has a true sense of his duties to his ancestors and to the House of Atreus."

It had been one of the last public works the King had engaged in before mustering his forces for Troy. The grave circle, which had always lain outside the citadel, had now been brought within it by the building of new walls and a new supporting terrace. The graves had been refurbished, the seals renewed and stones erected to mark the circle.

"You hardly noticed the graves before," Macris said, "when they were outside the walls. A stranger could pass by without even knowing they were there at all. Now you can't miss them. People come to make votive offerings and pour libations. All honor to your father, he has performed a great patriotic duty, he has shown that he understands what is due to his family."

These words were pleasing to Iphigeneia, for her father's sake and because she recognized the intention behind them. But she was watchful of her dignity, and the pleasure came mixed with the immediate decision neither to show it nor protract it. She smiled slightly and inclined her head a little and edged her mount forward, finally obliging the young man to give ground.

Sisipyla was preparing to follow when the gate behind them was again opened and a single rider came through, reining in a horse lathered with sweat. Seeing the princess, he instantly dismounted and went down on bended knee. But when he rose again it was to Macris that he spoke. He had ridden from the lookout post on the far side of the Arachneus Mountain. They had seen a party of riders approaching in the distance, from the north, on the more easterly road that came down through Tenea. Not a large party, perhaps twenty-five. They had still been too far away, when he had left the post, to see what colors they were carrying, or whether they were carrying any. He had thought it better to come at once, at first sight of them.

"Yes, you did well," Macris said. "You had better look to

the horse—you have ridden him hard. I will see that the message is conveyed."

His look and bearing had changed with the news. The times were dangerous, the garrison was understrength; until these newcomers were identified it was as well to take no chances; it was a small force, but there might be a larger one behind. He took leave of Iphigeneia, mounted the chariot once more and turned the horses onto the road leading up to the palace.

Iphigeneia and Sisipyla followed more slowly. They saw Macris turn off towards the staircase on the south side of the palace. They themselves took the broader road to the main entrance higher up. Here, in the small cobbled courtyard that lay immediately below the massive supporting wall of the terrace, they left their horses to the groom and made their way directly to the Great Court and from there to the royal apartments, taking the staircase that led up to the women's quarters. Because Sisipyla was accompanying her mistress, it was permitted to her to go by this shorter route. On her own, she would have been obliged to take a more roundabout way to the same point, through a maze of narrow passages and short flights of stairs. Her room was within calling distance of the princess's apartments, separated only by a narrow vestibule; but the routes it was possible to take were rigidly prescribed in accordance with rank. Sisipyla could spend as much time as her mistress wished attending her in the royal apartments, but on her own she could not approach the apartments by the main southward passage that led to the vestibule. It was in this vestibule now that, having made sure her services were for the time being not needed, she took her leave of Iphigeneia.

2.

Her room was small. The pallet on which she slept and the chest in which she kept her clothes took up most of the space. High in one wall there was a square aperture which let in light and air from an open courtyard beyond. A narrow, curtained opening gave access to the vestibule and the adjoining bedroom and dressing room that constituted Iphigeneia's apartments.

She took off her robe, folded it carefully and laid it in the chest. Then she put on the clothes that were still lying on the bed: the bell-shaped skirt and close-fitting bodice, open at the front to show the inner curves of the breasts. It was the usual dress of unmarried ladies of the palace and similar to, though plainer than, Iphigeneia's own; an unheard of privilege for Sisipyla, who was an alien and, technically at least, still a slave. It had been much resented in that narrow, jealous world of the palace;

but the princess had insisted on it, from the beginning she had wanted her companion to look like herself—it was the highest mark of favor she could show.

Even with leave to go Sisipyla felt uneasy, worried that Iphigeneia might require her for something, might want to talk. She was almost never out of sight or hearing of her mistress. But today she felt a certain need to be alone. Something in the combination of events earlier—the meeting with Macris, his words and looks, the arrival of the messenger with news of a mounted party approaching—had troubled her in a way she did not yet fully understand.

There was a place outside the walls where she had sometimes been before when free of duties and wanting solitude. She left her room and made her way through the narrow passages on the north side of the palace, emerging below the walls, near the precincts of the shrine. From here she followed the road to the postern gate. The men on duty there allowed her through without question. Beyond the angle made by the outworks of the gate a narrow terrace led onto a path that followed the contour of the slope. She passed above a disused kiln, with farther down the ancient gashes of quarries, half overgrown. It was from here, she had once been told, that long ago they had taken the great blocks of stone for the citadel.

The path descended and opened into a level area, planted with pine and holly oak. She sat where she remembered sitting before, in the shade of a pine, with her back against its trunk. From here she could look down over the hillside, steeply terraced with olive and vine and scattered with the beehive shapes of tombs, many of them neglected and invaded by scrub, resembling random clumps of vegetation, with the thatched huts of those who worked the terraces lying here and there among them. Far below this, half hidden in the haze, she could see a stretch of the road that came through Perseia and approached the citadel from the south.

She began to think again about the meeting with Macris. The princess had been aware of his admiration and not displeased by it. She had not returned his looks, but she had not been displeased. They had talked about the young man once or twice before. Iphigeneia was in the habit of confiding in her, though not always immediately. They had laughed together over his forwardness, his ardent looks. It was bothersome, the princess had said once, always to find someone's eyes upon you. But she had not seemed much bothered today . . . For her parents such a match would not be good enough, the son of a local chieftain bound by dues of clan service to Agamemnon. No, they would be looking for an ally more powerful, perhaps a prince from Crete or the land of the Hatti or even Egypt. But whoever was chosen, the day could not be so far off now. Iphigeneia would be given to someone, someone would come and take her away.

Strange that Iphigeneia too could be a gift. This was already in my mind, Sisipyla thought. Watching them together. Then the messenger came with news of visitors. Iphigeneia would take me with her, it is not that—she would not go without me. But once there, at a foreign court, she will have new claims upon her, there will be the family of the husband. Perhaps I am needed only here, only at Mycenae, a gift for childhood, for growing up, not for a new life.

She was swept suddenly by fear of abandonment. She had no life, no existence, without Iphigeneia. The princess's favor had isolated her, made her an object of jealousy and dislike among her fellow servants. Once again she thought about the day she had been given to the princess. The great people of the palace had been there, Iphigeneia's parents, her four-year-old sister Electra, the senior clan members and the high-ranking officials of the court. She remembered the men's darkly bearded faces looking down, how strange and fearsome they had seemed—the men in her native Lydia were clean-shaven. Within this ring of faces, on a level with her own, there was Iphigeneia's, glowing with excitement but serious, always serious. Sisipyla could close her eyes and see in exact detail the princess's excited face on that day of celebration, and her dress, dark red with a gold sash and tasseled sleeves. Thin gold bracelets on each wrist, her hair dressed high on top of her head, held in place by a gold net.

The slave dealer was there too, he who had been with them on the ship. He had brought her to the palace because of her prettiness, hoping she would take someone's fancy. This she had not known at the time—she had not known why she was alone, separated from the others. It had been the man's luck to have come just when the wild plum trees were flowering, the season of the princess's birth. While the flowers were on the trees a day was chosen to celebrate the event. It was thus that Sisipyla had come to the King's notice, thus that the idea of the gift had come into his mind.

She had been helped by the presence of the dealer. In the course of trade he had picked up some Lydian; he had been able to make her understand the questions. She had seen the pleasure on the princess's face, she had known at once that she was acceptable as a gift; but the questions she remembered as terrible, because she had not answered them well, and because of the laughter of the men that stood round.

"What is your name?" This was the first thing the princess

had asked her, and she had replied—when she understood—with the name that belonged to her then and which she had kept in memory since, as a sort of possession, like her memory of the sea: Amandralettes.

But it was too difficult. Iphigeneia had a hesitation in her speech at that time, a slight lisp, since overcome. She could not get beyond the cluster of consonants. And at her efforts the laughter came, like a wave lapping round their two serious faces that were so exactly level.

"Where have you come from?"

She needed time to answer this, never having had to consider the matter before. But Iphigeneia gave her no time, repeating the question immediately to the people around her.

"She comes from the country below Mount Sipylus in Lydia," the dealer said.

"I will call you by the name of that mountain," the princess said gravely. In her determination to get the name right she stumbled and began again, so it came out with the first syllable doubled: "Sisipyla." And this, to general mirth—in which neither child shared—was hailed as the new name.

"I will give you one of my dresses," Iphigeneia had said. "I will dress your hair and give you a ribbon for it, a red ribbon. How old are you?"

She couldn't answer this, she didn't know. And now at last Iphigeneia smiled, the tension of excitement dissolving in joy. "You are exactly the same age as me," she said. "This is our seventh spring, this is our birthday. That makes it perfect."

Thus she was given a name and an age and a promise of clothing. The words about perfection she did not understand, having no clear idea at the time of what she looked like. She had a mirror of her own now, an oval of polished bronze with a rim of ivory, a gift from her mistress; but until coming to live at the palace she had never seen a clear reflection of her face. So it was only later that she understood: Iphigeneia had been excited by the resemblance between them. Not only in height and figure and coloring but in feature too, both having the same shape of face and arch of brow, the same fullness of mouth, the same softly rounded molding of cheekbone and chin.

She thought of this likeness again now. It was her fortune, the reason she had found favor in the princess's eyes. She had wanted to keep it, to stay within it, like a shelter. As a child, she had watched Iphigeneia's every slightest movement and tried to copy it exactly, the way of sitting and walking, the expressions of the face, the gestures of the hands. The passage of time and the differences in character and station had lessened the resemblance, though it was still noticeable to the most casual glance. That childish softness of feature was no more; both faces were sharper now, more clearly drawn. There were differences in the cheekbones and setting of the eyes. The expressions were different too. The habit of authority, the expectation of being deferred to, had given a quality of deliberateness to Iphigeneia's regard, as it had to her manner. She was certain of things. And this Sisipyla felt to be the greatest difference between them. The certainty made her seem calm; but it had something tightly coiled inside it, something Sisipyla recognized but could not name, showing fiercely in the eyes and voice when she was disturbed in her view of things. Sisipyla herself was quicker in her glances, she smiled more than her mistress and noticed more. She had a way of looking round with an air of slight anxiety, as if there might be something she hadn't quite taken into account.

What she felt for her mistress she had always called by the name of love. She had been jolted that morning by a fear or a presentiment; and the reaction to it now brought back pictures from the past in a way that had become rare with her. She saw herself as she must have looked on that day of her new name and her new life, mute and bewildered. She saw the bearded, laughing faces and the serious, radiant one level with her own. The questions she couldn't answer, the pleasure of ownership in the other face, the red dress with its tassels, and the gold at the waist, at the wrists, in the net that lay on the dark hair.

It had been early spring when she and her mother were taken. They and some other women had been outside the stockade of the village, at the streamside, washing clothes. Talking and laughing together, beating the wet clothes on flat stones, they had heard no sound of an approach. In the flooded plain there were white wading birds with plumed crests. She remembered them with sudden distinctness, their movements, awkward and delicate, the way they thrust their heads forward as they walked. All this in the moment before the raiding party sprang upon them, before their cries were stifled and they were dragged away. Or perhaps not that day, she thought. The plain was always flooded at that time of the year. Memories or inventions, the eagles in the sky, the loud sound of bees? Elsewhere in the standing water great masses of white flowers with yellow throats and a scent of sweetness. And the whole expanse stirring with bees. No, it was another day, the scent belonged to summer, those were flowers of the marshland . . . On that note of decision she got to her feet. It was time she returned to the palace. She gave a final glance down the hillside and at that moment she saw the riders come into view, riding single file on the road below. They were half-obscured in the sun-shot dust cloud of their own making. But she thought she saw the lion standard of Mycenae held aloft in a clearer light for some moments before being again shrouded in the gilded haze. Whoever they were, one of them at least must be familiar with the ground; they had taken the rougher, shorter road, hardly more than a track, that led directly up to the citadel.

3.

When Macris had delivered the message at the palace, he made his way to his quarters and called a servant to bring him water. He washed and combed his hair and changed his tunic, sweated and dusty from the hunt, for a clean one. He wanted to make sure that the main gate and the sally ports were properly manned and the men there decently turned out; and he could not do so looking unkempt himself. Despite the openness and apparent nonchalance of his manner, Macris was a reflective and practical young man, much given to considering his situation and prospects. He took very seriously the duties delegated to him by his father, as he did all duties, not because he saw any inherent virtue in doing so, but because such things were noticed, they gained a man credit. In the same spirit he sought always to follow the precepts of his father that one should strive not just to command but to be living proof of fitness to command. One should always be an example to others, always to the fore whenever there was hardship and danger and the prospect of spoils, just as one should take care to be clean and well turned out, with weapons in good order, when requiring these qualities in inferiors. Not to do so might get you a black mark, it might be remembered against you. However, though Macris loved his father, he knew that these precepts were not enough. His father, in fact, was a living proof that they were not enough. Years of danger and service, and he was left here as Agamemnon's man of trust while everyone who counted was on the way to Troy to make his fortune. His father was too loyal, a fault which Macris did not intend to let linger on into the next generation. He wanted more than to be a man of trust, much more: he wanted fame, he wanted wealth, he wanted Iphigeneia.

He began at the main gate and adjoining guardhouse. There was a permanent guard of four men here, relieved every six hours. They took turns, in pairs, to do lookout duty at a roofed post outside the gate, beyond the bastion, from where the western approaches could be surveyed—this western limit of the citadel, though the highest in altitude, was the easiest to approach, the slopes being gentler. The guardroom was built against the wall and open on the side of the gate, but there was still a haze of smoke inside and a smell of frying oil. The men on guard, in company with the three resident hounds, had just eaten the midday meal of beans and eggs. With considerable severity Macris told them to clear out the dogs and make sure they were wearing helmets and carrying spears when they went to unbar the gate to the visitors. "I've told you about these animals before," he said. "And I've told you to keep that lookout post manned at all times. If you fail in it again I'll put the lot of you on punishment drill. First impressions are extremely important. We don't yet know who these people are. I don't want them to see bareheaded guards stumbling about, with dogs underfoot. I don't mean to say you should wear your helmets at all times, I realize they are hot in this weather. But you must wear them when you are in public view, they are part of your equipment."

The men listened to him without expression. They were disgruntled, he knew, because he had come upon them unexpectedly. The duty officer normally inspected them only at the changing of the guard. A ridiculous practice, in Macris's view; if they always knew when the officer was coming, what kind of inspection was it? The fact that there had been no war fought on Mycenaean territory in living memory was no reason for slackness. He kept such opinions to himself, however—no sense in making oneself unpopular when there was nothing to be gained from it.

Next he went to take a look at the sally port in the northern wall. It was from the guard post on the ramparts here that the famous eagles had first been seen, haunting the spear side of the palace walls. So his father had told him—at the time he had been at sea with his uncle, somewhere east of the island of Melos. The usual regret came with this thought, the sense of having missed a chance. He knew himself to be brave. He had been trained to arms since his boyhood. He did target practice with the javelin every day and had bouts with sword and buckler whenever he could find a partner. He made a point of doing fifty press-ups every morning and working out with weights to keep in shape. And here he was, checking guard posts, trying to instill some sense of discipline into men who basically couldn't care less.

Men without ambition, he thought. The worst fault of all. Men like that would end up on the scrap heap. Troy was where the action was, Troy was the opportunity of a lifetime; her riches were celebrated by singers wherever people were gathered together; she had provided an honorable cause for quarrel, blessed by Zeus through the eagles. A returning hero, laden with booty; it was his only hope of being taken seriously in the marriage stakes. With Iphigeneia as his bride there would come royal rank, large grants of land. After that, the way was open. Agamemnon might not survive the war. Orestes was the only son, and he was already, at the age of ten, showing marked signs of mental instability, talking to himself and seeming to see presences in empty rooms. At that rate he would be off his head altogether by the time he came of age.

No, the prospects were there for the man who was man enough to seize them. And that man he felt himself to be. Apart from everything else, she was a beautiful girl with a great figure. He thought of her again now, as he had seen her at their meeting near the gate, her face framed by the scarf, the way she had met his eyes and glanced aside, the smile she had given him, teasing, yes, but not only that, there had been kindness for him in it. Thinking of this, spurring his horse forward, he felt capable of anything. It was not too late. Some dream was clouding the mind of his father, or some bad augury. But the old man would come round, there would still be time to join the army. In his heart was the hope, naturally unconfessed, that the adverse wind might last just a little while longer, just until he could get to Aulis.

The men at the sally port had seen the mounted party pass below them, had seen the red-and-white banners of Mycenae carried by the foremost. The riders had already started the ascent, they would soon be at the gate. Learning this, Macris stayed only moments, just long enough to assure himself that all was in order. He was making his way towards the cluster of stone houses on the south side of the citadel, one of which was used as a mess for the officers of the garrison, when he met on the road a small detachment of his father's people, clan members from the home region of Dendra. Their leader told him they had been detailed to await the visitors outside the gates, where the road drew level with the bastion.

Macris accompanied them and waited there at their head. They heard the horses' hooves striking on the stone of the road. Then the first riders came into view and Macris at once recognized Phylakos, the commander of Agamemnon's personal guard. Riding beside him was a man he did not know, some dozen years older than himself, very erect in his bearing, with strongly marked, impassive features. Behind these two came others whose faces he knew, all men under Phylakos's command. The numbers were less than had been reported—he counted fourteen.

He waited there as they advanced, two abreast now on the narrow approach between the bastion and the outer wall. His own people waited in a group, slightly to the rear of him. So long as he was there, they would not move without his order. Phylakos raised a hand in greeting but did not immediately slacken his pace, and for some moments it seemed as if he were expecting those before him to give way without further ceremony.

But Macris, apart from returning the salute, did not move. There was a procedure to be followed with strangers, even when they came accompanied by people known. Macris believed in procedures, and he saw no reason to relax the rule for the sake of a man whom he neither liked nor trusted.

Phylakos was obliged to rein in his horse and displeasure at this was written on his face. The man beside him eased forward a little in the saddle but made no other move. He was dark-bearded, with a high-bridged prow of a nose and a curving scar on his forehead. The dust of the journey lay on the riding mantle he wore over his shoulders. "We have ridden far today," Phylakos said in his harsh, dragging voice. "We are in haste to see the Queen. Have them open the gate."

Still Macris did not move. The blood had risen to his face at the other's tone, at the implication that he was not important enough to have the identity of the stranger announced to him. He took care to show nothing of this, however. "I do not know who it is that is with you," he said.

"This is Diomedes," Phylakos said, anger still in his voice. He made a brief gesture towards the youth before him. "Macris, son of Amphidamas."

Both men laid hand on heart and slightly bowed their heads. Macris turned away quickly to order the gate opened. He was afraid it would show in his face, which always showed more than he liked despite all his striving, how impressed he was at this illustrious name, announced so brusquely. It must be a matter of first importance to have brought such a man from Aulis. Diomedes, whose father Tydeus had joined the expedition of the Seven against Thebes and been killed before the walls of the city. Diomedes, who at an age hardly greater than his own had marched against Thebes, together with the other sons of the Seven, the Epigoni, and razed it to the ground in vengeance for his father's death. Diomedes, who had provided eight ships, who headed the combined forces of Argos, Nauplia and Troezen. Macris was relieved to see that the men at the guardhouse moved briskly and were wearing their helmets and that there were no dogs in sight. It would be seen that he knew how to keep a guardhouse. It was not much to set against a record like that, but it was something.

The party passed through the gate and onto the ramp. Phylakos and Diomedes at once took the road to the palace. The remainder clattered down to the garrison barracks. Macris followed more slowly. He longed to know the purpose of the visit; but it would be a mistake to start questioning inferiors, to show oneself not only more ignorant than they but vulgarly curious into the bargain. These were points a man had to watch if he was in the business of establishing a reputation.

4.

The afternoon was almost over when the summons came for Iphigeneia. She and her younger sister, Electra, and Sisipyla and an older woman who had once been nurse to the princess were playing a game of throw and catch in the small open courtyard adjoining the south staircase. For the ball, Sisipyla had been sent to fetch an old cloth doll, a limp survivor of Iphigeneia's earliest childhood that still had a place in the box of old playthings in the princess's bedroom.

The nurse was on the heavy side and rather unwieldy, and she had not really wanted to play. They had found her spinning wool in a shady corner of the courtyard and Iphigeneia had coerced her into it. "We need four people," she had said. "Less than four is no use at all." And she had narrowed her eyes and looked intently at the nurse, in the way she had when meeting with opposition.

Sisipyla, watching this briefest of contests—the nurse did not resist long—had known at once why there had to be four players. The yard was square, the game had to be square too. She had long ago, while they were still children, recognized in her mistress an imperative need for things to match up and to be perfect; not only particular things, like her makeup or the combs in her hair, but forms and arrangements too, things you couldn't touch or really see, a puzzling matter for Sisipyla. She had watched, with the familiar sense of puzzlement, while Iphigeneia stationed the players in positions exactly corresponding to the angles made by the corners of the walls, forming an exact copy of the square.

The thing that gave the game its edge, however, was the opposite principle of disorder. None of the players could know whether the doll was to be thrown her way or not; it was permitted, it was even required, to make feints and pretended throws and to change direction at the last moment. The game had begun with a great deal of laughter but then deteriorated fairly quickly. Iphigeneia was getting crosser and crosser, first because the nurse dithered and fumbled, and this slowed the game down, then because Electra, in her eagerness to be tricky, would try to change direction at the very moment of throwing, and this made her aim erratic, so that the doll went flying at an impossible angle and could not be caught however quick one was.

"How could anyone be expected to catch that?" Iphigeneia demanded furiously, after the doll had come flailing at her knee-high. "Why don't you learn to throw straight?"

"Well, that's that," Electra said, she too flushed and furious. "I won't play this game anymore, not ever."

These words brought a certain pause; even at this early age she was known for one who kept her vows. The doll lay with arms outflung at Iphigeneia's feet. She had started life as an elegant doll, a luxury product, with black silk hair and slanting eyes made of dark amber and a cloth-of-gold dress with ivory buttons, naming-day gift of a vassal chieftain from the island of Cythera, off whose shores Aphrodite was said to have risen from the sea. But the doll was hairless now and she was blind—there were only the stitch marks where her eyes had been. Her gold dress was gashed here and there and the stuffing showed through.

Iphigeneia bent to pick the doll up. "You won't get your hands on Maia again, that's for sure," she said.

"Who cares?"

"You won't touch her again."

Sisipyla was swept by a rush of sympathy for her mistress. Whatever the others might think, she knew without needing to find the words in her mind that it was not Electra's erratic aim or scornful manner that was upsetting Iphigeneia now, but self-blame, the sudden sorrow of seeing her doll, the familiar companion of childhood, disheveled and defenseless, with her limbs sprawled out. She was trying, too late, to protect Maia and make things up to her.

"Whoever would want to touch your smelly old doll?" Electra said.

At this difficult moment, a woman named Crataeis, one of Clytemnestra's companions, entered the courtyard. She had been looking for the princess high and low, she said. The Queen required her presence immediately, was awaiting that presence even now in her apartments. Alone, the woman added, with a hostile glance at Sisipyla. What the Queen had to say was for her daughter's ears only.

Iphigeneia began to follow the woman across the courtyard, but realizing that she was still holding the doll, she turned back and handed it to Sisipyla. "Look after Maia for me," she said, exchanging looks with her sister that were unforgiving on both sides. "You can keep her with you till I get back."

Sisipyla, bearing the bedraggled Maia back to her room, thought how similar the sisters were in some ways, and wondered what Clytemnestra could have to communicate to her daughter so urgent that it could not keep till the evening hour, when Iphigeneia always attended on her mother. Something to do with the riders she had seen, half shrouded in dust, with the pennants flying above them. But they were from Aulis, she had heard. What possible message for Iphigeneia could come from men about to embark for war?

Maia lay on the narrow bed in an attitude of ruin and abandon. Light from the high window fell on the pale patches where her eyes had been and on her pulpy nose — Iphigeneia, when she was teething, had gnawed away at Maia's nose and reduced it to a mangled stump. After a while Sisipyla began to feel a certain horror at Maia, and did not want to look her way anymore. She waited, listening for footfalls, sitting on the floor with her back to the bed. While she waited the sun sank behind the horizon and the brief summer twilight came down. The old slave woman, whose task it was, came with a long-handled pan of fire and lit the lamps in the vestibule and in Iphigeneia's apartment.

Darkness had come when the princess returned, and she was accompanied by two attendants who had lighted her way with torches. Iphigeneia was standing between the bearers, and the torches were still burning when Sisipyla passed through into the vestibule, so that her first impression, coming from the dimness of her room, was of the leaping and trembling of reflected flame, on the walls, on the bronze standards of the torches, on the face of Iphigeneia and the silver threads of her bodice. The princess's expression was serious and exalted and she held her head high. She dismissed the torchbearers and waited till they had gone shuffling away in the loose felt slippers that all palace servants wore. Then she turned to Sisipyla and moved towards her, as if she wanted to speak low. Sisipyla saw her mistress's expression change, now that they were alone together, saw it become more openly and tensely excited, and was carried back in memory, in these moments before Iphigeneia spoke, to the radiant face of the six-year-old princess and the questions and the laughing men.

"They have come with a proposal of marriage," Iphigeneia said. "You will never guess who it is."

She paused for a moment, it seemed for effect rather than in expectation of guesses. In any case, Sisipyla made no attempt to reply. Her hand had risen in an unconscious movement to clutch loosely at the waist of her skirt.

"It is Achilles. He thinks of me day and night. He wants me—he can't wait till after the war. He wants me to come to Aulis and be married before the whole army. Just think of it, a thousand spectators. My mother is full of joy. That generation always exaggerates everything of course, but she says he is quite the most eligible hero alive today. And there is also the fact that he is of divine descent on the mother's side."

Becoming aware now of Sisipyla's silence and stillness, she looked more closely at her companion's face, and saw there an expression that she altogether misunderstood. "Do you mean to say you didn't know that? No, it's no use, I can tell from your face that you didn't. Good heavens. His father was Peleus of Phthia, and he married the sea goddess Thetis. All the gods came to the wedding, which was a great distinction because it is very rare where a mortal is concerned. When Achilles was a baby Thetis dipped him in the river Styx to make him immortal, but she must have been thinking of something else at the time, she kept hold of his heel, so he is immortal in every part but that. My mother says I must have made a tremendous impression on him when we met, though it was only once and I was only in my tenth summer at the time. You were with me, you saw him too."

Sisipyla had moved her hands to her sides now and she stood very straight. "I don't remember him," she said.

"Don't remember him? A marvelous man like that? You really are hopeless. I remember him perfectly. There was something in the way he looked at me, even then—you can always tell. What I think myself is that he must have been repressing it all these years and now he is about to go into danger it has come bursting out, no longer to be denied. It's very romantic. He probably thinks, you know, there isn't much time, make hay while the sun shines. We must start to get ready, there is going to be a banquet in honor of Diomedes, he is the one that brought the proposal, he is a close friend of Achilles. My mother offered to send some of her women to help me dress, but I said I only needed you."

5.

By virtue of his father's rank, Macris was seated in the upper part of the hall, in the area above the libation stone. Clytemnestra occupied the King's place in his absence, with the honored guest Diomedes at her right hand. Macris did not sit with his father, however, but lower down, as became his youth and relative obscurity. He was content with the place; from here he could observe and listen without anything much being required from him. Observing and listening were what he had vowed himself to, once the first shock of the news had passed. It was as near to action as he could come; and action, a refusal to languish or turn in on himself, was always his way of dealing with distress, had been so from his earliest years. Violent physical action, preferably; many were the setbacks and disappointments he had outrun, outwrestled, exhausted through the exhausting of his body.

This was not possible now. He did not want to combat his feelings because Iphigeneia was at the heart of them. But he could cultivate hostility for others, which was still better than lamenting and mooning about. Much better. Achilles first, the absent threat. The heart could not but falter at such a rival, so celebrated for his beauty and fleetness of foot and prowess in battle. Only a few years older than himself and so many killings and lootings to his credit.

Of course, a good part of this must be exaggeration; a lot depended on who had the ear of the Singer. This invulnerability business, for example—it was obviously something put about to scare people. Achilles had a heart and a belly and a gizzard, just like anyone else. I would be ready to put it to the test, he thought. At the drop of a hat. Then there was this matter of divine birth. Easy to say you had a sea goddess for a mother, but what about the proof? His own mother was Leucippa of Dendra. Anyone wanting to check up on him could go to Dendra and find her there, looking after the estates while her husband did his turn of service here. She would vouch for his birth, and woe betide any who doubted it. But how could anyone go looking for Thetis in her palace under the sea? What kind of an address was that?

He glanced across at Clytemnestra, who had calculated her effects well this evening, and looked spectacularly funereal among the festively dressed people round her, white-faced and raven-haired, with shadowed eyelids, in a black gown, the bodice tight and open down the front to show the dark borders of her nipples and the splendid depth of her cleavage. Pleasure at the news had warmed her face and softened the usual bitterness and hunger of her mouth. She had made the speech of welcome to the guests and poured the first libation, bearing the bowl herself to the altar. Seated on her left, across from Diomedes, was the mysterious Aegisthus, son of Thyestes and cousin to Agamemnon. His fair beard and florid complexion were in sharp contrast with the white-faced queen. He had arrived at the court almost as soon as the King had left it, and stories about him were rife. He was said to be the product of an incestuous union between his father and his half-sister Pelopia, to have been abandoned as a child and suckled by a goat. There were those who said, when they were sure of their company, that he was the killer of Atreus, Agamemnon's father, whose body had been found in a lonely place on the seashore, bearing many stab wounds upon it. But there were no stories, not yet at any rate, only insinuations, as to why, in Agamemnon's absence, he had received such a welcome at the Mycenaean court, why he lingered there, why the Queen kept him so constantly by her side.

Macris was glad for the wine, but he had small appetite for the soup of lentils flavored with cumin that was placed before him, still less for the quail's eggs and roast hare that followed. Nonetheless, he attacked the courses as they came with every appearance of gusto, in accordance with his principle of positive action. He saw Iphigeneia rise to take wine to the guest of honor. She was flushed and serious, conscious of being looked at as one about to change her state. Macris watched the tension of care in her movements as she poured out the wine, saw how intent she was on her duties, saw—with an insight unusual in him, born of his wretchedness—that she suffered, must always have suffered, at the fear of not getting things right, not being as she should. He had thought of her often, her face, her form, what it would be like to have her naked beneath him, the status and dignity it would confer on him to have her as his wife, how fertile she would be, whether she would bear sons. But it had not, until now that he was going to lose her, occurred to him to wonder what she might feel or think about things. He thought, She is one for whom nothing will ever be quite good enough, nothing will ever come up to the mark. As she stood before Diomedes waiting for the customary compliments, he thought he had never seen her look so beautiful, in her short-sleeved blue-and-silver bodice and long pleated skirt. A tress of her hair had been carried across the crown of her head and secured by gold pins.

Diomedes finished his words and drank, and Iphigeneia moved away. Aegisthus leaned his face forward to speak, the torchlight glinting on his fair brows. The Queen's eyes were lowered, she showed no sign of listening. She had thanked Diomedes in her speech of welcome, declared herself and the kingdom of Mycenae honored by the choice of such an ambassador. Achilles had sent his closest friend to show the value he placed on her daughter and on the alliance with the House of Atreus.

Was it Diomedes who had told her of this close friendship? It sounded to Macris like one more exaggeration. Hardly likely, he thought, that the two would have met before coming together at Aulis. Achilles was lord of Phthia on the borders of Thessaly, whereas Diomedes was an Argive. There was no story that connected them, none that he knew of. It was true that friendship could take quick root among men about to embark on war; but it was Agamemnon that Diomedes was more likely to be close to, they were neighbors, they had clan ties, they were close associates and allies in the war.

It was time now for the third libation. Iphigeneia rose and stood at her place and a silence fell among the people. She

raised her head and chanted the words honoring her absent father, Agamemnon. Her voice was not strong but it was clear
and pleasing. Macris watched the movements of her throat and
the pauses in her breathing and saw that she was moved. When
she ended and bowed her head there was a rustle of approba-
tion among the seated guests. Diomedes took the shallow, two-
handled cup to the altar, bearing it with both hands. He prayed
to Zeus the Guardian for blessing on the house, and poured the
wine over the stone slab. There was silence while they waited
for the prayer and the scent of the wine to reach the abode of
the god, which was the time required for the offering to run
along the grooves in the altar stone and down into the circular
basin at the foot. Then, at a signal from Clytemnestra, the flute
players began again and talk was resumed.

Macris's eye lighted on his father, Amphidamas, who was
saying something to Phylakos seated near to him. The contrast
between the two faces was striking, his father's good-humored,
with something mobile and expressive in the play of the features, the other's harsh and cold, with eyes that seemed always
to be aiming, calculating distances. There was no doubt which
was the better face. Macris felt an affectionate pride in his father, but it came accompanied, as usual nowadays, by a certain
caution. He had vowed not to be any more like his father than
he was already and could not help; he would not emulate a career that had consisted entirely of obedience to the dictates of
duty and fidelity, to the dues of military service, to the toilsome
patrimony of steep hillsides and narrow valleys. He had a better face than Phylakos, certainly; but it seemed a small reward.
His father was fond of saying that a man should give a good account of himself. But Macris had felt increasingly of late that
he wanted to be in that much smaller group to whom the ac-

counts were offered. Duty and fidelity were for apprentices. It was like the drill movements in swordplay: feint, thrust, side-step, disengage, once you know how to do it, you could use it or not, you could find your own rhythm, you passed into the zone of distinction. Macris liked this phrase and repeated it often to himself. His father did not know the zone existed, and this seemed to Macris like a mark of arrested development. One had to reach out, to go beyond . . .

This made him think again of Achilles, who must have entered the zone long ago. Where and when had he met Iphigeneia? In the time he himself had been at Mycenae Achilles had not been a visitor and Iphigeneia had not been away. If they had set eyes on each other before that, the princess must have been no more than a child. A sudden passion, after such a long interval, was always possible, but it seemed unlikely. It was more probably a political matter, a move to strengthen ties with the powerful kingdom of Mycenae. But in that case the proposal seemed oddly precipitate, lacking in ceremony, a hasty wedding far from home, on the eve of battle.

Then there was the delegation itself. Diomedes was a good choice as ambassador, he carried weight, he was a friend of her father's whom she might have seen at home sometimes. But who else was there? Half the escort were in the service of Diomedes and not from Mycenae at all; the rest were all members of the elite palace guard, personally chosen by Agamemnon and vowed to his service. Surely someone that really cared about the princess would have sent at least one or two people she knew well to accompany her, someone like Abas, who had been her singing master, or Penthes the gardener, who loved her and had pretended for years to comply with her instructions, generally wrong, for the cultivation of his vines and strawberries and walnut trees. Both men devoted to the family, who had volunteered for Troy when they might have stayed.

The princess would naturally want to take Sisipyla with her, and probably some other women. But where was the man she could completely trust, who would stay by her side? There was the long journey by land and sea, the unfamiliar atmosphere of a military camp. She would not even have the company of her mother—Clytemnestra had expressed her regret that the security of the kingdom would require her presence at Mycenae. The security of Aegisthus, more like it, he thought. Of course, once there she would be all right, her father would take care of her and supervise the preparations for the wedding.

He glanced again towards Iphigeneia, and in the moment that he did so Phylakos turned his head and the eyes of the two men met and locked into a stare, which for a moment neither was willing to break. There was dislike on both sides expressed in this, something which had been there before, but which the encounter at the gate had quickened. After some moments the older man looked away with a deliberate slowness, clearly contemptuous in intent. Something stirred in Macris, too vague to be called suspicion, a sense of incongruity, of elements that did not quite match up. By contrast, the words that formed now in his mind had a crystalline clarity and purity: *I will be that man.*

An amazing sense of freedom came to him with this resolve. He would be the man of trust. He would protect the princess's person and her interests. My own too, he thought, rather belatedly remembering the zone of distinction. It will get me to Troy, for one thing. Agamemnon will be grateful for my care of her, and remember it. And much can happen on a journey, she will see my worth . . . With or without his father's permission he would go. It would be easier with permission, so he would try to obtain this, urging the princess's need for protection—an argument likely to appeal to his father. If it failed, he would wait for them somewhere on the road below. He would take some of his own people, in case he met with any trouble, men who had come with him to Mycenae and would follow him to Aulis at a word—or anywhere else for that matter.

6.

It was not until the evening of the next day, when the face of the early summer moon was already showing, that Sisipyla was able to talk alone with her mistress. The princess had stayed late at the banquet, obliged to wait on the pleasure of her mother, who was noted for late nights and late mornings, and she had been too tired to talk by the time she got back to her apartments. And almost from the moment of waking next morning, Sisipyla had been anxiously occupied in seeing to the practical arrangements for the sacrifice, which were largely her responsibility. The ceremony at the time of the full moon, in honor of Artemis, was the most important of those that Iphigeneia had to conduct.

Sisipyla had been running here and there, making sure that all was ready, that those escorting the procession had their garlands at hand, that the water bearers

and the flute players knew their duties. The two girls who between them were to carry the incense burner had not done it
before, and they had to be carefully instructed. Then there
were the men who would lift up the goat at the altar; this had
to be done in just the right way so that Iphigeneia could have
free play with the knife. The throat had to be cut in one movement, and Sisipyla knew from experience that any botching in
this department roused the princess's ire. So it was important
that these men knew their business well; they would have to do
the skinning and butchering afterwards and see to the roasting
of the joints. The chosen animal she had prepared herself, gild-
ing its horns and marking its face with henna and twining
white ribbons in its coat. When, this done, she returned to the
women's quarters by way of the south staircase, she found
Iphigeneia waiting for her.

"What kept you so long?" the princess said. "I've been calling you, I've got some important news."

Sisipyla excused herself, but briefly, not wanting to delay
the news or add to the princess's evident impatience.
Iphigeneia expected her to be there when she was called, and
no amount of explanation could absolve her from the fault, self-
evident and beyond appeal, of having been absent.

"I wanted to tell you that my mother has given permission
for you to go with me."

"That is wonderful news." She was not really surprised,
however; it was what she had expected. She glanced quickly at
Iphigeneia's face, which had returned to calm now, the news
delivered. A kind of calm at least; something of the exaltation
of the night before, when she had come between the torchbearers with the news of the proposal, still remained. Sisipyla
looked always for the light in the princess's face—her moods

were expressed in light rather than changes of feature. Vexation dimmed her, happiness or pride was a radiance. It seemed the very quality of royalty to Sisipyla, this stillness of face — she was conscious of how quickly her own eyes glanced aside, how the corners of her mouth moved at any slightest thing. She thought, I was the first to be told, I will be the one closest to her of all who go there with her. "Then we will come back here, won't we?" she said, the words issuing, it seemed, before any intention had been formed to utter them.

"So I would suppose," Iphigeneia said. "What else should we do? They will hardly want us to go to Troy with them."

Sisipyla looked down, conscious that she had been in some way sloppy and unfocused again. From the moment she had heard of the proposal it had been her consolation that they would return, that Iphigeneia would not be taken from her. Achilles would go away to the war. People said the war would be over in no time once the army got there, but it might take much longer than anyone thought. And then, anything could happen in a war. Meanwhile she and Iphigeneia would return here and life would go on as before. In her gratitude for this, she had not much considered the feelings of Achilles, except to think it strange that a wind coming from the wrong direction should be the cause of his offer; he could not have intended it when he set out. Being forced to wait there, she thought vaguely, the desire of his heart had risen to the surface — she saw it as a silver fish in a dark pool, glimmering up to the light. And Iphigeneia had accepted, without a moment's hesitation, just one scoop . . .

"You have no doubts," she dared to say now, in the tone of a question, and saw an immediate shadow come to Iphigeneia's face.

"Doubts? Apart from being famous and well connected and

fantastic-looking, Achilles is one of the richest men in Greece. Did you know that? No, you didn't, I can tell. He is a copper magnate, he owns at least six copper mines in the region of Lamia. But that's not the main thing, not for me anyway. Through his mother he enjoys special protection and my family are in great need of that protection. There is a curse on us. You don't know the story of the House of Atreus, do you?"

"Well . . ."

The shadow on Iphigeneia's face deepened. "You can't possibly know it. No one outside the family knows it. No one is allowed to speak of it. It is not known to any Singer. I learned of it by accident, when I was very little, before the time I was due to be told."

The quantity of things Iphigeneia herself didn't know still sometimes surprised Sisipyla. The story was common knowledge, a matter of gossip, not only among the servants of the palace, the sweepers and washerwomen, but even in the town below the walls, among those who came with eggs and honey and cheese to sell. "I would very much like to hear the story," she said.

"Promise you won't tell anyone."

"I promise."

"The founder of the line was Tantalus and he had three children, Pelops, Niobe and Broteas. He got this idea of testing the omniscience of the gods. You don't know that word, do you? No, it's no use, I can tell from your face that you don't. It means knowing everything that there is to know. Tantalus invited the gods to a feast and he served them up with his own son Pelops."

She paused a moment, looking sternly at Sisipyla. "All mashed up in a stew, you know, and heavily disguised with spices, so no one should know what they were eating. It was his idea of a joke. Well, he was obviously unhinged. Of course, the guests saw through this trick at once, all but Demeter, she absentmindedly ate a piece of one shoulder. They were all highly offended, in fact they were furious. Well, wouldn't you be? They condemned Tantalus to starve and thirst in Hades forever, with all sorts of delicious things just out of his reach. That is where he is now, at this moment, all chained up."

Iphigeneia remained silent for some moments and Sisipyla saw that she was waiting for a question to spur the narrative forward. "That was the end of Pelops then?"

"No, they brought Pelops back to life."

"That must have been a difficult job when he was all chopped up like that. What about the shoulder?" She had not heard about the shoulder before and it had appealed to her imagination. "How could they put his shoulder in place when it had been partly eaten?"

"I've really no idea," Iphigeneia said impatiently. "You always seem to fasten on these unimportant details. Pelops went to another part of the country, Pisa, on the borders of Elis, and got married there to someone called Hippodameia. Her father didn't want anyone to marry her. I think he was, you know, keen on her himself. So Pelops had to kill him."

"How did he do that?"

"He bribed the king's charioteer, whose name was Myrtilus, to take the wooden pins out of one of the chariot wheels and put wax ones there instead. He promised Myrtilus half the kingdom and a night in bed with Hippodameia. Then he got into some sort of chariot race with the king and the wheel fell off and the king was thrown out and got entangled in the reins and Pelops killed him and then galloped away with Hippodameia by his side."

"What about Myrtilus?"

"Well, of course he lost no time in claiming his reward. But Pelops had no intention of keeping his promises now he had got what he wanted. He lured Myrtilus onto a boat and pushed him overboard somewhere near the harbor of Elis. Before he drowned this charioteer invoked a curse on the descendants of Pelops. This was the first curse that was put on our family, and it soon started to take effect. Pelops and Hippodameia had two sons, Atreus and Thyestes. Atreus was the rightful king of Mycenae but Thyestes tried to get the throne from him, so they quarreled, but then Atreus pretended that he wanted to make it up and he invited his brother to dinner."

Iphigeneia widened her eyes and stared solemnly at Sisipyla. "Guess what happened then," she said. "He did exactly the same thing, except that it was not his own children but his brother's three sons that he killed and served up to their father in a stew. It was history repeating itself."

"Three sons," Sisipyla said. "It must have been an enormous meal."

"When he had finished, Atreus showed him the heads and hands of his children, you know, just to drive the point home. Thyestes laid a curse on Atreus and his descendants, then fled into exile, taking his remaining son Aegisthus with him. That was the second curse. It is the same Aegisthus who has turned up again now and is being entertained by my mother as a guest here. No one knows where his father is. Someone sent a messenger to Atreus to say Thyestes had been killed—the man had a bloodied sword to prove it. Atreus was delighted. He went off alone to make a thanksgiving sacrifice and he was found dead next day with stab wounds all over him. Nobody knows who did it. The messenger can't be found. Atreus had two sons,

Agamemnon and Menelaus, my father and my uncle. That curse is still lying on them and all of us."

Sisipyla nodded. There were voices that named Aegisthus himself as the killer of Atreus, but she said nothing of this. Lots of stories went around. There were even those who said that Thyestes had raped his own daughter, Pelopia, and that Aegisthus was the child of this rape. She saw from Iphigeneia's fixity of expression and the thinning of her mouth that the princess had been affected by the grim story in telling it. It was hard to think of words of comfort. "It's always the children who suffer, isn't it?" she said.

"That's one thing," Iphigeneia said. "The other is tricks. Did you notice? These two things run through all the story. A chariot race, a boat trip, an invitation to dinner, a sword with blood on it. There's always a trick, and the trick always ends in a murder."

Sisipyla felt a return of anxiety about the sacrifice due soon to take place. It was late, darkness was falling. Those with parts to play in the procession would be already assembling in the courtyard below the main staircase. She and Iphigeneia would have to start getting ready soon. "What was the accident?" she said.

"Accident?"

"You said you only learned the story by accident."

"Oh yes, it was told me by a nurse when I was very little, before you came. She told me stories while she was bathing me and getting me ready for bed. All kinds of stories, but this was her favorite. Heaven knows how she found out about it. She had these huge eyes—or so they seemed to me then. She must have known she was frightening me. She made it seem like a secret, something just between the two of us; but I had nightmares, I used to wake up screaming, and so it all came out."

"What happened to the nurse?"

"She was sent away. Or so I was told—I never saw her again. But I still remember those eyes of hers and her mouth moving." She shook her head and her face relaxed a little from its former fixity of expression. "We are all the victims of stories in one way or another," she said, "even if we are not in them, even if we are not born yet. I wasn't born then, but Thyestes cursed me too."

"There might be curses we don't know about," Sisipyla said. "Then things would happen, terrible things, and we wouldn't even know why." As always, it was the unexpected that troubled her imagination most, the monster in the dark cave, waiting to pounce on the unwary traveler. If you knew about the curse, at least you could be on your guard. For some moments it had seemed to her that she shared the memory of the cruel nurse's face, but of course that was impossible. Just a memory of unkindness, she thought. Any face would do for that. She had not expected much from the story of the double curse, being already quite familiar with it; but then this new story of the nurse and the nightmares had sprung out from inside the old one. "Princess, we must prepare for the sacrifice," she said. "They will be waiting below."

"Yes, it is time." Iphigeneia made no move for the moment, however, but remained standing where she was, in the middle of the room. "The same things happen over and over," she said. "Did you notice? The story goes off in all directions, but it is always the same story. There is the trick and the shedding of blood and the outrage to Zeus the Guardian, protector of guests and hosts. Atreus is dead, but my father is alive, the curse is on

him too. But I can save him." Her voice had slowed and deepened a little and her eyes were shining. "By marrying Achilles, I
can save my father, I can lift this curse from the whole family.
Achilles is a great hero, there is no darkness on his name, he is
under the special protection of his goddess mother, Thetis, and
so of Zeus—it's no secret that Zeus has always had a soft spot
for her. Even if Achilles is killed in the war and I am left a
widow, it won't make that much difference, he can still use his
influence from the Isles of the Blessed, he is certain to go there,
being so well connected, you know, and they keep their bodily
forms and all their faculties there, not like those poor shadows
in Hades. I went to the shrine of Artemis this morning to make
a votive offering and I just stood on my own there and I felt she
was in favor and understood my reasons."

Devotion can still include irony towards the subject, and it
did not escape Sisipyla that her loved mistress talked as if she
had had the luxury of a yes or no, whereas, given the wishes of
her parents, it could only have been a choice between accepting gladly and accepting reluctantly. As they went together into
the short passage that led to the vestibule where their ceremonial clothes were kept, Sisipyla wondered if wanting to do what
you in any case had to do was a sort of choice. No one would
ever wonder about her in that way; no one would ever care
whether she did things willingly or not, so long as nothing
showed on her face. How marvelous and strange to be part of
a family, even one with a curse on it, to have a father to save,
to feel directed by the gods.

The white sacrificial robes, freshly laundered and scented
with coriander seed for purification, were in the vestibule
where Sisipyla had laid them out. She helped her mistress to
dress in the long-skirted, gold-trimmed gown, then the girdle

of virginity, then the bib and apron of thick felt, tied at the back, covering the front of the body from the neck to the knees and marked here and there with the bloodstains that made them always more sacred. Clytemnestra, when handing over the duties of priestess to her daughter, had offered the services of her own women, who had been attending her for years and knew the procedures; but Iphigeneia had wanted Sisipyla and no one else for her dresser.

The dressing done, Sisipyla applied to her mistress's face the white chalk paste, silky and lustrous in appearance, which she had mixed herself in a shallow bowl, smoothing the paste with her fingertips, following the lines of the brows and nose and cheeks, making a perfect oval. No one could easily have recognized Iphigeneia now. It was a gleaming mask that looked back at Sisipyla, not a human face at all, only the color of the lips and the dark pools of the eyes breaking that stiff composure. Sisipyla rubbed her fingers clean with a cloth, then went to the paint pot and brush standing on the low stone table. The moon mask was dry already; with the thin brush she made tiny vermilion circles on Iphigeneia's cheeks and chin and forehead, four in number, in token of the blood that was to be offered, and the phases of the moon.

When this was done, Sisipyla dressed hastily in her plain white gown, and they were ready. They passed from the vestibule into the corridor that led to the staircase on the south side of the palace, Iphigeneia walking in front, Sisipyla a step or two behind. The last part of the corridor, before the head of the stairs was reached, was a roofed terrace, open on one side. Beyond the stone columns that held up the roof, the perfect disk of the moon was rising, intensely bright but clear and definite at the edges, as though pasted on the night sky.

"Walk beside me till we are outside," Iphigeneia said, speaking over her shoulder. The voice was unrecognizable, without inflections, coming in a single tone because of the stiffening of the paste round her mouth. She had never asked this before, and Sisipyla, obeying, knew it was because they would never again make the sacrifice together in quite the same way. Nothing would be the same, even if they did the same things. At the next full moon, Iphigeneia would have laid aside the girdle, she would wear the tiara, she would be different. Sisipyla felt again the breath of change, the chill of loss. As they walked together side by side, stepping through the bars of moonlight cast over the pavement between the columns, Iphigeneia took her hand, they walked hand in hand together to the head of the stairs, and in Sisipyla's joy at this there was also the knowledge of loss.

In the cobbled yard below the steps the people of the procession were waiting, the gilded, beribboned goat in their midst, held by two men on leashes of corded silk. Moonlight lay on the upper wall of the terrace but the yard was still in shadow and the attendants had lit torches while waiting. All bowed low to the ground as Iphigeneia descended, but when they straightened up again Sisipyla gave them a sharp looking-over. The only ones that should be there, at least to start with, were the people who looked after the shrine and those who had a part to play in the sacrifice. Too many people who you never saw at other times tried to get in on the sacrificial procession for the sake of the roasted meat afterwards. Others would tag along while the procession was on the move, but that was different, more acceptable to the goddess—they weren't barefaced enough to pretend they had some official status.

Iphigeneia walked forward, leading again now, making no

acknowledgment of the people waiting. Sisipyla was handed the sacrificial basket, which she had prepared herself, with the knife concealed beneath the grains of barley. She placed the basket on her head, with her left arm upraised to support it. The torchbearers fell in on either side and the procession began to follow Iphigeneia across the yard and through an archway into the wider open area, unpaved and uneven and without enclosing walls, where the altar stood.

Here in the open they were in the full flood of the moonlight. The torches were extinguished and after this silencing of the flames there was at first only the scrape of their steps on the rough ground. Then came the wavering music of the flutes, eclipsing other sounds. Sisipyla was grateful that the goat remained silent. She had, as usual, mixed the dried juice of the poppy fruit into the mash of its last meal. This was a matter of careful judgment: too much, and the beast would stagger; too little, and there was the chance, when it came into this open space, that it would forget it was a captive, get a whiff of some exciting possibility in the night air or the stirred dust under its feet, utter some sound of complaint or belligerence which would sully the sacrifice and be taken as a bad omen. And this, since she had chosen and prepared the animal, would reflect on her.

She felt a slight shudder, the impending presence of the goddess. The soft darkness that lay within the light, the blended notes of the flutes, the scent of thyme and mint from the slopes beyond the walls, all things that, separate, were familiar matters of sense on a summer night, now flowed together into a stream on which her mind floated. She watched the slight sway of Iphigeneia's body, the rigidly held shoulders, the arms and hands motionless at the sides. The princess was walking with Artemis.

The sensation of weightlessness increased. Her ears were closed now to the sounds of the night. Her steps did not falter, but her judgment of the distance from the ground of her raised foot grew less certain, she felt a slight threat to her balance and knew these for signs of the nearness of the goddess, who took from those who approached her the certainties of the body so as to fill this unsureness with the sureness of her presence. She could scent now, acrid in her nostrils, the dead ash heaped around the altar, sweepings of old fires. The moonlight lay in intricate patterns on the stone of the altar table, bright where it was clear, darker where it was splashed with old blood.

The two youths who were sweepers at the palace and assisted in the care of the shrines marked out the circle that would contain all those present, beginning back to back and keeping the altar at the center. The flute players fell silent. Sisipyla followed round, holding up her basket, the water bearers keeping pace behind her. Now the circle was sealed off from the world outside. The people stood grouped around the altar and held out their hands for cleansing, and those with the water jars went from one to another.

All was now ready; but the goat gave no sign, neither looking down in submission nor looking up in eagerness, but staring straight ahead, its pale eyes unblinking, moonlight gleaming on its gilded horns, on the ribbons of white silk that Sisipyla had so patiently fastened in the long hair of its flanks. It was necessary that the goat too should signify assent; without this the sacrifice was marred. Iphigeneia was standing beside the altar. She turned on the water bearers the white, unchanging oval of her mask and raised a bare arm and fluttered her fingers rapidly, the sign for rain and the pouring of water. The nearer man stepped forward and sprinkled the neck and back of the animal, which still made no sound, but jerked its head with the shock of the water as if nodding up at the moonlit sky. It was the sign needed. Those within the circle took grains of barley from the basket and held them ready. Iphigeneia raised her arms to the moon and uttered the words she had learned from her mother, the prayer, the invocation, the wish and the vow. In the silence after her voice ceased there was no sound but the pattering of the grains as these were cast over the altar.

Then Sisipyla offered the basket to Iphigeneia, who took the narrow-bladed knife, now lying there exposed. The porters took the goat by its legs and turned it and lifted it up, exposing the throat. Raised thus, gripped in strong hands, there was no cry nor struggle. The goat looked up at the sky and the moonlight made amber of its eyes. Iphigeneia cut hairs from its forehead and let them fall, to signify that the life was violated, the victim ordained to the goddess. She raised the lustrous moon of her face to the face of the goddess, now high overhead. For a brief while sacrificer and victim both gazed upward, as if asking jointly for blessing. Then Iphigeneia looked down and her arm swept across her body in a single movement from right to left and the blade flashed and dulled and the blood came, as the men struggled to hold the beast in the convulsions of its death, spurting from the severed throat onto Iphigeneia, who still held the knife, and Sisipyla, who still held the basket, and over the men holding the beast, and over the altar.

Later, while the men were skinning the animal and building up the fire in preparation for the burnt offering and the feast that would follow, Iphigeneia did something that no one there had ever seen done before on the public occasion of a sacrifice: she slipped off her girdle from beneath the bloodstained apron and laid it on the fire and watched it burn.

Waiting

FOR

Iphigeneia

1.

At Aulis the burden of waiting was felt in different ways, as all such burdens are; but for everyone the nature of the waiting had changed, because it was known that the wind would not cease — could not cease — until Iphigeneia came. The wind itself had a different voice now, it was sighing or groaning or screaming for Iphigeneia to come. She occupied the thoughts and dreams of a thousand men, few of whom had actually seen her. Her face and body were imagined with intensity as the men lay through the nights of the growing moon; they saw her white throat, bared for the knife; and they felt the rigid blade, and the stabbing urge, in their own restless loins.

The knife was ordered early. First requesting the presence of Menelaus and Idomeneus and Chasimenos as witnesses — with the latter having the additional responsibility of close liaison with the Singer—Agamemnon sent for the bronzesmith, who entered with a single guard immediately behind him. He had come from his forge and wore the leather breast piece and long apron of his trade. He was squat of build and thick at the shoulders. His head and face were shaven and streaked with healed spark burns.

He stopped at some distance, abruptly, not waiting for an order, obliging the guard to stumble to a halt. He bowed his head briefly but said nothing, simply stood waiting, looking steadily at the King. He carried the power and mystery of the bronze with him and all felt it. The center of his forehead was tattooed with concentric circles of red and blue, the eye of Cyclops, emblem of his guild and cult mark of Hephaestus, the god of smiths. The smell of fire and metal hung about him, he was answerable only to the master artificer who was his god.

"His name is Palernus," Chasimenos said. "He is from Crete."

Agamemnon looked closely at the man, in what seemed an attempt to beat his gaze down. When this failed, he said, more loudly than was needed, "I want a knife specially made, made to order, a sacrificial knife."

"I understand, yes. A special knife for a special person."

Hearing this, Chasimenos felt a glow of satisfaction. He had primed the Singer with the promise of a warm cloak for winter, and the Singer had responded well: if the smith already knew who the knife was for, then everybody else would too. He glanced at the King's face in the hope of finding some awareness of this, or even encountering an approving glance.

But Agamemnon's attention was fixed on the smith. "It must be like no other knife that you or any smith has ever made before," he said. "No expense is to be spared, only the very best quality of materials is to be used, pure and unadulterated. The copper and the tin must be smelted by you personally, and they must be virgin metals. Nothing used in the making of this knife must ever have been used to make anything before. I have plans for the design. I intend both blade and handle to have expensive and state-of-the-art decorations. Chasimenos, you will report these words of mine to the Singer. No one will say I skimped on this, no one will say I failed in munificence, in honoring my house and my name."

"A special knife for a special person," the smith repeated, in exactly the tone he had used before. "That is what Agamemnon desires and that is what I will fashion for him. But only a god can fashion a knife that is unlike any other knife. This one is for a sacrifice, as I understand the matter?"

"Yes, I have said so."

"Your sacrificial knives, now, have certain things in common by virtue of their use. No one can make a sacrificial knife that does not resemble in some ways all other sacrificial knives. The King will desire a knife with a blade no wider than this." He raised a blackened hand and made a small gap between forefinger and thumb.

"Yes, I suppose so."

"A narrow blade is customary for your sacrificial knives so as to reduce accidental wounds if the victim happens to be struggling. Your sacrificial knives will need to be a certain length, not too short, a short blade may fail to find the vein, not too long, a long blade is dangerous in confined spaces, I have seen an innocent bystander get his eye put out."

"All these are details, I was speaking of the quality."

"Your sacrificial knives, now, must be single-edged, with a groove down the—"

"You may return to your forge," Agamemnon said. "I will pay you in gold for the work, if it is well done."

When the smith had gone he turned moody eyes on Menelaus. "There's an earthbound fellow if ever there was one," he said. "A mind that can't rise above petty details, incapable of taking flight."

"No vision," Menelaus said. "Bolshie too, he was talking as if one victim were as good as another. It's this new class of technicians, they have no respect for authority, no sense of tradition. For two pins I'd have given him a kick up the arse."

"You'd better get along to see the Singer," Agamemnon said to Chasimenos. "Just a general announcement, no need to go into details of design at this stage, I haven't worked them out yet. Just tell him the knife will be a masterpiece." He paused for a moment and something like a smile twisted his lips. "Calchas will take him my plans for the design. I'm going to make Calchas responsible for supervising the work from day to day."

And so the fashioning of the knife became an element in that longing for Iphigeneia which was the longing for release from pain and travail, puffed up and spread by the wind, which veered from north to northeast and varied in intensity but never died away, rustling in the scrub of the hillsides, whispering among the pebbles of the shore, slapping at the hulls of the moored ships. Sounds became rumors: the whole thing was just a story to keep people happy, Agamemnon was playing for time, the Mycenaeans were secretly planning to leave, Iphigeneia wouldn't come, she would come but only to sacrifice an ox to Zeus in token of repentance, it didn't matter whether she came or not because Palamedes was preparing a coup that would put an end to Agamemnon's leadership and the curse of the wind at one stroke. Dark glances and knowing looks proliferated. It was a good time for those who could claim to know more than others did, they were listened to, they dominated conversation; and there were some who remembered the importance they achieved at this time as a highlight in their lives.

In face of these contradictory stories, the priests of Zeus circulated among the army by day and night, with their oak staffs and insignia of eagle heads, their banners bearing the colors of blood and sky and their one unvarying interpretation of events: the justice of Zeus required the sacrifice of the witch, the wind would not abate until her lifeblood splashed the altar.

Such certainty at a time of doubt made easy converts. The retinue of Croton swelled from hour to hour until it formed a long double line that wound its way through the camp, at first to the sound of oboes and kettledrums only, but then a sort of choric chanting was developed, certain phrases were shouted loudly and repeatedly. Croton, in the lead, would raise his right arm at regular intervals, and when he did this all those following also raised an arm and shouted one of two things, either WE LOVE ZEUS or ZEUS HATES WITCHES. It happened quite often that some members of the procession shouted one slogan and some another; but this did not matter, it was volume and fervor that counted. For those at a distance the music and the shouting were strangely hollow and distorted, making it seem as if the wind had added one more to its repertory of voices; but those who were shouting felt that they were among comrades, they found the experience exhilarating and developed a taste for it. Croton was praised by the Singer, in a series of inspired verses, as the originator of civil liberty, the right to free assembly and the peaceful expression of the people's will.

The rumors, the slogans, the wind, the prospect of a spectacle, these became a state of things that might go on forever, might be the very nature of life itself—and indeed, those who survived and returned home remembered this period of waiting as much more protracted than it really was; it became in the minds of many the nature of life before the war.

There was no way of checking, no way of verifying anything. It was dangerous to ask. There were those in the army who had seen Iphigeneia grow up, those for example who had done regular guard duty at the palace. There must have been a desire among these men, among some of them, that the sacrifice might be averted. Certainly, no one could warn her, even if prepared to risk his life to do so. There was no way of commandeering a ship and leaving by sea, not without concerted action and substantial numbers, and these were lacking. A permanent guard was kept on the ships and checkpoints were maintained night and day on all roads leading from Aulis, manned by archers faithful to Odysseus or the Cretan Idomeneus, who had made themselves jointly responsible for security. Of course, if someone, alone or perhaps accompanied by one or two others, had slipped out from the camp by night, on foot, using mountain tracks that were loose-surfaced and treacherous even in daylight, they might escape detection. But traveling thus, how could they have vied with the official delegation, already departed, in their swift ship, favored now by the wind, how could they have reached Mycenae in time to prevent the princess's departure?

Poimenos, knowing the wishes of his master's heart, possessed by notions of heroic achievement derived from the Singer, offered to make the attempt. "I can find my way through the passes," he said. "It is summer, there is no snow. One mountain is like another. I was often in high places when I tended the goats and I didn't have such good strong sandals then, I didn't have any sandals at all, I wrapped my feet in rags. Traveling night and day, going by the sun, it could be done."

Calchas regarded his acolyte for some moments. The boy, in the glow of his idea, had turned to look eastward—the wrong direction. He had no idea of geography at all. He had no idea where Delphi was, and that was where he came from, let alone Mycenae. There was such radiant enterprise on his face, such a blaze of imagined glory, that the diviner felt his eyes almost shocked by it, as at the assault of some strong light. Simplicity like that burned away the accumulated fat of his own doubts and anxieties and obstinate logic, returned him to primal harmony and clarity, where the will of the gods and the meaning of their messages could be known with certainty. It was what he needed, it was what Poimenos gave him. Perhaps it was simply hope. Why was it that now, in these days of his isolation and the King's disfavor, when he most needed hope, he felt this impulse to destroy it?

"Judging by the direction of your gaze," he said, "you are proposing to jump into the sea from the top of Mount Ocha and swim across to the island of Chios." With gratification and sorrow he saw the light fade on the boy's face. "You should be looking that way," he said, pointing. "And ships travel night and day too, you know, especially with a favoring wind, and then they will have horses and a good road. Even on the moral plane you would be outdistanced. Those with the impulse to destroy will always travel faster than those with the impulse to save. That is a lesson life will teach you."

"I don't understand."

There was no inquiry in this, only a note of finality, a curtness of tone that Calchas had not heard in the boy before. Compunction came to him for the hurt he had given, the damage to the youthful sense of what daring and devotion might achieve. "I could not let you go," he said. "I want you with me, I cannot be without you, not even for a morning, let alone whole days and nights. You are my consolation."

This was the truth, more so now than ever, when Agamemnon no longer called for him, when he was held in contempt by all, when only the sacred duty of supervising the making of the knife gave him protection—the terrible protection of the King's hatred.

But the words had come too late. The boy's face was closed against him, the eyes were lowered. And now a certain kind of fear came to Calchas, and in the grip of this he blundered further. "There are lions on those mountains, you know," he said, attempting a jocular tone. "You would make a tender morsel. Those good strong sandals would be all that was left."

Poimenos smiled a little and nodded, because it was not in his nature to disappoint the maker of a joke; but he still had not looked at his master; and it was now, perhaps to avoid further claims on his understanding or sympathy, that he retailed the piece of news he had picked up earlier that morning. "The dogs dug up a body during the night," he said. "Farther along the shore, beyond the camp." He had been out early, at first light, to gather kindling for the morning fire, and he had heard this from others similarly engaged. "On that side," he said, raising a hand to point. "Towards the narrower water. He was buried in the shingle."

"It must have been a shallow grave," Calchas said. "I suppose it's the body of the Boeotian, Opilmenos, he who was killed by the dancer."

"The Boeotian was buried by his own people, not near the shore, higher up. They put stones on the grave, heavy stones that no dog would be able to move."

"Then who?"

"They say he is a Mycenaean." Poimenos paused briefly, then added, "He has been partly eaten."

The certainty of who this must be came to Calchas suddenly, like a memory, some knowledge possessed long before. "Let us go and see this offering of the dogs," he said, and thought he saw a shadow pass over the boy's face, something like reluctance or disappointment, as if he had been planning something else, or hoping for it.

2.

O dysseus was told of their leaving together, just as he was told of the un-
earthed corpse. Nothing that happened in
the camp escaped his knowledge; he ran
the entire Ithacan contingent on the lines
of an information and security unit. He too
had a good idea whose body it might be.
Obviously Phylakos had blundered again.
But there was nothing to be done about it
now, in daylight. In any case he was too
busy. He was in constant attendance on
Agamemnon during this period. The King
was not sleeping well and his moods were
constantly changing. The tearful self-
righteousness and patriotic fervor were all
right, all to the good in fact; but at times he
was sunk in a kind of stupor, deaf to any
voice; and every now and again—most
dangerous of all—he seemed to gasp for
air and look upward, as if seeking guidance from the gods. As far as Odysseus
was concerned, the gods had already deliv-

ered. He did what he could to keep the King isolated from any who might give him bad advice. It was fortunate that Agamemnon could no longer stand the sight of his diviner, Calchas.

It was a question, really, of substituting terms, and in a way Odysseus enjoyed the intellectual stimulus these encounters with the King provided. On the one hand there was the desire for power and loot, on the other the deliberate killing of an innocent. If you softened the first by mixing in notions of public service, the need for living space and wider markets to serve a growing population, and submerged the second in the heavy burden of command, the problem ceased to exist, they became the same thing, they blended into a single notion of painful duty. How Agamemnon loved it, this painful duty, how he drank it in, how it soothed him. Therapy, really. Of course, after a while things started to slide apart again, and the King became confused and sometimes gasped for air; then some further restoration work was required.

He was coming from the King's tent after one such maintenance session, on his way to check up on the Singer, when he had this thought and it stopped him in his tracks. It was just a question of concepts. It came to him like a shaft of light. *It's all conceptual!* The driving force in human society was not greed or the lust for power, as he had always thought, but the energy generated by juggling with concepts, endlessly striving to make perceptions of reality agree with them, to melt things together, iron out problems, harmonize warring elements, what was the phrase he was looking for? *Eliminate the contradictions.* They would rule the world who knew this and used it.

As he stood there, full of grateful wonder at the insight, he heard from somewhere ahead of him a hoarse, irate shouting interspersed with shriller tones, a double act that everyone in the camp was familiar with by now. Those two clowns again, he thought. It didn't seem possible to go anywhere without bumping into them. He resolved to go straight past the pair without pausing, but when he came in sight of them he was arrested by what looked like a superstructure of foliage on the smaller man's head, and he stopped, almost involuntarily, to see what it might be.

"My small friend and I are offering you the chance of a lifetime," Ajax the Larger shouted, looking furiously at the small knot of spectators. "We had selected precious cups and tripods and shining cauldrons as prizes for the winners of the Games. But then we thought, we thought . . ." He paused, his huge sun-reddened face fixed in concentration: he had forgotten for the moment the reason the two of them had agreed on.

As usual, his dwarfish companion came to the rescue. "We thought what the fuck can you do with cups and tripods and shining cauldrons?" A small trail of leaves had escaped from the containing band that circled his head and was obscuring the sight of one small round eye. But his face below was as melancholy as ever and the half erection that was so permanent a feature of his appearance was clearly defined below the kilt.

"I've told him about that language before. A man can't wear a cup or a tripod or a shining cauldron on his head, can he? People would think it strange."

"People would think he was off his fucking rocker."

"The result is, the result is . . ."

"You leave the cups and the tripods and the shining cauldrons at home and go out for a walk and nobody knows you're the fucking winner."

"Good grief, I was going to say that, why do you keep interrupting? Your mother should have washed your mouth out with soap when you said bad words, and your father should have beaten you and put cold compresses on your member when you showed signs of being a potential rapist. That's what my parents did and look at me now."

"It would take more than a cold compress," Ajax the Lesser shouted, twitching his pelvis and leering obscenely at the audience. "It would take more than a team of wild horses."

"So we have devised a much more valuable prize, a circlet of leaves that is worn on the head in the way that my small friend is wearing it now. Give these good people a demonstration."

The little man paraded back and forth, the wreath of leaves at a rakish angle. "You can wear it tilted back for the more casual look," he shouted in his reedy but penetrating voice, "or forward over the brow for when you mean business. The women will see you coming, they will see the wreath first, their legs will start loosening, no need for body language, the wreath will reduce them to a jelly."

"A man with a wreath on his head," bellowed Ajax the Larger, scarlet with vexation at his partner's lewdness, "a man with a wreath on his head—what was that?"

Someone in the audience had asked a question that Odysseus did not catch. A look of incredulity had appeared on the large man's face. "What happens when the leaves wither and start dropping off? Good grief, what kind of question is that? You must be as thick as two planks. You go out and get new leaves. That's the beauty of this prize we are offering, you can, it can be . . ."

"It's infinitely fucking renewable," Ajax the Lesser shouted at top volume. His head shuddered a little and the ragged crown slipped down further over his brows.

"I was going to say that, why do you keep —"

"No you weren't, no you weren't, shall I tell you why?"

"Tell me why."

"Those words are not in your fucking vocabulary, that's why."

Concepts again, Odysseus reflected as he proceeded on his way. Infinitely renewable, imperishable fame. These two buffoons had found a prize in keeping with the meanness which was just about all they had in common. Still, they provided some entertainment if nothing else; anything that took people's minds off the wind for a while was to be welcomed. So far all the volunteers for the Games had been either from Locris or from Salamis — hardly surprising, seeing that these were the contingents commanded by the dwarf and the giant respectively. It did not seem likely that this new offer would change matters much.

He heard the raised voice of the Singer and the vibrant cords of the lyre while still some distance off. It was the middle of the morning, not a time for peak audiences, but Odysseus was delighted to find that the Song was about the knife to be fashioned for Iphigeneia, this being just the sort of thing he had been going to recommend. He stood listening for a while, observing the faces of those in the audience. They seemed quite gripped, though there was not much to say for the moment, or so at least it seemed to Odysseus, the knife being little more than a project as yet.

The subject of the Song was the purity of the metals that would go to compose the knife. By a cleverly managed shift, this became identified with the virginal purity of the royal victim. This wondrous knife would be forged from a fusion of tin and copper, neither of which had been worked before, never probed, never pierced, never penetrated. Sheet of tin and ingot of copper, different shapes and substances, smelted together to make a third element, finer, stronger, more beautiful than either. A mystery, how things could transcend themselves by blending, only the gods knew the how and the why, but think of the clays from which the hyacinth springs, think of the clear dew left by the thick vapors of night . . .

He stopped here, raised his head as if listening to some echo, struck the lyre once and with the barest of pauses began the conventional preliminaries to the Song of the Argonauts, the heroes who sailed with Jason in the quest for the Golden Fleece.

Before he had time to get far into the episode he had chosen, Odysseus moved forward through the crowd. The Singer fell silent as he drew near, keeping his face averted with the usual air of listening rather than seeing — though Odysseus, always alert to subterfuge, was sure he saw more than he let on.

"I am Odysseus," he said, bending down towards the Singer and speaking quietly. "We had a little chat a day or two ago, do you remember? I am glad you saw reason on that occasion."

"I did not see reason," the Singer said, in his soft, rather hesitant voice — he was more fluent when he sang. "I was not given a reason. And in any case, there is no more reason in one Song than another."

"I can't say I agree with you there. Do you mean to say all Songs are of equal weight and importance, whether they deal with the past, the present or the future, whether it's a knife we are talking about or a hyacinth?"

"Yes."

"You can't be serious. Can one draw blood with a hyacinth?"

The Singer sighed audibly. He had been annoyed by the interruption; and now, it seemed, he was to be lectured on the nature of Songs by one who knew nothing about them. "Do you think it would be easier to find perfume in a knife? Tell me how I can be of service to you."

"Well, I don't want to interrupt your performance. I just wanted to tell you how pleased I was, in passing by, to hear you singing of this forthcoming sacrifice, it is exactly what is needed to maintain public interest in the event."

In fact he had been rather disappointed by the very brief treatment of the knife and by the way the Song had trailed off into poeticisms. No point in saying so, however. He had a close view of the Singer's face in half profile and the obscured crystal of his left eye. No one knew how much he could see, whether he could see much at all. Light and dark and the bulk of shapes before him he must be able to distinguish—he had no one to guide him. Odysseus felt a certain awe mingled with his repugnance. The man was god-possessed, there could be no doubt of that. How otherwise could you explain line after unfaltering line, and all in meter? But it was indecent to make far-fetched comparisons like that. A knife, a virgin, a flower, dew. Obvious falsehoods—a knife was a knife. He was himself no enemy to metaphor; the controller of concepts must be a master of metaphor too. But he could see no point in idle figures of speech like these. They were transparently untrue, which in itself was offensive to an accomplished liar like himself. And what was the use of them? Whose ends did they serve? And the obscenely casual ease with which the Singer had passed from the destined throat to the voyage of the Argonauts . . .

"Well, keep up the good work," he whispered to the unchanging face. "We are very glad to have you on the team and I am not alone in thinking that. Next time you return to this topic, which I hope will be soon, can I ask you to mention the fact that the smith has now received Agamemnon's instructions for the decoration of the knife? It's going to be fantastic, the last word in sophisticated ceremonial weaponry. The whole length of the blade will be mounted with silver and this silver mounting will be incised in a pattern of foliage and birds — doves actually — and the incisions will be fused with the black powder produced by melting copper and silver together and adding sulfur to the alloy, to make a striking overall design in silver and black. Magical stuff, this black powder, it deserves a Song of its own. The smith is a Cretan and they are masters of it there. You might also dwell a bit more next time on personalities. I must say I found your account deficient in that respect. You know, the extraordinary generosity Agamemnon is showing in this matter of the knife, after the sacrifice it will never be used again in spite of the expense, it will be thrown into the sea, he has vowed that in the presence of witnesses. It's very important that the army should have respect for the man at the helm. Unity and solidarity, that's the only way to beat this wind. You might also put in a phrase or two about the role I am playing, my loyal support for the Commander-in-Chief, you know the sort of thing, a man of few words but sterling virtue. You get it right and I'll see you are rewarded when we get to Troy."

The Singer listened to the words, heard the silence that followed upon them, sensed the speaker withdraw. Odysseus the trickster, the wrestler, the owner of the Great Bow. There had been the usual pattern: praise, detraction, the desired favor, the promise that always contained a threat. All who came to him with requests spoke with the same voice. Except the boy—he asked for nothing but the story. He had not come today. Perhaps he had been sent on some errand. He knew now that the boy belonged to Calchas, the diviner, and his name was Poimenos. Everyone else, however diverse the requests, always wanted something more than the story, something extra. It was not possible to keep everything in mind; some items were forgotten altogether, others were soon blended with old stories, yet others remained dormant for a time that might be long, like creatures waiting for the right weather. People like Odysseus never understood this underground life of Songs. He had sensed the other's dislike, heard the forced friendliness of the tone. Song was distrusted by people like that, because they saw everything in terms of utility and Song escaped their control.

There was some talking and stir of movement among the audience—his eyes were always strong enough to detect that. They were waiting for him to begin again. For a moment or two more he kept silent, passing his hand over the curve of the turtle shell that formed the belly of the lyre—a gesture of love. He raised his left hand to mute the two strings immediately below the yoke and struck the lower three with the bone thimble attached to his forefinger, allowing the strings to vibrate all through their length in a long, shuddering chord. When this died away he took up the story at the precise point where he had left it at the approach of Odysseus.

On its homeward journey the *Argo* came to the beautiful island of Anthemoessa, home of the Sirens, three winged women with bird feet whose singing had such allure that mariners who heard it forgot everything, went crazy, plunged into the sea and tried to swim to the source of that glorious sound, only to be drowned in the treacherous swirls of the current. Captains would wreck their ships on the jagged rocks that fringed the island in a frenzied attempt to land. That island was a death trap, its reefs and currents specially designed to destroy any who approached. All round there were bodies floating, and the wreckage of ships. Yet once you heard that amazing music, you couldn't resist, you lost all reasoning power.

The Singer paused, remained silent for some moments before plucking again at the strings. Pauses did not break the Song, they strengthened it, he knew this well, just as he knew he was singing the truth. Any song could be a siren song, any island could be Anthemoessa. Songs could make people believe anything, do anything, go from loving to killing and back again, to weep over the corpse.

The Argonauts too would have been destroyed, as so many before them, their bodies picked by the fish, their bones bleaching on the rocky shores of the island, had not quick-witted Orpheus seized his lyre, struck up a tune and burst into song, thus confusing the men's ears with conflicting sounds until they were safely past.

The Singer smiled as he sang, a thing very rare with him. It was one of his favorite episodes. Orpheus, the Great Singer, father of all singers, son of Oeagrus and the Muse Calliope, had saved them all, the music of life had prevailed over the music of death, it was a triumph.

But a greater danger still awaited them. Before long they were approaching the zone of the Wandering Rocks. On their left was the promontory where lives Scylla, she of the six ravenous heads on necks so long that she can stretch them out over the water and snatch sailors from the decks of passing ships. On their right was the whirlpool in which lurks the monster Charybdis, of insatiable appetite, capable of swallowing ships whole. Imagine the sight, the fearsome sight, the stretching necks and slavering mouths on one side, the menace of the vortex on the other. The smallest misjudgment on the pilot's part in that narrow strait, and you can guess what would happen: one of two things, neither of them very pleasant. They knew the odds were against them, they weren't stupid, but this was a crew of heroes, they sailed bravely ahead.

At this moment, just as they entered the strait, the white-armed sea nymphs appeared, swimming alongside, guiding the ship. The men were almost distracted from the danger, seeing these beautiful naked girls sporting below them. The nymphs were led by the goddess Thetis, silvery-footed daughter of the Old One of the Sea, and this was because her mortal lover Peleus was on board. As we all know, the fruit of this union was the incomparable Achilles, Sacker of Cities, who is here with us on this glorious expedition to restore the honor of Greece.

So the fair-browed nymphs stayed alongside the *Argo* as it now began to be tossed about in the turbulent waters that churn around the Wandering Rocks, in the shadow of smoke-crowned Aetna, where the god of smiths, Hephaestus, stokes his fires. As instructed by Thetis, they bore up the ship on either side so that it skimmed over the crests of the waves, avoiding the treacherous currents that would have dashed it against the rocks. And so, in a short while, the heroes were safely past and the nymphs, their mission completed, dived below the waves and disappeared from sight, though you can be sure that the Argonauts were sorry to see them go, having hoped they would come on board for a while and have a drink, now that the *Argo* was sailing in calm waters . . .

The Singer played a run of quiet notes to reinforce the notion of calm after storm. It was always a good idea to dilute a happy ending with a dollop of nostalgia. Restored to safety after danger has passed, the heart has leisure for regrets and desires; and those nymphs must have been quite something. The adventures of the Argonauts were always popular, a series of mortal perils surmounted in the nick of time, ideally suited to serial treatment.

His throat felt tired and he was hungry. A few gifts had been deposited on the square of felt before him, a wheat cake covered with sesame seeds, some figs, a small stoppered jar which might contain honey, a handful of terra-cotta beads painted in different colors and pierced to make a necklace. He needed a short song of praise to round things off, then he would rest for a while. The Ajaxes would do. Big Ajax had never given him the silver clip he had been promised, but the pair had come with two bronze arrowheads—one from each—and explained their new idea of a wreath of leaves worn on the head to honor winners in the Games.

They would do, yes, but what was one to say about them? The small one was a rapist of note. He launched into a list of Little Ajax's successes, all carried out in style, without once breaking the rules, no recourse to weapons, no maidens rudely seized and violated when they had taken sanctuary at the altar of a god. And his inseparable companion, Big Ajax, the Imperturbable, the Peacemaker, mighty in battle, the man who had dreamed up the idea of the Games Day. These two men had bequeathed to humanity a totally new type of headgear, the garland of entwined leaves, eternal symbol of victory.

3.

One man had remained to keep the dogs off. The corpse was lying with face to the sky, or what was left of the face—the eyes had gone, and the nose and most of the right cheek had been gnawed away. It seemed to Calchas, as he looked down, that these eyeless sockets had the same staring look of possession as when the living voice had spoken and the throat labored to bring out the goddess's words, tell of the devouring of the hare's young and warn the assembled chiefs. The dried blood was caked on his neck where the vein had been severed. This was no savaging of the dogs; his killers had slashed the throat that had betrayed them; he had been killed for speaking out of turn, for saying something that was not in the story, not part of the plan. But it was in the spaces between human plans that the gods conveyed their messages; he had been a vehicle for the goddess and in stopping his mouth they had tried to stop hers. The dogs were at the bidding of the Mistress, at her bidding they had brought this poor murdered creature up to the light again. For what purpose? Calchas felt again the ache of uncertainty, like a physical pain somewhere unlocalized in his body. "We must get back," he said. "I must talk again with the King."

At this moment, looking towards the sea, he saw a man running along the shore close to the water, sweat shining on his naked chest and arms. And now, as though to encourage the diviner in his resolve, the sun rose clear above the headland and was briefly defined as a perfect disk, containing its shape, a shape that lasted for moments only—already, as they began to return along the shore, it was lost, streaming off in a brilliance without form, not touching yet the western sky, which was cold-colored and hazed with thin mist.

"The summer is waning," Calchas said, as if speaking to himself. Did truth lie in the short-lived, perfect sphere? Or in this slow spreading of rays, this formless brightness? Was there one single, perfect thing to say to Agamemnon, if he could seize upon it?

Before they were back in the camp the sun had cleared away those lingerings of night in the west and laid a long stripe of silver across the water that shimmered as the wind moved it. The hulls of the chariots drawn up on the shingle flamed in the sun and the neurotic horses tossed their heads in the wind. And already Calchas was faltering. He would not go at once, it was never wise to speak or act precipitately, he would wait for the right moment, the right formula. Customary fears and doubts, customary quickening of self-contempt.

"Look, there goes the versatile Odysseus," Poimenos chose this moment to say. Odysseus, head lowered and seeming lost in thought, was walking slowly in the direction of Agamemnon's tent.

"The versatile Odysseus?" He looked at the boy's bright face, felt again the old conflict, the fear of losing this last resource, so precious to him, the bleak need for truth, even though destructive. Something else too, more recent: the jealousy of contested possession. "That is a term that belongs to singers. You listen to him often, our Singer, as you go about the camp?"

"Sometimes, passing by, I stop and listen for a while."

"Poimenos, you will never get the truth of things from Singers. They have interests to serve, their voice is a collective voice. Do you understand what I mean?"

"I think so, yes. The stories they tell belong to everybody."

"No, I mean their Songs are about what people already believe or what it is wished they should believe. Here at Aulis we have an army that must be kept together or the expedition will fail. Odysseus the versatile, the resourceful. Yes, these words describe him. But then come the words that don't, though they seem to follow naturally enough. Loyal Odysseus, faithful Odysseus, Odysseus who is using his great talents in the service of Greece."

The boy was silent; his expression had not changed but he had glanced aside. Calchas hesitated a moment, aware of the beating of his heart. This was not the way, he knew it. The specter of loss and desolation loomed between him and the boy's averted face. But he was driven to go on. "The loyalty and fidelity exist only in the Song. This Greece doesn't exist except in the Song. Odysseus is lord of Ithaca. Do you know where Ithaca is? It is over there, far to the west. It is a small island, very small. You haven't seen Ithaca, but I have seen it. When I first came to Greece, on the voyage to Megara, we ran into a great storm and the ship was blown far off course. We had to enter the Gulf of Corinth from the west."

He paused again, looking at the boy closely. Poimenos's eyes were on him now but there was no comprehension in his face. These names of seas and cities, these points of east and west, would mean little to him. The only sense of place he had was the place in a story, someone else's story. Calchas turned a little, into the wind, looked beyond the boy at the hills across the narrow water and the very faint striations of cloud in the sky above. Rifts in the cloud were smooth, not ragged, they made no shapes for him, only a strange confusion of liquid and solid. Again he sensed the waning of summer, cooler weather coming. Someone was grinding wheat not far away, he could hear the grating of the heavy stones, one above the other.

"I saw Ithaca from close by," he said. "It's just a rock standing up in the sea. There is nothing there, no great buildings, no industry of any kind. No stories belong to Ithaca, except only that it is the birthplace of Odysseus, son of Laertes. It has no past. On Ithaca Odysseus is nobody, lord of kelp-gatherers and swineherds and a few barren crags. Suppose, for the sake of comparison, we think of another island, let's say Lemnos. Lemnos lies in the northern part of the Aegean Sea. That is the sea we are looking at now, this one here before us."

He pointed, and with habitual obedience Poimenos followed the direction of his finger. "Has this island of Lemnos got stories belonging to it?" the boy said.

"It is rich in them. It is larger than Ithaca and more populous, it has fertile plains and wooded valleys and wide pastures. It has deposits of minerals and metals. But even more important than all this, it is in just the right place. It dominates the approaches to Troy from the west. One who could take possession of Lemnos and establish his rule there could control the trade that passes through the narrow water below the walls of Troy. That is where the gold is embarked, the gold that comes down from Thrace." He pointed again, northward this time. "Now don't you think that versatile Odysseus would rather be king of Lemnos than king of Ithaca?"

"Yes, I do." The boy's face wore again the look of innocent enthusiasm that Calchas loved and felt driven to discourage. "I would like to hear them," he said, "these stories belonging to Lemnos."

The diviner made a gesture of impatience. "I want to tell you meanings, not stories." This came out in a tone harsher than he had intended. With a strange feeling of helplessness he knew again that this was not the way, it would not hold the boy to him; Poimenos was outside the cage of meanings altogether, it was he himself who was imprisoned in it.

"Do you think this war is about Helen?" he said. "That's just a story. People intent on war always need a story and the singers always provide one. What it is really about is gold and copper and cinnabar and jade and slaves and timber. Great wealth will fall into the hands of those who conquer Troy and occupy her territories. Imagine what dreams of wealth would fill the mind of Odysseus, sitting on a rock far away on the wrong side of the sea. Agamemnon will want to come back, he is lord of a powerful kingdom. But why should Odysseus think of returning? He has a son, Telemachus, who can rule in Ithaca for him. His heart is set on conquest in the East. On his own, with the small force he has been able to muster, what can he do? But in alliance with Crete, Thebes, Pylos, Mycenae . . . you see? Then this wind comes, things begin to slip away, he must hold them together, he will do or say anything, it is his only chance. You see, don't you, Poimenos?"

It sounded like an entreaty. He fell silent, looking straight before him, away from the sea, towards the flatlands of the south. There was some different quality in the light, some thickening in the air above the lion-colored plain. After a moment or two he understood what it was. Here and there, across the whole expanse of the land, as far as the distant foothills, they were threshing the wheat, and the chaff was rising in pale gold puffs of cloud, lifted and scattered by the wind. He tried to discern shapes in these, but the blown chaff was too thin, too quickly dispersed. "That is the versatility of Odysseus," he said, "and it is something you will not hear from the Singer." He felt tired, defeated. This was just another story, after all, drabber, less entertaining, than those the boy liked. For some moments longer he studied the faint golden graining in the air above the plain. Then he said, "We must go and visit the smith now, to see how work on the knife is proceeding."

"If you will give me leave," Poimenos said, not quite meeting his master's eye, "I will not go with you. I have set snares for quail up on the hillside and I want to see if we have caught anything. The young are grown enough now, they are easier to catch than the older birds. But they flutter in the trap and crows can get them if they are left. I have seen this happen. Crows always start with the eyes, as if they must blind the birds before they can eat them. And then, there are plenty here in the camp who would rob the traps if they came upon them."

It was by far the longest speech Calchas had ever heard the boy utter. He hesitated a moment, then nodded. "Very well. We can hope for a brace of quail to roast on the fire when dark comes."

As he made his way towards the compound where the smith had his forge, he thought how strange it was that Poimenos should be so casually aware of animal and human rapine in the matter of quails, and yet take the Songs of Kings and Heroes with what seemed no smallest degree of question.

The smith had taken over the ruins of a building on the edge of the camp, originally a house of some kind, now no more than a shelter for goatherds, with broken-down stone walls and the remnants of a thatch. This last he had torn down to prevent fire, and he had set his shallow, clay-lined furnace in an angle made by the walls.

As he came forward now, Calchas noticed for the first time that he was slightly lame — his right foot dragged a little. He was dressed in his usual leather apron, but his thick arms were uncovered and his hands were bare. "So," he said, and grinned, revealing a mouth with not many teeth remaining and these not promising to remain long. "The diviner has been sent to make sure that Palernus the smith is doing his work properly."

"It is not that," Calchas said. "The King does not doubt you are a master of your trade." He felt always an uneasiness bordering on dread in the presence of the smith, with his shaven head and fire scars and the concentric rings of his guild mark set on his forehead like a staring third eye. One who could distill metal from stone, cast aside the dross, separate the elements of nature that had been joined since the creation of the world. This was magic, it set him apart. "No, it is not that," he said again. "Agamemnon takes close interest in the progress of this knife."

The smith nodded, still grinning. "And so he sends you, his diviner. Come round this way."

He led his visitor to the angle in the walls where the furnace had been set. Two slaves were crouched there, on either side of the brick hearth, shaven-headed like their master, naked save for loincloths. One was armed with pigskin bellows. The mouth of the bowl-shaped hearth roared with heat.

"It has taken me this time to set up the forge," the smith said. "The bricks, the sand, the clay for the lining, all had to be taken from the ship. We have got a good place for it, sheltered enough from the wind, not too much." He winked briefly with a bloodshot eye and made a slight movement of the head. "This wind serves us well, we will hardly need the bellows. You would say the wind wanted it."

"Wanted it?"

"Her death. First it maddens us, so she is summoned. Then it blows on the fire to make a good heat for the knife."

Calchas made no immediate reply. He heard the seething of the draft at the bottom of the hearth and saw the red pulse of the charcoal. The heat came against his face. He thought for a moment of what it might be like for the two naked men crouched so near it. "So the work has not properly begun yet?" he said.

"Brother, the work began when I heard the King's words and understood what was wanted. You can report that the fire is ready and the mold made and the copper and tin chosen. Come, see here."

He turned to a rough platform that had been made by pushing broken stones together and bent down to feel under a square of cloth that was lying there. After a moment he straightened and held out in both hands a short, reddish-colored bar with a soft shine to it. "I keep it well covered," he said. "Copper is soon corrupted, the damp of night puts a green coat on it. Tell the King how tender I am with his copper, even before it goes to the fire. This ingot came with us from Crete, it was smelted from weathered copper stone, as pure as ever you could find in a natural state, washed and washed again by the rain since first it pushed up from the womb of earth. Tell the King this."

"I will, you can rely on it."

The smith grinned again. "And he can rely on the knife. A special knife for the King's daughter, and also for his diviner, Calchas. Here is the tin." He moved aside, took from the base of the wall, against which it was leaning, a square sheet of metal. It gleamed in the light as he raised it and Calchas saw a brief, rippling image of his own face in the surface. "Tin has a voice," the smith said. He twisted the sheet a little in his scarred, thick-fingered hands, and it emitted a high, squeaking sound like some small mammal in fear. "This tin has never been mixed or alloyed, I swear by Hephaestus. We could not bring the ore with us, it is too heavy. And there is none to be found here. Besides, tinstone would be the devil to smelt on a makeshift furnace like this one. Has Calchas the diviner ever seen melting tin?"

"No, not that I can remember."

"Your tin is a timorous metal. It runs everywhere, it finds every thinnest crack to hide in, it flees away down slopes that look dead level to your eyes."

He tilted the sheet as if inviting Calchas again to seek his reflection; but the diviner looked sharply away. "I will come to-morrow at this same time," he said.

"Stay and see the work. You will see me smelt these two metals together and cast the bronze. Tell the King I will bond eight parts of copper with one of tin."

He twisted the sheet again, and again it made the sound of a small creature in some extreme distress. It seemed to Calchas that the heat was intensifying. The air above the furnace was blurred with it. His vision was momentarily affected, so that the rings of the tattooed eye in the center of the smith's fore-head appeared to turn slowly on their red center. Dread of the smith and what the smith seemed to know clutched at him. He thought of the half-eaten face and the slashed throat, the Boeotian squirming on the shingle as the dancer stepped round him, of his terrible failure to understand who must win that fight. It was then, he thought, while the life ebbed from Opilmenos, then that the gods withdrew their favor from me. He felt the beginnings of nausea.

"The best mix," the smith said. "Less tin than that and the bronze will not hammer well, Calchas the diviner will not get a keen blade."

The feeling of nausea grew stronger. "I will make this known to the King," Calchas said, and he turned and went half blindly out from the enclosure of the walls.

4.

The threshing of the wheat, which Calchas had seen as a haze of gold over the plain, continued in the days that followed, the days of waiting for Iphigeneia. Squads were sent out to seize the grain wherever it could be found; and the country people, faced with the prospect of starvation in the winter, grew cunning in concealment, leaving their granaries bare, carting off the grain in sacks during the night, hiding it in gullies and thickets. A man was beaten to death by his neighbors for taking a bronze incense burner, a thing he had no earthly use for and could not easily dispose of, to lead the soldiers to one such cache.

The straw was left, as always, in soft conical heaps, taller than a man, bright gold in the sunshine at first, soon bleaching to pale yellow. The wind swept across the open space, loosened the binding of the heaps, threw up the straw in clouds which rose and fell, drifting over a wide area, getting caught in ruts and hollows and in the short, sun-scorched grass of the plain. There was a period when the land seemed textured with it, as if this pale glinting yellow was the natural color of the earth. At this time too the foothills that lay beyond the plain had exactly this same shade of faded gold, so that the eye was carried on a single tide of color to the horizon. From the sparse settlements scattered over this great expanse the only sounds that could be heard above the wind were those of pain: the tormented braying of an ass, the squealing outcries of gelded hogs.

The altar was built under the supervision of Croton and his two assistant priests, who were allowed as many men as they needed for it. The crest of a short rise was chosen, beyond the confines of the camp, clear all round for maximum viewing, important both for the spectators and for Zeus himself, as Croton pointed out: in the open, under the wide sky, where the god could get a sweeping overall view, not in some thicket or cave or hole-in-corner place, haunts of Hecate and her devotees and all the obscene practices of the night.

It was no easy task to find stones of the right size and shape that could be fitted together and built up to form a waist-high platform. Lines of laboring figures, forced by their loads into attitudes of humility and supplication, toiled over slopes of thorny scrub that lacerated their legs. One man fell into a gulley and broke his collarbone, another dropped a stone on his foot, crushing the toes. However, stone by stone and hour by hour the work continued. At the end of the third day Croton professed himself satisfied; it was certain that Zeus would look favorably on such an altar. Now, however, what was needed was a road to it, broad enough for a ceremonial procession, naturally with Croton himself at the head—it was his ambition, and he had already petitioned Agamemnon in the matter, to be the one ordained to wield the knife. It was not of course possible to make a paved way up to the altar, but the track could be widened and stones cleared. Men worked in shifts to get the road ready for Iphigeneia.

There is a pattern, in periods of protracted waiting, made up of what is accustomed and what is singular. The figures of toiling men, the booming voice of Ajax the Larger as he shouted threats and promises to his squad of reluctant athletes, the soft, pervasive odor of excrement hanging over the camp, the sharper stink of the horses, the endless creaking and groaning of the ships as they rocked in their moorings, all these were things woven into the tissue of existence from day to day. But one afternoon a particular thing happened. A father and a daughter appeared, asking the way to the tent of Menelaus. They had with them a man from a neighboring village who had been recruited into the Euboean force under Elphenor and knew enough Greek to convert the local dialect into sounds intelligible to Menelaus and his Spartan guards.

These last had debated long and earnestly among themselves whether to disturb the king in his afternoon repose and so risk his wrath. The visitors did not look to be of much account, they were country people. The father was thin as a rake and vehement; the girl was broad-faced and stocky, with heavy breasts. Both had put on their best clothes for the visit, the father in clean white vest and loincloth, the girl in a high-necked bodice and long skirt decorated with paste glass beads of various colors. They would not say what their business was, conveying however that it was important, even urgent. Something affecting the security of the army, news of a plot they had somehow stumbled on? They might think Menelaus the commander most important and respected in the Greek host, the one to be told; it was not very likely that anyone should have that idea of him, but it couldn't be ruled out. If it was so, and these people were turned away, they would go elsewhere with their news and Menelaus would be absolutely livid. The guards hadn't much to occupy them, they were bored, ready to welcome any diversion. Besides, they were curious. They could put it to Menelaus that, considering him the most important and respected commander in the Greek host, they had thought it better not to take chances. In the end, having drawn lots, two of them went in to him, the visitors having resolutely refused to enter the tent.

The attempts to interrogate the pair and the subsequent discussion among the guards had aroused a good deal of interest, and when Menelaus emerged from the tent he found himself before a considerable crowd. "Well," he said to the couple, in his brusque way, "who are you? What have you to say to Menelaus? Come on, get on with it, I haven't got all bloody day."

The tone of this made translation unnecessary. The father's mouth worked in agitation and he began to speak in the soft, mumbling tongue of the region.

"What does he say?"

The interpreter hesitated a moment. "My lord, he says that this girl is his daughter and that you violated her yesterday afternoon when you passed by their house on a hunting trip."

Menelaus had been dozing inside his tent and his eyes were not adjusted yet to the strong light outside and the wind that came against his face. He blinked and craned his head forward a little to stare at the girl. "By Zeus, yes," he said after a moment. "Dead right. I knew I'd seen her somewhere before." A smile overspread his face. It was agreeable to have his prowess made public in this way, as it were accidentally, just a casual thing which a man like himself, accustomed to such exploits, hadn't found necessary to mention. "I didn't recognize her at first," he said. "She's got her glad rags on today. She didn't have so much on when I last saw her."

There were sniggers at this from Menelaus's followers, and particularly from the two guards who had gone in to him with the message and who now, seeing his good humor, were congratulating themselves on having done the right thing, and expecting a good reward.

"Well, lads, you know how it is," Menelaus said. "We've all been there, haven't we? On the way back to camp, it was. We'd been after boar all day and we were thirsty as hell, the dogs too. We stopped at this hovel. Water for the dogs, wine for us. These people always have wine, if you know where to look for it. We had to push this fellow around a bit before he got the idea."

Menelaus closed one of his small eyes in a wink and smiled round at his audience. "They kept the stuff in an earth cellar behind this shack of theirs. He sent the girl to draw some off for us. I followed her with one man, whom I set to watch at the door. She fought a bit and tried to cry out, just for form's sake, you know. I mean, she knew who I was, there's no mistaking a kingly bearing, breeding will always show. I stuck her up against a barrel. Fantastic. No one had been there before. Now they have come to ask me to acknowledge it publicly, and you can see why. It isn't every day that a girl gets that sort of attention. It will give them tremendous status in their community. Well, I have always been a man who accepts his responsibilities. I want you all to know that their claim is just.

Find out her name. I want the Singer to be told that this girl was raped by King Menelaus in person."

This was conveyed to the couple, but the expected smiles did not appear on their faces. The girl said nothing, remaining with eyes cast down, aware of the gaze of all upon her, aware that in the minds of all she was still being pushed up against a wine barrel and roughly penetrated. The father glanced at the faces round him, and after a moment broke again into rapid, mumbling speech.

"What does he say?" Menelaus, disappointed in the reception his words had been accorded, was growing testy.

The interpreter took time over replying. It could be seen from his face that he was no longer much enjoying the job. "He says he doesn't want the Singer to be told. He says it is already bad enough that everyone in the village should know his daughter is no longer a virgin. He humbly appeals to the laws of hospitality and would humbly like to remind the king that there was not only the wine but also the eggs, the oatmeal and a round of cheese. Plus the fact that the girl's marriage prospects have sunk to zero."

A scowl of mingled wrath and incredulity had come to Menelaus's face. "I can't believe what I'm hearing," he said. "Not want the Singer to be told? He's a liar, there were no eggs, we looked everywhere."

"My lord," the interpreter said unhappily, "he says they have been wronged, he will now have to find a much larger dowry for her, he asks for compensation."

"What?" Menelaus had flushed a dark red. In a voice choked with rage, he said, "I, Menelaus, eagle king of the House of Atreus, leader of the Spartan host, am required to pay for sex with a peasant girl? That would be something for the Singer to get hold of. My image ruined for all time to come. How dare they? Fetch me a javelin. I'll show the clod compensation, I'll shove it up his backside."

Several in the crowd, local men like the interpreter, closed round the couple and jostled them hastily away. By the time the guard came with a javelin they were some distance off and Menelaus was breathing heavily, in the way he had when his emotions were excited. He did not resort to the javelin but contented himself with shouting after them, in a voice broken by rage, "That was royal sperm, you bitch!"

When some measure of calm had returned and his breathing was back to normal, he sent for the two guards who had brought him news of the visitors. They came in fear and prostrated themselves before him.

"What a grotesque error of judgment," Menelaus said. "You should have known better than to disturb my repose like that. My nerves have been in pieces since my hospitality was abused by that lecherous wog, Paris. Anyone with an ounce of savvy would have seen at once that those two characters were not worth bothering with. I mean, I knew it as soon as I set eyes on them. Such dolts too, refusing my offer of free publicity. I'm tempted to have the pair of you soundly flogged. You'd better watch out in future. Go and report to Big Ajax for two successive days of latrine duties."

"Well, brother, that's the way the world goes," one guard said to the other as they trudged towards the Salamis lines. "You try to act for the best and you end up shoveling shit."

5.

---

hen there was the business of the Athenian, Leucon, who was found in possession of a gilded pendant in the shape of a beetle, the property of Achilles. After various denials and evasions he admitted taking this from Achilles' tent while the latter was with Patroclus having a massage.

This theft was regarded by all the chiefs as a very serious matter. It was the thin end of the wedge. If not checked in time, it could lead to widespread pilfering, with consequent ill feeling and collapse of discipline. It had to be stamped on until they could get to Troy. A tribunal was hastily convened, open to any who cared to attend. Achilles was demanding the maximum penalty, which was death. Both he and the accused had the right to make a statement at any point in the proceedings but they could have no other part in the trial. Achilles entrusted the prosecution to one of his officers, a man named Pleuron.

Leucon was defended by a fellow soldier, Calligonus, also from Athens, nimble of tongue and quick-witted, as the Athenians generally were. The final decision would rest with Agamemnon as Supreme Commander, helped in his deliberations by four chiefs who would act as judges—naturally none of them from either Attica or Phthia.

Pleuron began, speaking directly to Agamemnon, who sat immobile, hunched a little forward. This could by no means be regarded as an impulsive theft, he said. The accused man had waited, chosen his moment, a time when Achilles was away. He had taken advantage of some momentary inattention on the part of the guards. It was an open-and-shut case. There was no smallest doubt of Leucon's guilt. This was a deliberate, premeditated theft from a comrade in arms and deserved the maximum penalty.

This speech was greeted by cries of "no" from the Athenian contingent, a small but noisy group, and by a sustained growl of agreement from the Phthians.

Leucon's counsel began with the issue of impulse, crucial for the obtaining of a more lenient sentence. Passing by a tent, seeing it unguarded, entering it on the spur of a moment, if that wasn't impulse he didn't know what was. There was no momentary inattention on the part of the guards: they were playing dice in the shade, as everyone knew, but they were too frightened of Achilles to admit it. And what was this comrade business? Since when had there been comradeship between Attica and the Thessaly borders? Since when had there been comradeship between a great man like Achilles, lord of vast estates, rich and famous, with a goddess for a mother, and a common foot soldier like Leucon? It was a false and misleading term.

Pleuron was loyal and very steady in battle, but he was not

nearly so clever an advocate as Calligonus, who was not particularly loyal or steady, but whose last remarks had been greeted
with applause from all quarters. Feeling the case for the prosecution slipping away from him, with consequent loss of favor if
he screwed up, he decided at this point to invite Achilles to
make the personal statement to which he was entitled.

"Stand back, give me some air." Achilles twisted his ex-
quisitely molded lips into an expression of repugnance at the
nearness to him of unwashed humanity. His person was well
sprinkled with balsam, but darker whiffs got through to him all
the same. Though always scrupulous, he had taken extra care
with his appearance this morning. He was bareheaded, his fair
hair freshly curled, fitting thick and close round his neat ears.
His friend Patroclus, who was an expert in makeup, had
painted small red sunbursts on his cheeks. He was naked above
the waist save for a gold armband and the leather pads he wore
on the shoulders to emphasize their width. His bronzed, splendidly proportioned torso gleamed with oil. The linen skirt
showed off to advantage his shapely, strongly muscled thighs.
He stood with the ease, the power in repose, of the supreme
athlete, and his pale killer's eyes, very slightly astigmatic under
their level brows, looked coldly and intently across at the man
who had entered his tent and fingered his possessions and
whose death he was resolved on.

Possessed by this resolve, and inspired by the knowledge
that as the person wronged he would have the killing of the
man if the death sentence was brought in, he spoke with less af-
fectation of languidness than usual, explaining how great a
value he set upon this pendant, how it was among his most
treasured possessions, how distressed he had been to discover
its loss, how glad he was that punishment for the wrongdoer

was at hand, that justice would be done. "For what is justice, after all?" he demanded, coming to his peroration, turning his head gracefully from side to side so as to flex the marvelous tendons of his neck. "Justice is order and measure, justice is respect for rank and private property, justice is the safeguard of society as we know it. Without justice we would be delivered over to the rule of the mob."

The chiefs nodded solemnly at these sentiments, but they did not go down so well with the mob itself, and lost Achilles some considerable sympathy. Noting this and hoping to build on it, Calligonus called upon the accused to make his statement.

It had been a sudden impulse, Leucon said. He didn't know what had come over him. He had never done such a thing before. There was no one guarding the tent, the guards were a good fifty paces off, sitting in the shade playing dice. They were the ones who should be on trial: if they had been doing their job this would never have happened. Once inside, he had seen this pendant and taken a fancy to it. He didn't know why, he had just liked the look of it. He hadn't taken anything else.

Calligonus now had a good idea. "May this object be held up to public view? Perhaps Lord Ajax, as the tallest man present, could . . . Thank you. Now here is the treasure we have heard so much about. A thin chain of bronze links, a pendant in the form of a scarab, also bronze, washed with gold. A pretty thing, finely made, but not of such great value in the materials. Leucon took only this. Would a real thief take only this? There were things much more precious and costly lying here and there in that tent. Are we going to put a man to death for giving way to a passing fancy?"

There were prolonged shouts of "no" in answer to this,

coming now from every quarter. Achilles' brow was marred by a scowl. Pleuron, at his wits' end now, noticed that Nestor, accompanied as usual by his two sons, had joined the gathering. Some rambling and long-winded words from him, even if quite beside the point, might give the prosecution time to regain the initiative. "I call upon Nestor, wise in counsel, to give us the benefit of—"

He was interrupted by a shout from the back of the crowd. "I know that pendant!"

Heads craned round at this. But only those nearest could make out who had spoken. "Can that man be brought forward?" Calligonus shouted over the hubbub. This was done, to the accompaniment of some backslapping and words of encouragement. The interrupter was revealed as a person of short stature with luxuriant eyebrows and a habit of frequent blinking. He peered up at the pendant, still held aloft by Ajax. "I thought as much," he said. "This pendant belonged to my mother's brother, I'd know it anywhere. He always wore it. He said it brought him luck."

"When did you last see it?"

"He was wearing it when I saw him last. He went on a trading trip and never came back. None of the party came back. That's two years ago now—we've given him up for dead."

"Your uncle's name?"

"Dalgon of Thebes. He was a merchant, he exported pottery from the workshops on the mainland to Thrace and the islands of the north."

"And where did this particular trip take him?"

"To Pteleon."

Eyes now turned towards Achilles, who had taken his small ivory-handled fan from a pocket in his skirt and was fanning himself slowly with it, looking over the heads of the crowd. This was impressive, it was somehow menacing: only Achilles could have thought of fanning himself in a wind. Everybody knew that Pteleon, and all the region east of Mount Othrys, formed part of his lands.

Calligonus risked a smile. He was entering the danger zone, but the passion of the pleader had him in its grip. "He said it brought him luck? His luck ran out when he got to Pteleon. Someone else saw a pretty thing and liked it."

"I must protest against these innuendos," Pleuron said. "There is no scrap of proof that this is the same pendant. And even if it were, everyone knows that objects taken from a slain foe constitute legitimate booty and add to the honor of the victor, whereas what we are discussing here is a case of vulgar theft."

Agamemnon nodded slowly, his face showing ashen against the dark hair of his beard. It was his first public appearance since the waiting for Iphigeneia had begun. Chasimenos had prevailed on him to attend, pointing out that allowing someone else to preside over the tribunal would be taken as a sign of weakness. "Does this nephew of this uncle wish to make accusations against some particular person?" he asked. "Does he seek to avenge some slur on the honor of his family?"

The Theban's eyes rested briefly on Achilles, whose splendidly articulated biceps rippled below the oiled skin with each slow movement of the fan, and who chose this moment to turn his head lazily, not as if looking but listening.

"We are waiting," Agamemnon said.

"Well, now that I look again, I'm not so sure. I could be wrong. One pendant is very like another after all."

"We understand perfectly," Calligonus said, casting significant looks here and there. He was coming to the end of his plea and he wanted it to be strong. He felt the sympathy of the crowd and it led him now to think—a bad mistake, as it turned out—that he could get Leucon off altogether. "It is the wind that is to blame," he said. "This terrible wind that keeps us cooped up here. Consider the case of this poor Leucon. Consider it well, because it is the case with all of us. When he first came here he was full of ardor and enthusiasm, determined to distinguish himself in battle, get his hands on a pile of loot and move up some notches in society. Then what happens? He lies awake night after night listening to the voices of the wind. He feels the constant touch of it, on his face, on his body, always picking him over, giving him no peace. Round the headland he knows it is a gale. Day by day his hopes wither, all that youthful idealism crumbles away, he is not far from a nervous breakdown. Like us all, he is waiting for Iphigeneia. Like us all, he must believe his leaders when they tell him that the sacrifice of the witch will bring an end to the wind. He must have faith. But faith is a variable, not a constant. It goes up and down. Anyone who denies this is either a fool or in bad faith. On top of everything else, this poor Leucon is hungry. It's getting harder all the time to screw anything out of these miserly people. And there aren't enough whores, Leucon has to stand in line. Waiting half a day in the wind is guaranteed to take the edge off anyone. Is it so surprising that his morale, his sense of solidarity, should be undermined? Is it so surprising that Leucon, in his frustration, should become bewildered and confused, should lose his sense of the distinction, a valid distinction as I am the first to agree, between pilfering and pillage? He took only one small thing, not very valuable. It was a gesture, a token. My friends, this was not a theft at all, it was a cry for help. Let our great commander Agamemnon, tamer of horses, show mercy to this poor confused man and give the blame to the wind."

Even before he came to the end of this he saw a certain sort of stillness settle over the judges and knew he had blundered. There was silence for some moments, then Agamemnon said, "How can a wind sent by Zeus be a cause of crime?"

Odysseus, one of the two judges on Agamemnon's right, now spoke for the first time. "You would have done better to stick to the issue of impulse and beg for leniency, without bringing the wind into it. But you are in love with your own voice, Calligonus, and you have gone too far. Do you not see that you have forced us to an extreme judgment? If we make the wind an excuse for this theft, we make it an excuse for any wrong that is done here. Murder, mutiny, desertion, failure to keep your weapons in good order, you name it. It's a formula for anarchy. Above all, and this is where you have really fouled up your case, it reduces everyone to the same level. We are all exposed to the wind. If Leucon is a victim of the wind, so are we all. In that way we lose the vital distinction between a contemptible instance of petty thieving and the noble and altruistic readiness of our Commander-in-Chief to sacrifice his nearest and dearest for the sake of the common good." He paused for a moment, glancing towards his fellow judges. "I hope I take you with me on this," he said. "It seems to me absolutely crucial."

No way round it, this Leucon would have to die, he thought as he watched them nodding. An even more dangerous precedent lurked behind this one of declaring that the wind was to blame. He had seen how cleverly Calligonus had swayed the audience, made his appeal to the common man; he had noted the easy rhetoric, the sense of theater, the readiness to run into danger for the sake of winning. That touch about it not being a crime but a cry for help, so bold and original. He could hardly have done it better himself. This Calligonus was a dangerous man, he would need watching carefully. An error of the first magnitude to give him the victory now, or any slightest concession that could add to his prestige or strengthen his influence among his fellows.

"One might just as well say the sound of the sea maddened me, or the cawing of the crows, or the voice of a neighbor," said Agapenor, leader of the Arcadians, the judge on his left.

"Zeus sends the wind to show us our past crimes, not lead us into new ones." This came from the Lapith chief, Polypoetes, on the other side of Agamemnon.

"We are agreed then. Guilty with no extenuating circumstances." Odysseus looked towards Agamemnon as he said this. One could never be quite sure of the King's responses; that reference to the sacrifice had been a calculated risk, it could have released a flood of self-pitying bombast. "Great King, we wait for you to pronounce the sentence," he said.

Agamemnon showed no hesitation. "It is our judgment that Leucon the Athenian be delivered to the sword of the man he has wronged."

The remaining moments of Leucon's life were few. In spite of his tears and the loud displeasure of his countrymen, he was taken and made to kneel and his hands were tied behind him. He begged for mercy as he knelt there, offering himself as bondsman to Achilles, swearing to serve him all his life long without wages.

Achilles paid no heed to this. He exchanged the fan for a short sword, very heavy in the blade, which had been fashioned specially for him; having set his feet in just the right position to the side of the kneeling man he performed one or two preliminary passes to show how he could make the blade whistle. Then, with a beautifully coordinated pivoting movement of shoulders, arms and trunk, all below the waist remaining planted and immobile, he made a perfectly judged slicing cut, drawing the blade in an arc so cunning that Leucon's head, though completely severed, yet remained on his shoulders, and his eyes continued to stare ahead. There were even those among the bystanders ready to swear that Leucon had continued pleading for his life and offering his services free for some appreciable time before he toppled over and his head jumped away.

6.

Sitting in his accustomed place, the
Singer mingled past and present and
future together, strands of a single rope.
He sang of an ancient conflagration,
flames that burst through the roofs of the
caverns under the sea because they had
stoked the fires too high in the workshops
of Poseidon, burst up and made a mountain with a burning mouth, and the discharge from this mouth destroyed the
island of Thera and made the sea boil,
killing all the creatures of the deep, rearing
up in a scalding wave as high as the palace
of Pylos, that ran against Crete and destroyed all the ships in the harbors of
Knossos and Cydonia, and the ashes of the
fire covered all the land and nothing would
grow and the people starved.

He sang of the consummately skillful
blow that had decapitated Leucon the
Athenian, who had gone on begging for
mercy without knowing he was a dead

man. He gave out news of the knife, repeating the details of design and emphasizing the costliness of the materials. Then, for the fourth time that day, he traced the itinerary of Iphigeneia on her way towards them. This, he had discovered, went down very well—it brought her nearer; his audiences had doubled since the idea came to him. Indeed, so popular had the item proved that there was no need to bother with metrical form. He concentrated on cadence, chanting Iphigeneia's journey as a litany of place names. Many of his listeners, especially those coming from the places mentioned, joined in with obvious enjoyment. It was the first time in his career that the Singer had experienced audience participation on anything like this scale.

Overland to Corinth on the good road, then by ship through the Saronic Gulf, steering between the islands of Salamis and Aegina, rounding Cape Sounion, hugging the shore to escape the wind, passing on the lee side of Macronisi, entering the mouth of the Euboean Strait. Then Brauron, the looming shape of Pendelicon, Rhamnus and the temples of Nemesis. At Rhamnus there were those waiting and watching, ready to light the bonfires as soon as she was sighted entering the narrow water. From Rhamnus to Aulis, less than a day's sail . . .

How eagerly she was awaited, how happy they would be when she came, what a glorious future awaited them once the sacrifice had been made and Zeus had released them from his displeasure, what undying fame would be achieved by the Greek heroes. The war would soon be over. Their leaders were men of high caliber, men to be trusted, and they had announced that Troy could not stand a long siege, lacking adequate supplies of water. The Greek heroes would return to their homes and the arms of their wives, laden with honor and precious

cups and tripods and shining cauldrons. Their children, and
their children's children, gathered round the fireside in the
evening, would be able to ask them: "O Father," or "O
Grandfather," as the case may be, "what did you do in the
war?" And the answers would bring a flush of pride to those
fresh young faces: "Yes, I fought in the Trojan campaign. I im-
paled so-and-so on my spear and held him aloft, wriggling like
a worm on a pin, for all to see. I got so-and-so through the
throat with an arrow at five hundred paces, a shot that is still
remembered round the campfires. We surrounded so-and-so
and, having first stripped him of his armor, we cut off his arms
and legs and rolled him downhill like a bobbin, what a laugh.
Then we quarreled over the armor, and guess who was the only
survivor of that quarrel, yes, it was your own father, or grandfather." As the case may be.

He had liked the zeugma, and tried a variant of it now, to
round things off. "Freighted with fame and the glorious tro-
phies of conquest." He made a brief pause and was about to begin on the story of Cadmus, founder of Thebes, he who sowed
dragon's teeth and had a crop of armed warriors, when he became aware of the face of a boy near his own—a face which,
even to his impaired vision, was revealed as beautiful. This face
leaned towards him, whispering: *"Will you sing me the stories of
Lemnos?"*

7.

Calchas waited still for the right moment, the right form of words, a message to take to the King that should be true
and compelling, like that perfect shape of
the sun, so briefly seen above the headland
before it streamed away and mixed its fire
with baser elements, mist, the spume of the
sea. He was alone more now, Poimenos
was away more often and for longer. In
these periods of solitude he kept mainly to
his tent, but was sometimes seen walking
slowly along the shore, beyond the camp,
eyes lowered as if studying the ground before him. Sometimes he would stop dead
and remain fixed for several minutes. All
the energy of his mind was consumed in an
endless reviewing of his failures and mistakes, a seeking to find, at least here, some
pattern, some meaning. His slowness to
discover the sender of the wind, his failure
to understand that Stimon's dancing and
the leaping flames had been symbols of

life, and that life, whether of man or fire, is purchased by destruction. Why had Pollein misled him? Agamemnon's dream of the tongueless nightingale, he had lost an opportunity there to sound a warning. He might have told the King about his own dream, that tide of bronze that bore away the helmeted warriors, Greek and Trojan tumbled together in the bright flood, then drowned and lost in that strange silver peace of the horizon. Poimenos had wanted him to speak of this, had been disappointed at his failure to do so. Looking back now, it seemed to Calchas that this had been the boy's first disappointment in him, the first shadow. He had tried to conceal his fears and doubts so as to keep the boy's regard, this too a mistake — Poimenos no longer observed him, no longer imitated his movements, though he could not remember a definite time when that had ceased. If he could, even now, convince the King that Artemis was the sender, then Iphigeneia might be saved and the crime and the bloodguilt averted. For why should the goddess desire the death of her priestess? Why was there no help for him in smoke or cloud or embers or the light on water? The gods had deadened his eyes.

He continued to visit the smith and make his reports; he was becoming an expert in the manufacture of knives. The King wanted to know the progress of the work in detail, and this detail Calchas faithfully supplied. An exact model of the knife had been made in wax, then covered in clay and heated so that the wax melted and drained off while the clay hardened, forming the mold — a process that Agamemnon knew well enough already but still wanted to hear related. Calchas praised the mold's sharpness of detail, described how it was grooved on both sides to make strengthening ribs for the blade.

He was no longer allowed to attend alone upon the King —

that mark of favor had been withdrawn. He did not apply for audience now, he waited until sent for, and there were always others present when he came. When Poimenos accompanied him, he left the boy outside the tent, where he was subject to the indecent proposals of the guards.

"Such a mold is used only once and must then be thrown away," the diviner said, and saw the King nod with satisfaction.

"And the casting of the bronze?"

"Lord, it is done already." It had been a source of fearful wonder to Calchas, whose mind was so fluid in its connections, almost helplessly so, how the King's close interest in this knife detached his mind from thoughts of the wound it was designed to make, the blood it was designed to spill. It was as if the weapon were being made for its beauty alone. When he saw Agamemnon's deep-set eyes, dark-ringed below the prominent ridges of the brows from the nights of his insomnia, light up at some detail to do with the knife's fashioning, saw this all-consuming interest in the technical process, the impression returned to him that the King was mad, that the gods had taken away his capacity for imagining.

I am mad too, he thought, to lend myself to this game. He said, "Molten bronze has a special property, or so the smith tells me. It chooses the final moments before solidifying to enlarge its body in the mold, and so it picks up all the fine detail. As it cools it dwindles again so as to be the more easily extracted. This property of swelling and shrinking is possessed by neither of the parent metals. It is a gift to the alloy from the god Hephaestus."

The King's eyes glistened. "He knows my design for the decoration of the blade?"

"Your instructions have all been made known to him."

The King said nothing for some moments, chin sunk on chest as if pondering. Chasimenos, the only other person present on this occasion, also remained silent, his thin face stiff and expressionless. Calchas became aware again of the insistent, petulant snapping of the wind in the folds of the canvas, the seeping hiss of the air below the edges of the walls. Overhead, where sunlight trembled through the membrane of the roof, he counted four tortoiseshell butterflies fluttering together, and heard or imagined small thuds of collision among them. All the tents now were haunted by butterflies and moths and small creeping things that had taken the only refuge they could find against the unceasing onslaught of the wind. Even the men sleeping in the open would be troubled by beetles and lizards and mice that crawled under the covers with them or hid in the folds of their clothing.

As the silence continued it seemed to Calchas that all his experience of patience, all the times in the whole of his life when he had longed for release, was summed up in these few moments of waiting for Agamemnon to make known his further wishes regarding the knife, moments which lay clasped and enclosed within all the other things there were to wait for: a sign to guide him, the courage to speak, the arrival of Iphigeneia, an end to the wind, an end to this cold fever of his life. Like square boxes of juniper wood, one fitting within another, that he had once seen on a market stall in Miletus, seen and wanted at a time of poverty when he had nothing to tender in exchange. Fashioned in the far north, the Thracian traders had told him; wood from the lands of snow. But the scent of the wood had come warm to his nostrils, like a breathing of the sun . . .

"I want the inlay of silver to go the whole length of the

blade from the haft to the point. I want the width of it to be so."
Agamemnon held out his right hand with thumb and forefinger
a little extended. "Come closer, priest," he said.

Calchas approached and looked down at the hand. "Yes, I
see," he said.

"You will tell the smith. This is the width I want for the inlay."

"Lord, I will deliver your instructions." The required width
of the inlay had been conveyed to the smith once already; due
allowance had already been made for it.

"He will be well rewarded. I have some ideas for the incis-
ing of the inlay, but we will talk of that later. One thing at a
time, eh?" The King's mouth formed into a thin smile. "You too
will be rewarded," he said. "When the time comes."

Calchas emerged from the tent with these words still in his
ears. There was no sign of Poimenos. He heard a booming
voice that carried over the sound of the wind and saw Ajax the
Larger below him on the shore, watched him lower from his
face and then raise again a long, cone-shaped object. He set the
narrow end to his mouth and the strange booming came again.

"What is that?" he asked one of the guards.

"He is getting them lined up for a footrace."

"No, I mean the thing he is shouting through."

"Palamedes invented it, they say. He calls it a voice-booster.
Both the Ajaxes have one. The voice is made bigger—down
there they have the sound of the water as well as the wind to
contend with. But they mainly use them for shouting at each
other."

Calchas glanced round in search of Poimenos. "Why is
that?"

The guard spat delicately aside. "They don't see eye to eye on anything, those two. These Games won't come to anything, if you ask me. No one is going to burst his lungs for the sake of a few bloody leaves."

Tension broke from Calchas in a short, barking laugh. "Those two will never see eye to eye, that much is certain." He lingered some moments, glancing at the guard's face. It was rare that anyone spoke so freely to him these days, and this man had even accompanied him a little way as he was leaving the tent. The eyes that regarded him expressed no friendliness, but there seemed nothing of hostility in them either, small in the big-chinned, weather-roughened face, red-rimmed and sore-looking from the constant pressure of the wind.

A sudden recklessness came to Calchas, akin to the laughter that had just broken from him. He said, "Does it not seem to you that this world of the camp is a world turned upside down? Two champions of unity always divided, a god who blesses and curses us in the same breath, a victim whose innocence takes away our guilt?"

The guard said nothing. No particular expression had appeared on his face. Calchas turned away, already regretting his words. "It takes some understanding, doesn't it?" he said.

He was beginning to make his way back towards his own tent, but before he had gone far it came to him quite suddenly where Poimenos must be. He changed direction and went towards the open space on the shore side of the camp, where the Locrian lines began. As he approached he heard the short twanging sounds of the lyre when the strings are plucked and at once stilled. Then the Singer's voice came over to him in snatches. He was singing of the eighth labor of Heracles, the capturing of the four mares that fed on human flesh. Drawing nearer, he saw Poimenos sitting very close to the Singer, a little behind him. The boy was motionless, listening with head tilted upward in an exact replica of the Singer's pose. He was lost in the story, spellbound, as sightless in his way as his new master.

8.

Agamemnon's pious habit of including the senile Nestor in all councils and consultative assemblies meant that nothing, however small the gathering otherwise, could remain a secret for very long. Sooner or later it would find its way into one of the old man's interminable monologues about the highlights of his life, especially the one about his youthful exploits as a rustler in Elis, when he had disemboweled the king's son and got away with fifty cows. So it came about that one evening Agamemnon was visited in his tent by an Achilles incandescent with rage, accompanied by his inseparable companion and lover, Patroclus.

Rage in Achilles was not much expressed in outward motions. Rather, his movements became slighter, more contained, as if he was saving energy for the moment of the kill. There was a glowing paleness about him, his eyes were wider than usual and the line of his jaw more prominent, somewhat marring the perfection of his profile.

Agamemnon was with Chasimenos and Odysseus when the two visitors entered brusquely without depositing their arms at the door, as custom demanded. Meeting that murderous gaze, he thought for a moment that these two were the leaders of a coup, an event he dreaded day and night, arriving to put an end to him. He started up and his hand went to the sword at his side. He might at least put paid to that vain dimwit Patroclus before Achilles' sword found his heart. He was stayed by calm words from Odysseus, who also feared a coup, but not on the part of Achilles, whom he considered too coldhearted and narcissistic to have much popular appeal. Besides, he had instantly reasoned, they would have moved faster, there would have been more of them.

"Good evening, gentlemen," he said. "Is there something the matter?"

Tension about the jaws did not allow Achilles much range of sound. His words came out flat and uninflected. "Whose idea was it to use my name?"

"I'm sorry, I'm afraid I don't—"

Achilles looked at Patroclus, who said, "Lord Achilles has formed the intention of challenging to mortal combat the person responsible for putting forward his name, without his knowledge or consent, as a suitor for Iphigeneia's hand in marriage."

"My name," Achilles said, grinding his teeth. *"My name."*

"An illustrious name was needed, or she might not have agreed to come," Chasimenos said. "What name more illustrious than yours, O mighty Achilles, goddess-born."

He received in reply the full homicidal blaze of Achilles' eyes, which caused him quickly to lower his own.

"It was you then?"

"Er, no."

Agamemnon felt unutterably weary, weary to the marrow of his bones. Wasn't it enough that a man should be bearing the heavy burden of command without having a maniac like this to deal with? "It was a collective decision," he said. "I forget how many people were involved. A dozen at least. You can't kill us all, you would leave the army leaderless."

"That's a lie. I know you, Agamemnon. You would have kept it close and secret, just among a few, schemers like yourself. Do you think I'm a fool? By Zeus, I'll show you different."

"We'll really have to stop including Nestor in these meetings," Chasimenos said.

"Is it only this?" Odysseus's smile concealed a vast surprise at the depths of human stupidity. Here was one who could not see beyond vanity and bloodlust, even in a matter that concerned his reputation and public image. He felt a preliminary pang of pleasure at the thought of bemusing this brute and taming him with words. "I will tell you the truth, Achilles," he said. "As you know, it is not my habit to go beating about the bush. It is true that we put you forward as a suitor for Iphigeneia without telling you. We were afraid that otherwise you might refuse. And if you had refused and we had gone ahead after your refusal, that would have been worse still, wouldn't it? And we would still have had to risk it."

"I don't follow you."

"Well, look at it this way. If you had been asked and refused, that refusal would have been a very public one. You would have made sure it was public, wouldn't you? You would have wanted there to be no doubt, no smallest doubt, about your attitude. And what would the result have been?"

"The army would have known I set a value on my name, the army would have understood what it means to be Achilles."

"Forgive me, it would have had an opposite effect, your name would have been irredeemably tarnished. The army would simply have thought, mistakenly of course, that self-esteem was more important to you than the Greek cause, that you were lacking in the spirit that unites us all in this great enterprise, making us forget petty differences, making us gird up our loins, set our shoulders to the wheel, share and share alike, what's the word I'm looking for?"

"Civic sense."

"Civic sense, brilliant, you can always count on Chasimenos for the *mot juste*. Of course, you might not have refused, but how were we to know? Now, as things are, you have been saved from a total disaster in public relations, for the simple reason that the matter is not public at all. Agamemnon, understandably enough, exaggerated a little. The only people in the know are the people in this tent now, at this present moment in time. Nestor's sons waited outside on that occasion and nobody takes the old man seriously, it's a well-known fact that he doesn't know his arse from his elbow."

"I have always found him a great support in times of trouble," Agamemnon said.

"Well, you are alone in that. Even Diomedes, whom we chose as our ambassador, doesn't know. We were obliged to tell him that you had agreed. He is a simple man, with a very rudimentary moral sense, and would not be convincing if he didn't believe what he was saying."

Achilles' jaws had slackened appreciably in his puzzlement at these words that issued so easily, in such impeccable order, from the slightly smiling mouth before him. "You mean to say he believes the offer of marriage is genuine?"

"No, no, not that, but he believes that you know the offer is being made."

"But if he knows the offer is fake he is lying through his teeth."

"My dear Achilles, that is a secondary matter, another unit as it were. Life is made up of units. Units of action, decision, choice. We try to associate them together, to discover the essential relations between them, to see them as links in a chain, what's the word —"

"Making connections."

"Absolutely brilliant, bravo Chasimenos. Now some of us are not so clever at making connections and Diomedes is one such. He has outstanding qualities, he is a first-rate charioteer for example, but he does not think in terms of links. It doesn't concern him that the offer is a fake, all he needs to know is that you actually made it. Otherwise, you see, he would be misrepresenting a comrade, and that would seem dishonorable to him. Chasimenos, you always have a lucid grasp of detail, perhaps you could sum all this up for us?"

"Certainly. Since nobody in the army except us knows that you didn't know, and since nobody in the army except us and the members of the delegation, who in any case think you knew, knows that the proposal is being made at all, and human assumptions being what they are, the view that you had full knowledge from the beginning will prevail over any other possible view."

"That's supposed to be lucid?"

"My dear fellow," Odysseus said, "it will prevail because it is the way we look at things. When it comes to the conduct of affairs, people are far readier to see purpose and design than ignorance and accident. We are all basically on the side of the operator because we see how he succeeds."

"We're talking human nature now," Chasimenos said.

Agamemnon entered the discussion at this point, with a cloudy sense of playing his part, and very nearly ruined everything. "It is true, Achilles," he said. "People are more likely to think one a twister than a dupe."

"Anyone who calls Achilles twister or dupe will soon find himself feeding his entrails to the crows."

"No, no," Odysseus said, "these are not the right terms at all. The King has a lot on his mind, as we all know. No, it will simply be thought that, suppressing all personal feelings, acting for the common good, Achilles lent his illustrious name to our enterprise. The common good, what a wonderful, all-embracing concept that is."

Achilles pursed his lips and glanced at Patroclus, who shrugged. "But what if one of you should go round telling people that I didn't know, that I was fooled? It would ruin my image."

"Why on earth should anyone do that? What purpose would it serve, other than to suggest discord and disunity at the very time that we want to convey the opposite impression? In any case, we would not be believed. It would simply be thought we were trying to blacken your name, make you out to be a simpleton, when all the world knows you are a shrewd fellow."

"How can I be sure?"

Odysseus paused, savoring the moment. He had kept the most clinching argument to the last. "Because, my dear

Achilles, your greatness of soul, your patriotic readiness to forward the cause of the Greek Expeditionary Force, will be made official as of today, it will be told to the Singer immediately, and he will insert it into his program of entertainment for this evening, at a time when the audience is at its peak, and he will repeat it at intervals during these coming days until it is common knowledge. Once a thing is common knowledge, there is no power on earth that can put it into question. I will see to this myself, in person, you can rest assured. He and I have an excellent understanding. Of course, it's always a good idea to give him a sweetener, it seems to increase the power of his performance. Perhaps you could provide me with something? Some trifle . . . That pendant of yours, the one that all the fuss was about, that would be just the thing."

9.

Poimenos did not return. Thenceforth he cared for the Singer, foraged for him, made up his fire and slept beside him in his shelter of skins, while Calchas, lonelier than ever, lay grieving for his loss, remembering the foreshadowing of it on the boy's face, portents he had not fully appreciated, trapped as he had been in his role of mind-former, advocate of the critical spirit, corrupter of simplicity. The boy had chosen fictions and the choice was final; he would not come back—this Calchas knew with certainty, as he knew the fault was his own.

In the nights of his desolation he tried to find sleep through a discipline of the senses, striving to shut out the greater sounds of the wind and hear only the lesser ones, noises not audible except to the imagination, the manifold frictions along the surface of the earth, the tumbling or hopping or sliding of minute particles. He would drift away on this, only to wake in fear as the wind roared its anger at being cheated.

Meanwhile the life of the camp continued. Big Ajax, in the course of training for the javelin-throwing event, which, like the weight lifting, he had every prospect of winning, as so far there were no contestants but himself, made a throw so mighty that it brained a member of the Arcadian contingent, who was crouched two thousand paces away—or so the Singer was to give it out—waiting at a rabbit hole in the hope of braining a rabbit as it emerged. This man turned out to be a second cousin of King Agapenor and the blood price demanded was high. On the grounds that they were both in this thing together, having been partners in the enterprise from day one, Big Ajax tried to get his small partner to pay half, which led to furious quarrels, a serious crisis in their friendship and a total and indefinite suspension of the Games.

The knife was finished and hammered into keenness, and the smith, who was an artist in his way, made a beautiful job of the silver inlay and the incised decorations, using a mixture of his own, lead and sulfur and borax, powdered and fused by a process he guarded jealously. Odysseus and Chasimenos continued to attend on the King, keeping careful watch over his swings of mood, which were quite unpredictable. The knife was a case in point: having taken such an intense interest in the making of it, he now showed no desire to see it. For everyone the tension of waiting was great. Iphigeneia was expected from hour to hour. All looked for the fires that would signal the first glimpse of her ship as it rounded the headlands of Attica and entered the sheltered waters of the Euboean channel.

Then, on a morning like any other, when the wind had low-

ered a little, quietening into gusts like sobs, as it quite often did
in the first light of the day, it came to Calchas what he must say
to the King. He lay still as the light strengthened, and the
words came to him in the sobs of the wind. When the sun was
over the horizon he went to Agamemnon's tent and asked the
guards to announce him. He had come prepared to wait but
was admitted almost at once. The King was seated on his
throne chair. His face looked swollen and his long hair was
lank and unkempt, hanging below the thin gold band that circled his head. There was only Chasimenos with him, sitting on
a cushion at his feet. "Well," he said, "what has Calchas, the
priest of Apollo, to say to Agamemnon?"

"Great king, live forever," Calchas said, and hesitated a moment, only now aware of having used the ceremonial form of
address common among the Hittites. In his solitude he was reverting to foreignness, to the outcast state. He said, "I have
kept vigil and prayed for light to Pollein, whom the Greeks call
Apollo, giver of ecstasy, god who dwells in light, and I have
come to announce the meaning of that eagle feast the King was
told of." He paused on this. The moisture had gone from his
mouth. He heard Chasimenos make a muttered exclamation
which seemed derisive in intent.

"You have hesitated long," Agamemnon said. "Too long.
You are one who will always hesitate too long, which is something I did not know when I took you for my diviner."

"You are wasting the King's time, in any case," Chasimenos
said. "The whole army now accepts the meaning of the omen as
given to us by Croton."

Without looking at Chasimenos, Calchas said, "Croton's
meaning allows the King no way but one. It was here, in

this place, that the man told us he had witnessed the eagles devouring the young of the hare. This was something that was not true before, it became a true story only as he spoke it, there was no knowledge of it in anyone's mind before. And because of this, because this new story was unwelcome to the others, or even just unexpected, his mouth was stopped. Croton knows, and all of us know, that Zeus does not concern himself with the creatures of earth and their young. Zeus lives above, he governs from above, his justice is not something you can see or touch, it does not live in concrete things or have a particular shape, like a hare that is killed by eagles in the morning, a hare with young. The creatures are in the care of the Lady, who has different names in different places, Rhea, Potnia, Cybele, Artemis. She spoke to us through the man's mouth."

Chasimenos had risen to his feet and now stood close to the King. He said, "We have reason to think that this man is in the pay of our enemies. We Greeks worship Artemis as the daughter of Zeus, but the Trojans deny she is the daughter, they say she was here before, that she has always been. It is now clear that this priest has been bribed to spread the Asian cults among us and so undermine the war effort."

Calchas felt fear at this; there was no mistaking the menace in it. But he had gone too far to retract; the only way now was to convince the King, recover his favor. He had good hope of this; he had come with a gift for Agamemnon, something deserving of gratitude. He said, "Those on guard with him, the other witnesses, why did they not immediately deny the man's words? When he said they had seen what they had not seen, why did no one speak? There can only be one reason."

"The King has heard enough of this raving," Chasimenos said.

"No, let him speak." Agamemnon fixed on the diviner a look of somber and deliberate patience. "Tell us the reason."

"They could not deny it without discrediting their own story too. There was no hare, this was an invention of some here who wanted to raise the army's morale by promising a glorious end to the war."

He paused again and after a moment bowed low to Agamemnon, a deep reverence from the waist, knees flexed and head lowered, following—deliberately now—the practice of the Hittites. He said, "Lord King, I am still your diviner. You have shown me your love, do not take it from me now. The wind is sent by the goddess, she who planted the words of warning in the man's mouth, the Mistress, however we call her, the protectress of the innocent. It is sent to give us pause, to tell us that for the slaughter of the unoffending she will exact a price."

He raised his head, struggled to control his breathing. He was about to do the bravest thing he had ever done in all his fearful life. "She will exact a price," he said again. "Not now, not in the present, not by requiring the blood of an innocent. How can she be propitiated by the shedding of blood now, when she is warning us against it in the future? The gods are not like us, they cannot contradict themselves."

His breathing had grown calmer as he spoke. He had reached the moment of the gift, the moment that would redeem him, restore him to trust. For the first time he met the King's eyes. "No crimes are yet committed," he said. "The goddess gives us time to reconsider. And this is the message brought to the King by his diviner, which I said once before and was not heard. But now I see further. If the King will accept the goddess as sender, he will be free from necessity. The justice of Zeus and the compassion of Artemis will make a single path for him if he can find it. Since there is no offense, there can be no punishment. With the fear of punishment lifted, there can be no constraint. This is the gift of the goddess to Agamemnon, through the words of his diviner. She offers him the greatest gift that mortals know, the power of choice."

He fell silent and bowed his head and waited. Then Chasimenos spoke and there was a note of genuine incredulity in his voice. "A seer from Asia who denies that Artemis is bound in obedience to Zeus, who believes the snake and the eagle to be equal in power, this upstart tells the King to reconsider."

Agamemnon said nothing for some moments, his head lowered on his chest. Then he looked up and Calchas felt his heart contract at the hatred on the King's face and knew in that moment that he had been led again into error, that in offering freedom he had snatched away the comfort of necessity from the King's heart.

Chasimenos said, "We have it on good authority that it was this man who encouraged Iphigeneia to put Artemis above Zeus. Now he is seeking to undermine the King's authority and his dedication to the heavy burden of command. Further proof, if any were needed, that he is a Trojan spy. Let me call the guard and have him shackled."

"No." Agamemnon's mouth seemed to smile a little. "No, I have other plans for Calchas the diviner. Not one hair on his head must be harmed. Do you hear me, Chasimenos? I make you responsible for his safety."

"I will obey you in this, as in—"

While he was still speaking a guard entered hastily and
sank to his knees before Agamemnon. "Lord King," he said,
"the word has come, the ship has been sighted."

In the moments following upon this announcement, all
those in the tent felt a strange deafness descend on them, like
the humming aftermath of some crash or collision. This they
thought at first was due to the momentous nature of the news;
but then, in a collective moment of realization, the true reason
came: the wind had ceased. The guard remained kneeling; no
one moved or spoke; the first sounds that came creeping back
were still, at first, like symptoms of deafness.

Afterwards, everyone in the camp asked himself the same
question: Where was I, what was I doing, when the wind
ceased? People stopped in their tracks and stood stock-still, listening to the silence. Those sleeping woke abruptly, with a
sense of insecurity and alarm. After the first deafness there was
the illusion that one could hear the very slightest of sounds,
sounds never heard before. Those on the hillside thought they
could hear the straightening of grasses or the clicking sounds
made by the movements of insects' antennae; others swore that
they could hear the breathing of the horses, even though they
were far away on the other side of the shore; others claimed
that they could hear the winking and bubbling as the suds of
the last waves burst and webbed the pebbles.

Odysseus, as a person of authority and unrelated by family
to either of the Ajaxes, was trying to arbitrate in the dispute between them, which had grown more embittered with time. All
three were sitting in the shelter of some dunes, well away from
the camp, so as to avoid any spreading of the quarrel among
the rank and file.

"Do you not think," Odysseus said to Ajax the Larger, who had just threatened once again to leave the expedition and return home, "that it will be very bad for your image if, having introduced these Games as a means of peaceful and healthy competition, in order to avoid quarreling and disunity, having had yourself widely publicized through the Singer as Ajax the Unifier, the man who held the allies together, you now abandon those same allies because of a dispute with your closest friend? See what I mean? Does it not seem contradictory to you?"

Ajax the Larger's huge face bore no detectable expression. His greenish eyes under their sun-bleached brows looked more than usually blank. "Share and share alike," he said. "Through thick and thin. That's what friends are for."

"Thick and thin my arse," Ajax the Lesser said. "How come I always get the thin end? I wasn't even there when you threw that fucking javelin, why the fuck should I pay anything?"

Odysseus sighed and cast around in his mind for further arguments. Both men were stingy and obstinate, but the basic trouble was that Big Ajax was not intelligent enough to keep incongruous elements present together in his mind. Far from thinking his attitudes contradictory, he appeared to believe that quarreling with his friend over the blood price was quite consistent with his role as peacemaker. Arbitrating between them was a thankless task; however, some further effort would have to be made. "Look at it this way," he was beginning when suddenly the wind ceased, leaving all three of them staring at the sea as if in expectation of a storm.

Odysseus was the first to gather his wits. This calm came to him as a serious threat. "I must get back," he said, and he got to his feet and moved away, leaving the other two sitting there. When he reached the first lines he learned that Iphigeneia's ship had been sighted and would soon be entering the strait. Heralds were already crying through the camp, summoning the chiefs to an immediate assembly.

10.

roton and his assistants were included in the summons and so was
Calchas. The same obscure wish, or need,
to mark himself out, assert his foreignness,
had made him want to appear looking his
best, in full priestly regalia; but he had
grown accustomed to the ministrations of
Poimenos, especially in the dressing of his
hair and the applying of his makeup. These
things he now had to do for himself and
hastily, with the aid of a hand mirror. He
felt conscious as he arrived that he was in
disarray, the fringes of his skirt hanging
too low, his hair not properly pinned up,
the kohl on his eyelids smudged.

Agamemnon opened the proceedings,
briefly thanking the assembled chiefs, re-
marking on the strange coincidence of the
calm falling just as the ship was sighted.
What could this portend?

By common consent, the first among
the chiefs to speak was Idomeneus, com-

mander of the Cretan contingent, which was second in numbers only to the Mycenaean. His support was essential, whatever the ultimate decision. He was known as a pragmatist, with both feet firmly on the ground, and his words now bore this out.

"I think we should make immediate preparations to leave," he said. "The wind has dropped, that's the salient fact, there's no need to look beyond it. For whatever reason, it has pleased Zeus to release us from this misery. We've waited long for this moment. For heaven's sake, let's take the opportunity that is presented to us, let's welcome Agamemnon's daughter as befits a princess of Mycenae, and embark her for home again as soon as possible. Meanwhile let's start work breaking camp and loading the ships. If there's a calm in the narrows we can use our oars to get out into the open sea. Once there, we'll be all right. The breezes will be southerly, as accords with the season. We've lost time enough already, are we going to lose more days while she is got ready for the sacrifice? I am for setting out immediately."

"Send Iphigeneia home again?" Achilles said. "I'm surprised to hear you suggest that, Idomeneus. I thought you were my friend. Don't you see, it will be thought she changed her mind about marrying me. As you all know, and as the Singer has given out, for patriotic reasons I allowed my name to be made use of as a means of persuading Iphigeneia to come here. No name but mine could have brought her on such a journey. What sort of figure will I make now if she turns round and goes straight back home again? Think what future generations will say. Think of my image. A girl arrives, looks Achilles over, decides he doesn't come up to scratch and promptly leaves again. No, I can't allow that to happen. I'll kill her myself first. Then at least it will be supposed that she didn't come up to *my* expectations. With all due respect, Agamemnon." On this he bowed slightly to the King, who made no answering sign.

"We must rise above personal issues and think of the needs of the alliance," Chasimenos said. "As it happens, I agree with Achilles, though not of course for personal reasons. Let me state my credentials. Let me speak as what I am, what I am proud to be, a top civil servant in Agamemnon's service. In fact, not to be needlessly modest, I am the head of the whole palace bureaucracy. Mine has been the overall responsibility for arranging this sacrifice. Sending Iphigeneia back again would be both illogical and sinfully wasteful. In fact it would be an absurd thing to do. The knife has been fashioned at considerable cost, in accordance with daily instructions from the King. The sacrificial altar has been built at enormous labor under the personal supervision of Croton, priest of Zeus, who has done a marvelous job. I am sure that all here share my sentiments of gratitude to him for the time he has put in and for his dedication to this project."

Shouts of "Hear hear, well done, Croton" came from various quarters and the priest raised his staff in acknowledgment. "Not only that," Chasimenos continued, "but a processional way has been laid up the slope to the altar by levies of men working day and night, without remission. In the course of these works five men have been injured, two of them seriously. Think of the planning and organization involved, the sheer human cost in blood and sweat. The knife, the altar, the road, these things have been brought into being for one purpose only. They must be used for that purpose. To divorce the product from the purpose for which it was produced undermines the logic on which our civilization and all its values are based.

It makes nonsense of everything. It is unnatural, it is perverse, I might even say it is inhuman." Chasimenos looked earnestly from face to face. Beads of sweat had appeared on his high and narrow forehead. It was plain to all that he was deeply moved. "It would leave us with a deficit on the books," he said. "There is no way it could be justified in terms of cost-effectiveness."

Chasimenos was not very well liked among the chiefs, being a known intriguer; but one or two bravos were heard at the end of this speech and Achilles went so far as to send Patroclus over to say a word of thanks. In the brief silence that followed all heard the querulous voice of Nestor suddenly raised: "I remember a similar case many years ago now. It was in the land of the Lapiths. I was young then, I could hold my own with anyone, as a wrestler and spearman my equal was hard to find. My companions were men like Caeneus and Exardius, men such as we don't see nowadays, more like gods than men, or was it Caenichus? I'm sure of his name when he was a girl, he was called Caenis when he was a girl, he was raped by Poseidon, or she, I should say, she was still a girl then, afterwards she asked Poseidon to change her into a boy so it couldn't happen again, but of course that doesn't follow, he didn't know much about life, she, I should say, she was still a girl then, Poseidon liked the look of him as a boy and did it again. I was one of the guests at Peirithous's wedding when the fight broke out between the Lapiths and the Centaurs, we were all drunk, I killed three Centaurs single-handed, this was after that famous cattle raid in Elis when we got away with fifty—"

"Father, where is this leading?"

"Don't interrupt me. My sentence is for death."

"Death for Iphigeneia?"

"Fool, how does she come into it? The penalty for stealing from a comrade is death. I demand the death penalty."

"Father, the man whose death you are justly demanding was decapitated the day before yesterday."

While the old man was still being shushed into silence by his dutiful sons, Calchas raised his hand and waited for Agamemnon's nod. Like Croton, he had no authority deriving from command and therefore no automatic right of speech. He had not been sure whether he would speak or not—it was unlikely he would be invited to do so. But after all he had been sent for; and he felt some of the recklessness that visits fearful souls when their fears are realized. No immediate harm could come to him, he knew that: he was protected by the King's hate. Listening to Idomeneus, a practical man and not god-vexed like himself, it had occurred to him that others might see it in the same way and be inclined, after so much waiting, to go at once. It was futile now to argue against the war. But at least the folly of the sacrifice, the offense to Artemis, might be avoided.

"Surely," he said when the nod came, "we do not think of sacrificing a king's daughter only because arrangements have been made to do it? If we go so far along a road and find it is the wrong one, do we continue along the road and make the error worse and weary ourselves to no purpose, or do we stop and look about us and try to find the right way? O Kings, the wind has ceased, is it not signal enough? The meaning is plain to see. There was contention between Zeus and Artemis; but there is contention no more and that is why the wind has ceased. What could better show reconciliation than a calm? Idomeneus is right. The way to Troy lies open to us. Why should we wait here a single day longer?"

Now Croton raised his staff, shouting as he did so, barely waiting for the nod of permission. "Lies! How dare you speak to this assembly in such a manner, as if Zeus and Artemis were on an equal footing, as if they could quarrel as equals, be reconciled as equals? False diviner, where are your friends here? Zeus sent the wind and Zeus has lifted it. There is only Zeus. Now that the witch is approaching and he sees us ready to fulfill our vows and perform the sacrifice, he shows his trust in us by ending the wind. If we betray that trust, he will send the terror of his bolts against us, he will destroy us utterly."

At the sight of Croton's contorted face, Calchas felt his body stiffen with a passion of rage stronger than any he could remember, stronger far than caution. "Madman," he said loudly, "we live in a world of movement and you try to understand it by casting dead things on the ground, bones and stones and entrails, and so you see only death. Your Zeus stands for death. Who truly sent the wind, who stopped it, what do you care? You call the woman a witch and kill her in the name of Zeus and so you gain power for the priests of Zeus." He ceased and hung his head to hide the trembling of his lower lip—he had never, even as a young man, been robust enough to contain anger.

"I say we wait a day or two and see what happens," Ajax the Larger said in his loud, clotted voice. "You know, sort of test it out. If the wind doesn't come back we're in the clear. That way we could get to the finals of the javelin-throwing and weight-lifting events, and in the meantime I could hope to bring my small friend here to see reason over this blood-price business."

"See reason? I see the reason well enough, you want me to pay for your fucking blunders."

Odysseus smiled very slightly and raised a hand. He had

been waiting for the right moment to intervene. It was always a good thing to follow upon fools, they gave one a chance to drive things home. "Croton has a point," he said. "What if Zeus has ended the wind because he takes it on trust that the sacrifice will be performed? How can we be sure? There is no sense in trying to test it out, as Ajax suggests. It's Zeus who would be playing the waiting game, not us. The gods are immortal, they have all the time in the world. If Zeus is holding the wind over us, as seems very likely to me, he will obviously wait till we are at sea before bringing it back, because embarking without performing the sacrifice will be taken as the final proof that we don't intend to perform it. If that happens we'll be worse off than ever, there'll be nowhere to run to, the fleet will be wrecked, we'll all be drowned. The only way to be sure is to hedge our bets and carry out the sacrifice as planned. Then we are safe either way."

The saliva of pleasure had gathered in his mouth as he spoke, slightly thickening his words. Here they were, discussing the sacrifice of a man's daughter. And there was the man himself, the one most vitally affected, wordless, helpless, all trussed up—precisely because he *was* the father. It was neat. Agamemnon could not speak against the sacrifice now, he would risk being overruled and thus losing what shreds of authority he had left. His voice had been needed once and once only. He had given it and could not take it back. He was superfluous now and he knew it; but the fiction had to be maintained, there had to be a figurehead, a vehicle for the general will. Agamemnon knew that too. Agamemnon, the Commander-in-Chief . . .

Odysseus swallowed, clearing his mouth of excess saliva. "There is one circumstance that nobody has remarked on. Only one man received news of the ship and felt the wind cease at precisely the same moment. We can't count those with him, the message was not delivered to them. The men on lookout knew of the ship but only felt the wind drop later, and this applies to any they told on the way. The man I refer to is Agamemnon. It was granted to our Commander-in-Chief to understand the intimate connection between the two events, making clear the necessity for the sacrifice and at the same time confirming his place as the supreme leader of this great expedition."

"There's the moral aspect too," Menelaus said. "I've been thinking about this for some time now. I've been doing some soul-searching. I think I may have been too hard on the Trojans because of Paris carrying off my Helen, who is a very valuable woman, in fact she is unique, being the only woman currently alive today who can claim to have been born from a swan's egg. Now it is true that the Trojans are Asians, but they can't help that, can they? Most of them have never had a chance to be anything else. I mean, there they are, they are stuck with it. They are kept in ignorance and superstition, they live in the midst of squalor and bad smells, they are unhygienic, they have the wrong gods. Now we could save them from that, we could bring light into their darkness. I mean, we are streets ahead of them, especially in metalwork and catapults. We have a duty towards these people. Once the territory has been occupied and the troublemakers rounded up—I don't believe in leniency towards those responsible for the war, I have every intention of personally hanging Paris up by his balls—we could set about civilizing the population and changing their ways. Nothing must be allowed to get in the way of this. I see it as a mission. I am with Odysseus, we should take no chances."

The clinching voice, however, came from one of the least important of the chiefs, a man named Nineus, who had brought a small force from the island of Simi. "You really amaze me," he said. "You are all talking as if we had the luxury of choice. Do you really think it is we who decide? If so, you are out of touch with reality. The whole army is waiting for Iphigeneia. They have seen the knife made, they have labored to erect the altar and make the processional way. The one thing that has kept them going, kept them cheerful and joking among themselves, is the prospect of this colorful and unusual spectacle, a king's daughter on the slab. They may believe this will bring an end to the wind, but that is an abstract matter. It is the prospect of the show itself that has held them together, given them something to look forward to. They are only human, they have to have some color and excitement in their lives. If we cheat them out of it now, we'll have a full-scale mutiny on our hands. No, let's face it, if we want to save our own skins, she'll have to be sacrificed now."

Dressing
Up

1.

Early in the morning, soon after first light, as the ship rounded the headland of Attica and passed into the open sea beyond the island of Ceos, the hostile wind suddenly dropped and a period of calm descended. Then a breeze from the southeast sprang up, bearing them forward, to the great relief of all on board. By noon they were well into the Euboean channel and Sisipyla was sent to ask the captain how long it would be before they came to Aulis. Soon, she was told. Perhaps before the dark.

It was time to prepare the princess for her arrival. Her litter, and an awning to protect her from the sun, and a tent improvised from canvas and spars were in place already on the high poop of the ship. Here, while the ship was propelled smoothly forward by the auspicious breeze—surely sent by Artemis in favor of the nuptials— under the skillful hands of Sisipyla, the princess was dressed for her meeting with the groom. She wore a long skirt, hooped with copper wires to make it bell-shaped, and made up of numerous small strips of different colors falling in flounces and decorated in half-moon patterns in honor of the goddess, and a red jacket brocaded in a darker shade, open at the front from throat to navel, with the breasts lightly veiled by a high-necked diaphanous vest. Her cheeks were touched with rouge and her eyelids darkened with a dye made from the black poplar, Hecate's tree, symbolizing the renewal of the moon.

It was a beautiful and stately stranger that was at last revealed to view. Aware of her finery, she bore herself more deliberately, and she seemed taller to Macris, waiting below, because of the high chignon on the crown of her head, rising above the rows of small curls before and behind the silver headband. Seeing her thus, dressed and scented and painted for another, he felt a thin phlegm of bitterness rise in his throat; he did not speak the compliments that had risen to his mind and after a moment or two he moved away into the waist of the ship.

The light was failing when they came within sight of the Greek ships lying at anchor, and it was dusk when they disembarked, Iphigeneia carried on her litter by four men through the placid shallows, Sisipyla wading with the others, raising the hem of her narrow skirt. Waiting with lighted torches on the shore was a group of men, no more than a dozen, their faces not yet distinguishable.

Macris offered his arm to the princess as she descended from the litter, and remained at her side while she stood there, motionless on the dark beach, waiting, with a sure instinct of dignity, for those meeting her to advance. The flickering light of the torches still made vision difficult. A man detached himself from the group and came some paces forward, followed closely by one of the torchbearers. He bowed and straightened himself and the light fell on his dark-eyed, handsome face. "Welcome, princess," he said. "Achilles sends deepest apologies at not being here to meet you. He has been delayed at the hunt."

"Who are you?"

"I am Patroclus."

"And my father? Why is he not here to meet me?" Iphigeneia spoke calmly, without haste. Perhaps only Sisipyla, standing close behind, knew the effort this cost her.

"An unfortunate indisposition. An attack of colic that came upon him suddenly."

Iphigeneia took a step forward. "I will go to him."

"No, no, he is in some pain, he would not wish to receive you in that condition. He expects to be recovered by morning. It is late, you will be tired, our orders are to escort you to your quarters."

"Your orders?" Macris said. He too, for quite different reasons, found it difficult to keep his voice on an even keel. Iphigeneia's beauty and loneliness in the torchlight, the wasted splendor of her dress, something too brusque in the manner of this messenger of Achilles had distressed and angered him in equal measure. He glanced briefly round for Diomedes, who as chief ambassador was most responsible for the princess's reception. But he had disappeared into the darkness. Phylakos was there still, but no appeal could be made to him. He said, "Your orders will need to take account of the princess's wishes and of her natural disappointment at finding neither bride-groom nor father to welcome her after such a journey."

"And who may you be?" Patroclus said.

Macris left the princess's side to move forward so that his face could be clearly seen. He was close to Patroclus now, and looked directly into his eyes. "I am Macris, son of Amphidamas."

He continued the close regard and for some moments it was like the game he remembered from childhood, played with sticks instead of swords, the game of who strikes first at the signal; and he knew he would win this contest against the man before him, whether it was in play or in earnest. He said, "You must have sighted our ship in early morning. Lord Achilles did not think of forgoing his sport on this day, when his bride was arriving?"

"Macris, you go too far and too fast, as usual," Iphigeneia said. "I have not asked you to quarrel on my behalf."

"This one is always ready to quarrel," Phylakos said, and he came forward, crossed to the group with the torches, passed into the shadows beyond them. Macris saw now that of those who had landed with the princess there only remained the women and himself and the six he had brought with him. "He is a boy that needs a lesson," Phylakos said from somewhere in the shadowy haze beyond the lights.

Macris suppressed the retort that rose to his lips. He would have been ready enough to quarrel with Phylakos too, for all the older man's strong build and the tricks he had picked up in the years of battle. All his suspicion, his sense of the general wrongness of things, first felt at Mycenae, was redoubled now at this scrambled reception, at the rudeness to himself when he stood by the side of the princess as her escort. Patroclus had not even bothered to find a convincing form of words. How could Achilles convey regrets when he was still somewhere out in the countryside?

"Permit us to accompany you to your quarters," Patroclus said. "We have made everything ready for you."

"I will need my women with me."

"There is no need. There are women here who will be within call."

"Women of the camp?"

"Lady, we are far from the luxuries of the palace here. There would not be room for people in constant attendance."

Iphigeneia had been allowing herself to be guided forward, but now she stopped. "I will keep Sisipyla with me," she said.

"You can send for your slave girl at any time you need her, but our orders —"

Iphigeneia remained motionless. "I am not interested in your orders," she said, and there was the faintest quiver in her voice. "Perhaps you didn't hear me properly. Macris, will you make my wishes plain to this man?"

Without needing instructions, the small squadron under Macris's command had formed in close order round the princess, and Macris now positioned himself directly in front of her, right arm resting loosely across his body. He said, "The princess desires that her companion Sisipyla should accompany her and remain in attendance. If this desire is not met, she will return under our escort to the ship."

For some while nobody stirred or spoke. They could hear the faint hissing of the water as it moved among the pebbles. Somewhere inland a dog barked and others joined in. Macris watched Patroclus come to the only possible conclusion. He could sense the calculation going on behind the other's eyes:

Better to yield in lesser matters . . . Why did they want to isolate her?

"Lady, by all means keep the girl with you. Forgive me, I had not realized that it mattered so much."

On this, Iphigeneia moved forward once again with Sisipyla beside her. Macris, following close behind, saw the lighted tent that they were led to. He had hoped for a word of farewell, or even just a glance, but none came. Iphigeneia had not looked at him or spoken to him again after that one request. Six armed men had been stationed round the tent. Light fell on the faces of the two at the entrance as they stood aside for the princess to pass, and Macris recognized them as members of Agamemnon's palace guard. Six seemed a lot; but of course the King would want to give his daughter what state and consequence he could in the rough conditions of the camp. Surely Agamemnon would take it amiss, as a slight upon himself, that the husband-to-be had failed to be present at his betrothed's arrival?

The two girls moved here and there inside the tent and their shadows were cast on the canvas wall. Macris tried to distinguish between them, tried to determine which one was Iphigeneia's, but they were identical in form and movement, it was impossible to tell which was the princess and which the slave. Then they vanished altogether as the two passed into the central part of the tent where the woven hangings blocked the light.

Sick at heart, he turned away, turned his back on the lighted chamber where Iphigeneia would wait for Achilles. He dismissed his men with orders to find quarters in the Mycenaean lines and report to him next day at sunrise. He had no desire for rest; in the agitation of his feelings even the thought of remaining still was intolerable to him; he had no gift for passivity, no saving instinct to seek shelter from unhappiness by retreating into the self. It was dark outside the confines of the camp, the light of fires and torches making the world beyond seem vast and featureless. He would walk along the shore until he felt tired enough to think of sleeping.

The descent of night had stilled the sea and the ships at their moorings made no sound as he passed. The light was strong enough for him to make out the gleam of the waterline, and he kept just above it, on the shingle. Somewhere out to sea a lost gull uttered desolate cries. Macris walked until the way was closed off by rocks, the scattering of some ancient landslide. On his return, as he came up to the outskirts of the camp, he saw a low light burning above the shore and heard the high chant of a singer and the ruffling wingbeat sound of a lyre.

He mounted towards the light and the sound and came upon men grouped in a semicircle round a singer with a bird-like tilt of the head that suggested blindness. Seated close behind him was a boy with a beautiful rapt face.

It was the story of the Boeotian king Athamas, and Macris had heard it before, it was in every singer's repertory, always in demand because of the dramatic changes of fortune in it and the element of horror. Macris found a place a little apart and sat down to listen.

Athamas was a very unlucky man, though rich and powerful. This bad luck he brought upon himself by his folly in taking a second wife while the first was still living. The new wife was named Ino, a Theban woman, one of the daughters of Cadmus. She was a potent sorceress, and very grasping and greedy, the kind of person who wants everything and wants it now. She was immediately jealous of the first wife, whose name was Nephele. She was tormented by the thought that Nephele's son Phrixus would inherit the throne, taking precedence over her own children. This thought allowed her no rest by day or night. She couldn't think of anything else, she felt she was going mad.

She didn't dare to do any harm to Phrixus directly, much as she would have liked to. But she brooded over it and in the end she hit upon a plan. By her black arts she maddened the Boeotian women so that they secretly parched the corn seed intended for the spring sowing. As a result the crop failed and the specter of famine loomed over the land. Just as Ino had expected, Athamas sent messengers to consult the oracle at Delphi and bring back word as to how the catastrophe could be avoided. This was the springing of the trap, the moment this diabolical woman had been waiting for. She was ahead of the game at every point, for now with her spells she turned the brains of the returning messengers and made them commit a horrible crime. They falsified the words of the oracle, they reported to the king that if the famine was to be averted his only son Phrixus must be sacrificed at the altar of Zeus.

Macris felt a prickling at the nape of his neck. Never before had he heard the story told in such a gripping manner. It was as if the Singer were himself a witness, as if he were trying in his own person to warn or persuade. The boy had assumed his exact posture, shoulders held back and head tilted. The people listening were rapt in silence, no smallest sound came from them.

It was a lie, a lie, but the king believed it. He had no choice but to believe it. And that is the important thing, not the truth or the lie but the belief, the readiness, that is what pleases Zeus. It cannot be immediate, there must always be struggle, but in the end the king must agree, so as to save his people. Otherwise, how can he continue to be king? The welfare of the people is more important than the life of the child. Some say Athamas was concerned only to save his throne, but this is to take the view of the snake, not the eagle. There will always be cynics. How can our great leader, Agamemnon, tamer of horses, think only of one life when a thousand men are waiting on his word, how can he pause to wonder whether the messenger is under a spell? He leads his child to the altar and makes everything ready for the sacrifice. He takes up the knife . . .

The Singer paused, waited a moment, then struck a shuddering chord on the lyre for the killing stroke. When he resumed, it was on a quieter, more measured note. It was related by some that at the very moment the knife was raised a ram with a fleece the color of gold appeared from nowhere, sent by merciful Zeus, and Phrixus climbed on its back and it rose with him and flew off to the northeast and neither the boy nor the ram was ever seen again. The northeast, where the wind that had so plagued them came from, the wind that was now stopped . . .

Once more he made a pause. And now he did something very rare with him, almost unprecedented, he turned his face towards the vague, glimmering shapes of his listeners and spoke directly to them. "Now that the wind has gone, it is difficult for a blind man to know north from south. Now that the wind has gone, it is difficult for blind and sighted alike to know the will of Zeus. Some say this, some say that. There is always another story. Perhaps there was no witchcraft, perhaps the messengers spoke the truth. Perhaps Ino was innocent, pursued as some say by the jealous wrath of white-armed Hera, consort of Zeus, because her lord had once been in love with

Ino's sister, Semele. There is always another story. But it is the stories told by the strong, the songs of the kings, that are believed in the end."

The Singer's voice had lost force and fervor now, he sounded tired and rather confused. He made some effort to return to the miraculous ram, offspring of Poseidon and Theophane, which not only could fly but had the gift of speech, and whose golden fleece was later to be the object of the Argonauts' quest. But his phrasing was halting and mechanical and after a short while he fell silent.

In any case, Macris was not much interested in the ram. He had always found miraculous interventions hard to imagine. It had been the verve of the narrative, the drama of treachery and falsehood, the terrible gullibility of Athamas, that had gripped him. What could have been meant by the reference to Agamemnon? There had been no wavering in the voice, no sense of an incongruous or discordant note, no seeming distinction in the Singer's mind between Athamas of Orchomenus and Agamemnon of Mycenae. Then the change in tone, the direct address, the overlaying of one story with another. Perhaps not weariness, as he had thought, but something else. Perhaps caution . . .

The boy had risen and was helping the Singer to his feet. The members of the audience were dispersing. Macris got up and went to the Singer, who was standing now, the boy supporting him with a hand under his arm.

Macris took the torch from the ground where it had been set, and held it up. "What did you mean?" he said. "How does Agamemnon enter into this story of Athamas and Phrixus?"

The Singer's face was stretched over the bones and deeply

marked by privation. He turned in the direction of the voice, and Macris saw that one of his eyes was without focus and useless to him and the other was unsteady, as if affrighted by the nearness of the torchlight.

"You see nothing?"

"Some light comes on this side." The Singer raised a hand. "I see the shapes of things. I see you are tall and hear you are young. I have the boy's eyes to help me. This is Poimenos, a gift to me from the gods. Have *you* come with some gift?"

"I have nothing about me that I could give you. I have just arrived here. Tomorrow I will bring you a gift. What did you mean in the Song just now?"

"Young man, the meaning is inside the Song, and I have finished my singing for the night. If the meaning could be told so easily, what would be the use of the Song? You have just arrived? So you have come with Iphigeneia? You are of her party?"

"Yes."

"You have spoken to no one?"

"Only to those who came to meet us at the shore."

"But the princess was with you then."

"Of course." Macris was growing impatient. "I have just told you that I came with Iphigeneia."

"Naturally, in her presence . . ." The Singer lowered his head as if talking to himself.

"What are you talking about? What is all this mystery?"

There was a short pause while the Singer seemed to ruminate. Then he said, "I do not tell things that are outside of the Songs, or I would not last long as a Singer, not here at least, and probably not anywhere. Calchas the priest would be the one to ask."

"Calchas? I know him. I saw him sometimes at Mycenae. He is the King's diviner."

"Not any longer. He has one task only now."

"What is that?"

"He will tell you. Calchas has become talkative, he speaks to anyone who will listen, telling his wrongs. Poimenos will show you the way."

2.

nside the tent Iphigeneia was silent for a while, not quite looking at her companion, not quite looking at her surroundings, as if still waiting for something more, something to save her from the burden of being alone here, dressed for a different sort of reception.

Sisipyla felt the loneliness of her mistress, seeing her stand there motionless and lost in her bridal clothes. She remembered how she had dressed the princess in the improvised enclosure on the ship, and how docile the usually impatient Iphigeneia had been, raising her arms, turning her body this way and that, offering her face for the makeup, eager for everything to be just so, wanting to make a splendid impression. Now, if Achilles did not come soon, these beautiful things would have to be taken off again, the rouge sponged away, the hair released from its elaborate dressing, the nightgown put on.

But it occurred to her now that this couldn't be done yet, the chest with their things in it had not been brought up from the ship.

"I know these hangings," Iphigeneia said suddenly. "They are from the walls of the royal apartments at Mycenae. That design of foliage and doves, it's been there as long as I can remember." She was smiling and a faint flush of color had come to her face. "My father brought them for tent hangings to use during the siege of Troy, then when he was getting things ready for my arrival he had them hung here, something familiar so I wouldn't feel too far from home. Even with all these affairs of state in his mind, all that responsibility resting on his shoulders, he found time to think of his daughter's welfare."

"He is truly great," Sisipyla said, glad that the princess had broken the silence, as it meant that now she could speak herself and perhaps be of some comfort to her mistress. She thought of Agamemnon, for whom she had never felt anything but a sort of dread, picturing his face in the brief glances she had had of it, the narrow eyes, the bitter pride of the mouth. "The truly great are so in small things also," she said. "If they would only bring our chest up I could get you ready for the night. You will need your sleep to look your best tomorrow, when Achilles —"

"Achilles will come tonight, I know he will come tonight, as soon as he returns from the hunt. He will not want to let a night pass without coming to bid me welcome."

"But lady, if he has been overtaken by the dark somewhere, or gone astray in some difficult place, he too may have to wait for morning before returning to the camp. Besides, excuse me, if he is going to be so very late and come expecting interviews in the middle of the night, since it is his own fault, even if accidental, it will show better judgment for the princess to send me to tell him that she has retired, that she will see him in the morning. It is always good to begin well and get things clear from the start. In that way the man does not take things so much for granted. I could ask one of them outside if we could just have the chest brought up."

"I forbid you to mention this chest one more time. How is it that you occupy your mind with small things, like chests and getting ready for bed? Do you think I don't know yet what suits with my dignity, that I have to go in for tricks and false modesty and pretended offense?"

Iphigeneia had spoken angrily, but her face softened as she looked at Sisipyla now. "I know that you like everything to be done in the proper way, and that you are concerned to guard me against incautious behavior, but there are times in life when we have to take a broader view. Naturally, looking as you do from the commonplace, everyday perspective, you cannot possibly understand the nature of a man like Achilles. We met only once, but it stayed in his memory forever, from that moment I was his predestined bride. We are both of noble birth and that puts us on the same wavelength, we have the same sense of special destiny. And then there is this splendidly reckless proposal of marriage on the eve of battle. Do you think a man like that will feel he is scoring points because I am ready to receive him in the middle of the night? He is far above such petty egotism and vanity. Call it intuition if you like, I just have this very strong sense of what kind of person he is. I feel as if I know him through and through. He is brave and strong, but he is gentle and forbearing too. I know that when he enters this tent he will not seem a stranger to me. He may arrive at any moment and I intend—"

At this moment they heard a man's voice outside, speaking to the guards. "What did I tell you?" Iphigeneia drew herself up and raised her head and gestured to Sisipyla, who went forward to the entrance and passed through, returning after some moments followed by a dark-bearded, broad-shouldered man of average height with flecks of gray in his hair. Iphigeneia went some paces towards him. "Achilles," she said, "you have come at last."

"No," the man said, shaking his head a little. "I am not Achilles, I am Odysseus of Ithaca, son of Laertes. I have come to call you to a higher destiny than even the noble Achilles could offer. Will you ask your attendant to leave us alone together for a little while?"

3.

Poimenos indicated the tent at some twenty or thirty paces' distance, then turned abruptly and disappeared into the night, giving Macris the impression that he wanted to avoid going any closer. The tent was small, closed across the front. There was a light inside and the shadow of a hunched form. Macris called out his name and his father's name, and after some moments there was a fumbling with the strings of the flaps inside and then a man emerged, crouching low at the entrance, holding a small and reeking oil lamp in one hand.

"What do you want with me," he said, in the Greek of the Argolis but with accents markedly foreign.

Macris remembered the priest as he had last seen him at Mycenae, perfumed and expensively dressed, in close attendance upon Agamemnon as his diviner. But even in a better light he would not easily have recognized him in this disheveled crouching figure, with the long, matted hair falling in disorder round his face, the black smudges that made caverns of the hollows of his eyes. He wore only a loincloth and a sleeveless vest, and there was a heavy odor of wine on his breath.

"Macris, Macris," he said. "Yes, I know your father. Is he well?"

"Thank you, yes, he is well."

"What brings you to me? No one calls for Calchas now."

"I was sent to you by the Singer. He said you were the one to ask. Things have happened that I don't understand. Why wasn't Achilles there to—"

"Did he have a boy with him?"

"No, he didn't have anyone with him. How could he have anyone with him when he wasn't there himself? That's what—"

"I was robbed of that boy. While I had the ear of the King, while I could still read the signs, he admired me, I was his model. I would catch him imitating my smallest movements. The Singer took him away from me with stories."

"I am sorry to hear of this loss," Macris said, as politely as he could manage. "Just now the Singer was telling the story of Athamas and he brought Agamemnon into it, as if they were somehow in the same situation." A presentiment of horror came to him as he spoke, and his mind flinched away from it. "What is the meaning?" he said.

Calchas's eyes rolled strangely in their darkened sockets. "I don't feel well," he said. "Shall we sit down? Outside here is better—everything's in a mess inside." He set down the lamp and squatted near it, but after a moment lost his balance and sat back heavily. "I tried to tell him meanings," he said from this half-recumbent position, "but he didn't want that, he wanted only stories."

Macris watched the diviner struggle upright again. "Something is wrong," he said. "I sensed it when we landed, the way we were treated. Has Achilles changed his mind?"

"Achilles hasn't got a mind, he has only certain attitudes. Nor has Poimenos, in a different way. That was what I valued in him, that beautiful absence of thought. I am always so caught up, so harassed. Then the gods withheld their messages. How terrible to lie night after night listening to a wind that was only a wind. It all began with my failure to see the truth about the dancer and the flames."

Macris felt his patience giving out. He reached forward and took the thin arm of the priest and gripped it hard for a moment. "What is all this to me?" he said. "I have just come here to Aulis, with the party that accompanied Iphigeneia. What is this talk of sacrifice?" Again he felt the fingering of horror along his spine. "But the wind has dropped," he said, as if answering a suggestion someone had made to him. "Has he brought her all this way only to humiliate her? If so, I will call him to account were he invulnerable twenty times over."

"Achilles is not invulnerable," Calchas said slowly. "He will kill a certain number of times, then he will be killed. And that will be all his epitaph, at least all the epitaph that he deserves. It is only his heart that cannot be touched because it is made of stone." He looked at the pale expanse of the face before him. "You are her champion?"

The question, in its gentleness, took Macris by surprise, robbed him of defenses. "She fills my mind," he said huskily, and immediately regretted giving so much away to no purpose.

"I see, yes." Calchas felt the fumes of the wine clear a little, leaving the beginning of desolation. He reached forward in his turn and laid a hand on the young man's tensed forearm. "This will not be easy for you," he said. "There is a strange logic of reversal that rules among us here. I spoke against the sacrifice, so I will wield the knife. There is not even the wind now to explain why we are killing her, how this madness has come about. The madness has outlasted the wind because it was there before, it belongs to us."

4.

ext morning, soon after sunrise, Odysseus, accompanied by Chasimenos, made his first report to the King. It was rather like the business of the knife. Agamemnon had to be kept, not informed exactly, but reassured that the details of the design were being carried out, that his daughter was being persuaded of her high destiny. What he didn't want to hear about was suffering; he would have found it intolerable that any suffering should be added to his own.

A careful touch was needed, and Odysseus was tired this morning. After this first session with the girl he had not been able to sleep, his mind had been so stimulated. There had been the shock to be managed first of all; he had known from the very beginning, while the whole design was still on the drawing board, that the shock factor would be very important. It was the opposite technique from breaking bad news gently. The shock had to be used like a battering ram to crash through the girl's defenses, break down her accustomed sense of being cared for and protected, lay her world to waste, open it wide to the argument of a patriotic destiny, in the way that relief brought to a devastated city is grasped eagerly, even amid the ruins.

That was the ideal; but this first meeting had been far from easy. He could not feel he had got far yet. The girl was spoilt and obdurate and there was no immediate self-interest that could be appealed to, as had been the case with her father. As he had earlier remarked to Chasimenos, having your throat cut before a large crowd of spectators was hardly something that could be presented as materially rewarding, even by a hugely talented advocate like himself. No, they would have to go directly, at a leap, to the abstract, there was no other way. Still, a beginning had been made; he had talked the girl through the first white-faced, horrified disbelief, denied her demands to see her father, scored the direct hit of informing her that she was there on the orders of that father. When the tears came, he had left. Tears were good, they softened the mind . . .

"No," he said, "I can reliably report that a start has been made in opening her eyes to the high, I might even say glorious, role she has to play."

"It is not given to every girl," Chasimenos said, "to hold the fate of a whole army in her hands. And at such a tender age too. I mean, most girls of that age have scarcely finished playing with dolls."

Odysseus suppressed a feeling of irritation. There was something distinctly insensitive and tactless about Chasimenos, he had noticed it before. He was looking forward to the time when their collaboration would no longer be necessary.

"Mycenae was not built in a day," he said. "We must gain ground by degrees, we must remove petty notions of complacency and self-regard from the girl's mind, all sloth and egotism, in their place we must put worthwhile goals and objectives, we must get her to raise her sights, aim high, what's the word I'm looking for?"

"Incentivize."

"Incentivize, there you go again, Chasimenos, absolutely brilliant. What it is to have a solid culture behind one. We must incentivize her, but it will take a little time. We have made a good start, we are making progress. In fact, this first report can be summed up in that one word: progress."

Interested in words as he was, he had always liked this one. It had magical properties if properly applied. Any movement, in any sort of direction, could be called progress. It was a notion that blunted present discontents, directing the thoughts to a future of greater prosperity, higher consumption and a more equitable distribution of wealth for oneself. "It's not where you start from but where you finish that's the important thing," he said. "I can promise the King that his daughter will be brought to embrace her high destiny and walk with light steps and a willing heart to the altar, having accepted the will of the people and the gods."

Agamemnon nodded at this and even smiled a little, it being exactly the sort of thing he wanted to hear. As the bronze had been docile and the knife made beautiful, so would Iphigeneia be docile, even happy, and make a beautiful end. "She was always a high-minded girl, and one who knew her duties," he said.

"She takes after her father in that." Odysseus wondered briefly why he went on bothering to salve Agamemnon's conscience, when it was perfectly clear that the King was trapped. It was not only a matter of greed and ambition. The problems at home that had driven Agamemnon to embark on the war would be waiting for him much aggravated if he returned discredited and stripped of his command. Rivals to his power in the royal house, jealousy among kinsmen, the constant drain on the state of maintaining an army strong enough to protect him against an uprising. Odysseus was well informed about the situation in Mycenae. The textile workshops in the Argolis were on half production, exports of pottery had been declining for many months, the weapons industry, and in particular the sale of bronze swords to Egypt and Cyrenaica, depended on supplies of copper and tin which had to come by complicated routes, sometimes from far away, from Cyprus or Sardinia, with loss of cargoes from weather or piracy, and consequent shortages and increased prices. The ravishment of Helen by a Trojan prince had come as a godsend to him, the perfect pretext . . . It must be the artist in me, Odysseus thought, the desire for excellence, that makes me want to keep him smiling in the sticky web. "It is there in her," he said. "Nobility like a fire burning within her, that sense of responsibility which is such a dominant characteristic of your own, that readiness to sacrifice herself for the common good. Mark my words, Agamemnon, your father's heart will be proud of her on the day."

At this moment, Menelaus and Diomedes entered the tent and for once Odysseus was glad to see them: they would swell the numbers for the scene he had in mind. "I think we are ready for the girl now," he said. "Has she been brought?"

"She's waiting outside, under guard," Menelaus said. "We passed her as we came in. Nice bit of stuff."

"Let's have her brought in. I think you'd better leave things to Chasimenos and me, we are used to working together by this time. You others just maintain a sort of imposing silence and keep staring down at her. That will be enough to impress the gravity of the situation upon her, I should think. Iphigeneia is fond of her, that much we have seen. But after all, she's just a little servant, used to scuttling about in the corridors of the women's quarter. She won't have had much experience of being alone among men. Ah, there you are, my dear. Come forward, you are among friends here, don't be afraid."

Sisipyla, left near the entrance by the guard, advanced on her own, taking short, shuffling steps, keeping her arms pressed to her sides, her head inclined forward and her eyes on the ground before her. It was the slave gait, not used when she was alone with Iphigeneia, but adopted whenever she was attending the princess in company. From the moment of the summons—which she had half expected—she had given careful thought to how she should bear herself during this interview. When she was close to the group of men she crouched forward in a reverence, hands on knees.

"This is Sisipyla," Odysseus said. "You are a pretty girl and you have a pretty name. Did you have it from your parents?"

Sisipyla glanced up for the first time at the faces of the tall bearded men that stood close around her, and she was six years old again and lost and looking at a face closely resembling her own, and a childish voice was asking her questions, stammering on the syllables of her new name, and the bearded mouths were laughing, but these now were not. This time she would get the answers right. "The name was given me by my mistress," she said. "The lady Iphigeneia gave me my name. I do not remember the name my parents gave me." This was a lie; but a lie told deliberately, one beyond detection, was good at the outset, it steeled her, it separated her from the purposes of these men, whose purposes she must seem to serve.

"You are devoted to your mistress, aren't you?" Chasimenos said. "You want to serve her best interests, don't you? I suppose you still hope her life can be saved?"

"Yes, lord."

"It is not possible to save her life," Odysseus said. "We have brought you here so you can understand that. Within two days, at the outside, the thing must be done. There are a thousand men out there waiting to see the will of the gods fulfilled so they can set sail for Troy under clear skies, with a clear conscience. Her own father has accepted the absolute necessity for her death, though of course it has given him a good deal of personal malaise."

He paused and Sisipyla saw him swallow at something, some impediment as it seemed, in his throat. "A considerable amount of malaise," he said.

"You must keep this one basic fact in your mind," Chasimenos said. "The sacrifice must and will take place. No power on earth can stop it now."

"The key to the whole thing lies in recognizing that," Odysseus said. "Now you are a bright girl, I can see that, you will understand that what it boils down to is not *whether* your mistress will die, but *how*."

A pause followed upon this and Sisipyla sensed that some response from her was expected. "How?" she said. "Why, at the altar, by the knife, as we sacrifice to Artemis."

"No, no," said Chasimenos, who could not forbear chuckling at such simplicity. "We are talking about the manner of it, not the means."

"Chasimenos, you are confusing the girl. My dear, it comes down to style. What would be the right style for Iphigeneia, royal princess and priestess of Artemis? Struggling in the hands of her captors, gagged to stifle her shrieks, drugged to the eyebrows and hardly able to walk? Would any of these be the right style?"

He paused, enjoining caution on himself. He was enjoying this too much, he was talking too fast. The girl was no fool, he could see it in her eyes. All the same, it was neat, it was stimulating, persuading love to be the agent of death. "Hardly, eh?" he said.

"No, lord."

"Well then." Odysseus straightened his shoulders, pressed back his head and gazed at her expectantly. "What would be the best style?"

Sisipyla looked seriously at the shrewd and humorous face before her. The eyes were full of life but there was no kindness in them. This was the man who was talking to Iphigeneia, he was the moving spirit in all this. She felt the force of his will and his cleverness, which was greater than hers. Something else too: this was pleasure to him, it was a sort of game. "The victim must assent," she said. "She must go of her own accord. In that way Artemis is the more honored and the omens will be good."

"It is Zeus she will be honoring," one of the other men broke in harshly.

Sisipyla cast her eyes down, "Yes, lord, for you it is Zeus, but my mistress will not so easily be persuaded to offer her life to Zeus. She will need to feel it is the will of the goddess."

"Bravo!" Odysseus looked round at the others as if inviting

them to share his admiration. "We were not wrong about this girl," he said. "By all means let it seem to Iphigeneia that she is carrying out the will of Artemis."

"The princess listens to you, doesn't she?" Chasimenos said.

"I have served her since we were children together."

"If you love your mistress you will want her to make a good end. You must do your part, you must help us to prepare her mind."

"I see, yes." Sisipyla paused for a moment, then said slowly, "When Iphigeneia is gone I will have nobody. All my service in the palace has been with her. What will I do, alone and unprotected, a slave, without possessions."

She had spoken without looking at any of those around her; but when she looked again at Odysseus's face she saw that he was smiling. "But of course," he said. "We have given that aspect of things some thought already. Devotion is all very well, but a girl needs to think about her future." He glanced at Chasimenos. "This can be taken care of, can't it?"

"Certainly. I will make the arrangements personally. You will be set free from slavery and given a grant of land in a place of your choosing, terraced already and planted with olives, five hectares we had in mind, with a timbered house built on it free of charge."

"With a dowry like that, and a pretty face to go with it, you won't wait long for a husband," Odysseus said. "I will throw in a few trinkets that you can wear at your wedding."

"Excuse me, I am only a poor girl, how will I know that I can count on these promises?"

"My my," Odysseus said, and the admiration now did not seemed feigned. "Here is a young lady with her head screwed on the right way."

"I will give you a papyrus, signed by my hand as chief scribe, with the royal seal on it, that you can present at the palace when you return. Will that satisfy you?"

"And how will I return?"

Chasimenos had assumed a look of patience. "We will arrange for your passage home."

"Escorted?"

"Certainly, yes."

"I am afraid of the Queen's hatred if I return without my mistress."

"Have no fear, we will take care of everything."

Sisipyla allowed time for an appearance of consideration, then nodded. She felt the approval of the men now, their faces had lost that sternness of regard. "I will work to bring the princess to a proper frame of mind," she said. "There is one thing that might help."

"What is that?"

"If she could be allowed to walk with the goddess."

"What do you mean?"

"If she could be allowed to honor Artemis by wearing the moon face when she goes to the altar, that is a white paste we make from gypsum and use at home when we offer sacrifices at the time of full moon. More than anything else I can think of this would help the princess see the way she must go."

"And you have this paste?"

"Yes, we had thought it might be needed for the wedding. We use it sometimes in powder to whiten the face so that the red coloring on the cheeks will show up better."

Odysseus glanced at Agamemnon, who nodded with eyes averted. He himself could see nothing wrong with the idea. If it could reconcile Iphigeneia to her lot, and avoid unseemly and ill-omened behavior on her part, so much the better; and he felt sure it would please Croton and the fundamentalists, who now formed a considerable faction in the camp. Like all people interested in power, Croton understood the importance of symbols. The moon mask would bring the princess into the semblance of the goddess, it would seem to the mob that the goddess herself was being put to death for daring to compete with all-powerful Zeus.

"We have no objection to that," he said. "In fact it strikes me as a very good idea. You are a girl with a lot between the ears. I can prophesy a bright future for you."

5.

rom first light Macris had been waiting and watching not far from Iphigeneia's tent, himself closely observed in his turn by two men from Phylakos's squadron. He saw Sisipyla escorted from the tent by a guard. He saw her return alone some time later. Then Odysseus entered the tent and almost at once Sisipyla emerged again.

He went forward to meet her. The scarf she wore over her head came down low enough to shade the eyes, but her face looked ghastly in this morning sunlight, drained of all color. Her manner, however, was composed, and when she spoke the voice was clear and controlled. "I was hoping to meet you," she said. "There is something I want to talk about. I expect we are being watched, but we could walk by the shore where there would be no danger of anyone hearing us."

"Very well." Even in the anguish of his spirit he was impressed by this directness and the unfaltering gaze of her eyes; impressed and in a certain way almost taken aback. He could not remember exchanging words with her before, his attention had all been for the princess. Now this slave girl did not look at him or talk to him as if his permission for anything might be needed.

The sea was calm, there was a light breeze from the land. They walked for a while in silence. Then Macris could contain himself no longer. "I have no following here," he said. "The people from our lands are with my father at Mycenae, making up the garrison. The six I brought are with me to a man, but six is very few. The tent they are keeping her in is in the middle of the lines, surrounded on all sides. We would have to get her out, kill the guards without making any sound at all, then bear her away through the camp to some safe place. We would need horses. There are six men on guard, changed every four hours. And there are others at a greater distance, keeping watch. It would have to be done in darkness."

He walked along in silence for a while, then something between a sigh and a groan came from him. "There would be some danger to her life," he said. "But that is not the main thing—they would avoid harm to her if they could. It is that even with the advantage of surprise the odds are heavily against us. And if we fail we die, and her last hope dies with us."

It was what she had expected. She heard it in his voice. He would not make the attempt, the chances of success were too slight. In the night, in the desolation after her weeping, the knowledge had come to her, sum of what she sensed and surmised about him. He was brave enough and resolute, and he wanted Iphigeneia; but he would always be one to weigh up the odds. He would take a calculated risk, but he would not stake everything—for Iphigeneia or anyone. She had intended him to begin, she had hoped for this note of discouragement. It would make him the more ready to listen to her, perhaps remove some of the distrust he might feel for the plan of a servant. She had arranged this conversation carefully in her mind, lying near her mistress through the terrible sleepless hours.

She said, "Iphigeneia and I have the same height and the same figure. The general shape of the face is the same in both of us. When we were little we were so alike, everyone remarked on it. It was the reason I was given to her. Over the years there have come differences, but the general likeness is still there."

"It's true, there is a likeness," Macris said, it seemed reluctantly.

"You won't have been so aware of it because you see royalty in her face and you see your desires mirrored in it. This gives a different cast to the features. Forgive me, I speak in a way that I shouldn't, but I want you to see that the likeness is closer than you have been used to thinking. At a distance, dressed in the same way, it wouldn't be possible to tell us apart. Walking to the altar, wearing the robe of the victim, everyone would believe it was Iphigeneia."

Macris stopped dead and turned to look down at her from his considerably greater height. "What are you saying?" His tone was angry almost, and a kind of wondering surprise had come to his face.

"It wouldn't be Iphigeneia, it would be me."

"You would die in her place?"

There was disbelief in his voice; and Sisipyla saw suddenly

now that her first task would not be, as she had thought, to convince him that her plan was sound, but to persuade a man who thought first of the odds that she was firm enough of purpose to carry it out.

She turned to look out across the water, at the low hills that rose above the opposite shore. They were paling as the sun climbed overhead, every day the noon sun stole their color and gave it to the sky, a deep burning blue now, cloudless to the horizon. Above them, in the coarse sand above the shingle, there were thistles with pale blue flowers that stirred as she watched in a sudden breeze, soon spent. She saw tiny newborn crabs, the color of cinnamon, scuttle for cover. She paused a moment longer, as if to gather all this, the air of the morning, the clear light, the movement and the stillness, gather it into herself and gain power to make herself believed.

"I was given to her," she said. "My life belongs to her. Everything I have and am I owe to her. My life has no meaning without her. How can I explain? If I die she continues to be Iphigeneia. If she dies there is no person called Sisipyla." For the first time her voice trembled and her eyes were threatened with tears.

Macris nodded but there was no real comprehension on his face. He could not imagine the fear of abandonment, of being left alone in a dark place, like the straw children, the eyeless doll in the box of old playthings. A simpler explanation would work better with one who had never questioned his right to exist. "I am her slave, she is my mistress," she said. "She became the owner of my life when she became the owner of my body. It is only right that I should save her body with my own."

"Yes, you are right, it is your duty," Macris said. Duty he understood well, and also that it could take different forms.

"They will know it is not the princess," he said. "All eyes will be on her. Those nearest the altar will know her face well. Calchas, who makes the cut, he knows her. Chasimenos also. Her own father . . . Before you ever get to the altar people will see through the deception. A royal princess has a way of walking, a carriage of the head."

"Do you think I have not seen Iphigeneia walking? I walk behind her every day. She keeps her head up and her back straight and any girl who is not ill made can do the same."

She was speaking too hastily, too bluntly, she knew that. It would seem shocking to a young man of family to imply that the head and back of a princess were much like anyone else's. But she was indifferent to his sense of propriety, such things were no longer important; and somewhere within her there was a sort of surprise at this indifference of hers, something she had never felt before, which had grown with the growing of her plan. "No one will know it is not Iphigeneia," she said. "The victim will be wearing a mask."

She told him then what she had told Odysseus earlier, the white clay, the moon mask covering the features, so that the priestess of Artemis could walk with the goddess. "They have agreed," she said, "they have given permission. Iphigeneia will make up my face with the paste. When they come for her, I will be the one with the white mask and the saffron robe. Iphigeneia will be dressed in the clothes of Sisipyla, the slave girl. When they are taking me out she will hide her face in grief. No one will pay any attention to her. When we begin the procession towards the altar, the people will be flocking to see me die, the camp will be deserted. The princess will make her way down here, to the shore, where you will have a boat waiting."

"But afterwards, when your . . . when they wash the body to prepare it for burial, when the chalk is washed away, Agamemnon will know, he will see it is not his daughter."

"A face so changed in death, after such loss of blood? How well does Agamemnon know his daughter's face? How much time has he spent with her in these recent years? Besides, even if so, what will he do?"

This too she had mulled over, lying on her back straight and still, hands by her sides for concentration, a habit of childhood, while the light slowly strengthened and the first songs of the birds sounded from the hillsides all round the camp. She said, "Iphigeneia will be safe by then, you will be at her side, she will depend on you for support. And Agamemnon will be looking down at my dead face. The fleet is ready to sail, success awaits him, he has satisfied all the conditions."

She paused, aware that her heart had quickened, aware of the need to breathe deeply. It was exhilaration she felt, not doubt or dismay; and still that same surprise at her indifference to everything but his agreement. Never had she spoken words so unhesitating, in such clear order. She was not the person she had been, at the altar she would die a different person. "What will he do?" she said again. "Will he declare to the army that there has been a mistake, that the wrong person has been sacrificed? He will keep the knowledge buried in his heart. And how can there be a wrong person, in any case? Surely it will be enough for Zeus that Agamemnon believed it was his daughter at the time of the killing. It is not a matter of bodies. My mistress and I are the same age, our bodies are the same. It is the belief of the King that matters."

"That is true." A light had come to Macris's face. "It's the thought that counts," he said. But the light had not come only from this comforting truth. He would be the princess's savior and protector. He would stand alone with her against the world. She would be grateful to him. There were no rivals now. The day would come when Agamemnon too would be grateful for this substitution, grateful to the man who at a single stroke had confirmed him in his command and saved him from the shedding of a daughter's blood. And with the gratitude of kings there came very tangible benefits. "Yes," he said, "yes, it could work. We could be across to the other side in no time. The current runs that way, I noticed it yesterday when we came off the ship. Yes, I will do my part, I will wait with the boat."

He stood still a little while, looking down at her in silence. Perhaps it was her closeness to childhood that moved him at this moment — she was not yet full-grown. He reached out and laid a hand on her shoulder. "You are made of good metal," he said. "The goddess will be with you, she will make things easier."

On this she left him, returning alone. She was armed with two assurances now. Macris believed in the scheme, he would see to the boat; Odysseus had swallowed the idea of the moon mask. She found Iphigeneia alone — Odysseus had just left, promising to return shortly.

"He gives me no rest," the princess said. "He tells me constantly that my death is certain, that I must turn it to account, that it must not be a death wasted." She was dry-eyed now, and seemed composed, but the voice was toneless and she held her lower lip folded inward as if to keep the mouth firm. "He says the deaths of great persons must not be wasted, their deaths must be in keeping with their greatness."

"Odysseus is clever," Sisipyla said. "I felt it when he spoke to me. But he is wrong when he says the princess's death is certain."

With this, in a voice not much louder than a whisper, taking great care to get everything in order, she began to outline the plan, whose marvelous simplicity had come to her, a shaft from Artemis, in the dawn of that morning. It was a better plan now for the double assurance contained in it. She had no way of knowing, as she spoke, how Iphigeneia was taking it, because the princess, after the first look of fixity, kept her face averted.

In the silence after she had finished, Iphigeneia turned to look at her and there was something in the princess's eyes that made her feel the prickle of tears in her own.

"You would do this for me?"

"Princess, you gave me my life, I am ready to give it back now if you will favor me and take it."

Iphigeneia made a quick movement towards her and she found herself clasped in a close embrace. She felt a shuddering within the princess and this was transmitted to her own body and for these few moments their two bodies were a single vehicle for grief. Then Iphigeneia drew away and already her face had changed, there was a kind of sharpness in it. "But how could you be mistaken for me?" she said.

"With the makeup, the moon paste . . ."

"Even masked, it would be seen that you were not the princess."

"But lady, how could it be seen?" It was the same objection that Macris had made. What would have been easy for her — recognizing that she could be confused with another — was hard for Iphigeneia, and this was something she had not fully taken into account. As if the princess bore a sign always about her, like a light round her head, or something like music, something everyone would recognize and know. With a firmness that came as a surprise to herself, she said, "With the mask that makes the face round and white, with the robe of the victim, with the way I will walk, everyone will think it is Iphigeneia."

It was the first time in her life that she had taken such a tone with her mistress, and she felt a kind of alarm at her temerity. But Iphigeneia showed no displeasure, merely compressed her lips and nodded once, as if considering.

"But are you sure you can go through with it? What if you lose your nerve halfway through?"

Sisipyla felt a flood of relief at this. Not a question at all really, only a doubt. It meant that the princess would agree. She had not thought for a moment that Iphigeneia would refuse the offer of a slave's life to save her own, fond as she knew her mistress to be of her; but she knew also that the princess had no high opinion of her powers of concentration, thinking her sloppy and unfocused—she had said so often enough. She said, "Once I step outside in the mask and the robe, once I take the first paces towards the altar, my death is certain. If they find out I am only Sisipyla, they will kill me. Why would I lose my nerve, knowing I am dead in any case?"

Iphigeneia was silent for a time that seemed long to Sisipyla. Then, in a tone in which there was no finality, only a sort of reflectiveness, she said, "So I will prepare you for the sacrifice, dress your hair, spread the moon mask on your face. You will be my substitute, you will honor the goddess in my name."

"Yes, lady. And you will live to honor the goddess many times over."

"The sacrifice will not be in keeping with your destiny, you have no destiny."

"Lady, I am nothing, I am less than your shadow. This talk of destiny comes from Odysseus. He is clever but he is a bad man and he sees only what is bad in others. So he can be deceived. He will come again to persuade you. But now you will be stronger than he, you will know something he doesn't know. It will be better if you seem to be yielding, if you let him see that he is gaining ground. Not all at once, of course. Then he will be glad, he will want to fix the time of the sacrifice as soon as possible, so as to be done with it, so the ships can sail. In that way we can be ready with our plan. They talk of Zeus, and for a sacrifice to Zeus they will come just before sunrise. We will keep the light low inside here, when they come you will hide your face, you will be Sisipyla, overcome with grief. When they have taken me from the tent you will wait a little time and then make your escape. The boat will be waiting at the edge of the camp, at that side where the rocks have fallen. Everyone will be up on the hillside, waiting for the sacrifice. Macris will take you across the water, he will keep you safe."

6.

"mazing, absolutely amazing," Odysseus said. "You can talk for hours,
for days, and not a flicker. Then you say
the same thing again in slightly different
words and hey, presto, you see a change in
the eyes, you hear a change in the voice,
you know you are on the way, you know
you've struck the right note, you see light
at the end of the tunnel . . ."

"Breakthrough."

"Breakthrough, brilliant, what I would
do without you I don't know. I must admit
that I feel pleased about the way things
have gone. Of course, I spared no effort to
make her see reason, I am capable of dedication when there is need for it. I mean,
this business has taken two days and half
of one night and given me a sore throat.
There were times when I felt irritated,
times when I felt like giving her a good
spanking. The heavy-burden-of-command
argument was no good, for obvious rea-

sons. The sense-of-responsibility argument, which worked so well with her father, didn't really go down very well. I mean, she isn't responsible for anything, is she? She doesn't see herself as a witch, naturally. She is devoted to Artemis, it would have ruined everything to reflect on her duties as a priestess, it would have set her against us, made her more intractable than ever, lost ground already gained . . ."

"Counterproductive."

"There you go again, brilliant. I lost a lot of time initially, talking to her about greatness, what is due to her station and so on. But she isn't old enough to know what greatness means. It only started to have effect when I linked it up with destiny. She didn't show any sign at that point, but I am pretty sure that's where her resistance began to break down. Yes, our little Iphigeneia is interested in the idea of a noble destiny. Already, last night, I was getting some response. But it wasn't until this morning that I hit upon the right connection. Believe it or not, she thinks it is her destiny to save her people. She wants to take on the burden, discharge the debt, redeem the wrongs of the world . . ."

"Messianic complex."

"By all the gods, you are excelling yourself today. Yes, once I understood that, we got on like a house on fire. She began to confide in me—there couldn't be a clearer sign that she was caving in. She told me the story of the blood curse on her family, which of course I already knew, but she seemed to think it was a secret. She actually thought that by marrying Achilles she could lift the curse. Now the groom she will meet will be more irresistible even than he and the salvation factor much greater. Not only the family, you see, but everything else too. She declares herself ready to die, and she means it. I know sincerity when I see it. We can notify Croton immediately and set things going. The sacrifice will take place at sunrise tomorrow. It's odd, isn't it? We used the same basic argument of a noble destiny with both father and daughter. It succeeded with the father because he hasn't got any nobility, it has succeeded with the daughter because she has too much of it. I call that really neat. We must remember to keep our promises to that pretty little slave girl, what's her name again?"

"Sisipyla."

"I think we owe a lot to her. She's obviously been working behind the scenes to bring her mistress round. And she gave me a clue, something I might not have thought of—we all have our limitations."

"What was that?"

"Well, this moon-mask business. Everything is conceptual, that's a discovery my experience of life has brought me to. I thought, you know, if it was so important for Iphigeneia to walk to the altar with the goddess, she would be open to the idea that the goddess wanted it, had always wanted it, that it was the will of Artemis that she should die."

7.

I t was still dark when Sisipyla started
to prepare. The robe had been
brought to them the evening before; cut
from new cloth and dyed saffron by women
of the camp, it had been scented and folded
and kept ready for the princess's arrival.
Sisipyla put it on carefully in the dim light
of the lamp and Iphigeneia adjusted the
folds at the shoulders and tied the narrow
sash behind. Now it was time for the mask,
and here Sisipyla had to instruct her mistress, who was new to this task. First,
slowly and carefully, the outline of the oval,
beginning across the forehead, curving
down through the temples, meeting at the
center of the chin. Then the filling in of
the shape, smoothing the paste evenly over
the brow and nose and cheeks, taking care
not to go too close to the eyes and lips and
nostrils. Under her fingers Iphigeneia saw
the face she knew disappear and that of an
immaculate stranger take its place.

"Now the hair," Sisipyla said. "It must be dressed high on the head if we are not to cut it. It must be kept well clear of the neck." How strange it seemed that her mistress should now be making her up, getting her ready, acting the servant. When they were small Iphigeneia used often to dress her up, tie her hair with ribbons, put various outfits on her. She had served as a live doll for a while, perhaps a year, until the princess had grown tired of it. She felt fear like a knot in her stomach, and the palms of her hands were moist. She saw or imagined a faint light straining through the canvas, contending with the lamplight. It was not ceasing to be that frightened her, only the manner of it, the violation. She had struggled to keep the fear from her mind while she concentrated on the instructions to her mistress. Now that she was dressed and ready, the fear came at her more strongly for being held back, and she felt a quick, involuntary contraction of the throat.

Iphigeneia stepped back suddenly, putting a distance between them for the first time since the dressing-up had begun. And now, just as suddenly, through her own unchanging mask Sisipyla saw the face before her change, pass from a look of appraisal to a different kind of scrutiny, colder, somehow stricken.

"You are me," she said. "If you are me, what am I?"

"You are always Iphigeneia."

"They will think you are me, they will think your blood is mine."

"Only for as long as needs be. Then you will—"

"No, the time when they think your blood is mine can never be got back again, because the blood is shed forever."

"Lady, we must be ready, it will soon be light."

"You are my dear companion but our blood is not the same.

My blood is royal, yours is that of an Asian slave girl. You will
steal my destiny."

"Destiny?"

"Only great people have destiny, common people cannot
have it. Odysseus explained this to me."

Sisipyla felt a trembling within her as at some prophecy of
ill, not believed, now fulfilled. She made an effort to overcome
it. To Iphigeneia's face there had come a radiance she knew, exalted, remote—it was the look she had worn when she spoke of
marrying Achilles.

"I wanted to save my life," the princess said. "I pretended
to agree, at first I pretended, but then it was pretense no longer.
When he said it is my destiny to save my father and my people
I knew he was right. I said the words again inside myself and I
knew he was right. It is what I was born for."

Sisipyla's trembling grew stronger. She tensed her body to
control it. "This destiny costs you your life, it costs Odysseus
nothing but breath. Where is it, this destiny? It is only a word."
She paused, struggling with unaccustomed thoughts. "It is not
like love or the feeling of being grateful. It is only a word. The
knife makes the same stroke, whether it is you or me or a goat
or a rabbit, and the blood is the same color."

As if she had not heard, Iphigeneia said, "I didn't realize it,
not fully, not until I saw you standing there in my gown and my
mask. It was like a dream when you are doing something you
don't want to do but some force makes you go on with it. All the
time it was in my mind. Sisipyla, you came from nowhere to be
my friend. But how can the blood of a person from nowhere deceive the goddess? Will she not know whose blood it is? How
can the blood of a person from nowhere save the name of my father and strengthen his command, how can she save this great

expedition and forge the Greeks into a single nation, how can she be remembered in the songs as the savior of a whole people? She cannot. Artemis has called me to this work of salvation. I want you to make me ready for the sacrifice."

"You are using their language. They have put their language into your mouth."

"Do you hear me? I want you to make me ready. Take off my gown."

Wordless now, Sisipyla obeyed. She untied the sash behind, slipped off the gown, handed it to her mistress. Iphigeneia undressed, dropping her clothes here and there on the floor of the tent. Sisipyla hastily dressed in her own things again. Her trembling had ceased now, but there was a weakness in her limbs and in the movements of her hands as she began to apply the chalk paste to the face of her mistress. She made a last effort. "Lady," she said, "don't believe them, please don't believe them, it is only words, they care no more for your life than for mine."

But Iphigeneia made no reply, holding herself stiffly, mutely offering her face for the masking. As Sisipyla spread the gray-white glutinous paste, taking the usual care to make a perfect oval, as touch by touch the known and loved face of her mistress disappeared below the featureless mask, it came to Sisipyla with a force that strengthened and steadied her that it was not she who was being abandoned, left among the playthings. She had been ready to give her life for a reason that belonged to her, a life to save a life. Iphigeneia's reason did not belong to her, it belonged to Odysseus and the chiefs. Her throat would be severed for reasons that belonged to other people. This was to be like the straw effigies in the dark grove that had always oppressed and frightened her so, left dangling and helpless there, with no reason that belonged to them, to sway or be still as the wind bade them.

When Iphigeneia was ready they faced each other for some time in silence, mask regarding mask, all expression concealed beneath the stiffening paste. The light of early morning was coming through the canvas. There were shadows of men at the entrance, and then voices.

"Sisipyla, I thank you for the love and service you have given me. Now I leave you behind, I go to fulfill my destiny and perform the will of Artemis." The voice was composed, without a tremor.

"My true name is not Sisipyla. That name dies with you. I had another name before, my own name. It was Amandralettes. Now I will be Amandralettes."

These were the last words spoken between them. It was Calchas who came, haggard in the morning light, flanked by guards. Iphigeneia went forward to meet them, head held high. No one gave more than a glance to the slave girl crouching in a corner, her head averted in grief. When they had gone she waited where she was for a short while. There was no time to remove the paste, even had there been water enough inside the tent to do it. At the last moment, at the entrance, she turned back inside, took the gold shoulder clasps from Iphigeneia's dress and the necklace of silver and ivory. These she tied up in her shawl, holding the bundle close under her cloak as she left the tent.

She met no one as she went down towards the shore. Macris would be waiting at the place arranged, but she did not take this direction. Below the camp there were always boats. No one would be guarding them now. The current would help her . . . Behind her, as she went, she heard a great shout. Then there was silence.

Calchas, accompanied by a watchful Chasimenos and two armed men from Phylakos's squadron, himself took a boat not very much later, and according to instructions cast the blood-stained knife into the sea where it ran deepest. And as he watched the knife cleave the water and disappear from sight with only the slightest of sounds and no visible marring of the surface, his talent returned to him and he saw radiant circles spread outward from this plunge of the knife and he was at the heart of these ripples of light and at their most distant borders, together with the meanest of crawling things and the mightiest of gods. He was pierced through with the wonder of existence and everything he could think or know or experience lit up this wonder and darkened it and the light and darkness were one and the same. He trailed his hand in the water and his eyes filled with tears and he prayed for the safe passage of Iphigeneia's soul.

And so the fleet set sail and the army landed at Troy. The war lasted ten years. Greeks and Trojans alike were borne away on that tide of metal the diviner had seen in his vision. Agamemnon returned, only to be murdered, together with his concubine Cassandra, by Clytemnestra, in revenge for the killing of their daughter Iphigeneia. Not long after this, within the lifetime of some who survived the war, the power of Mycenae collapsed, citadel and palace went up in flames and the inhabitants were put to the sword. This destruction, from which the kingdom never recovered, is said to have been the work of wandering marauders called the Sea People, but who these people were and where they came from is still disputed.

The girl was remembered by a fisherman out early, who saw her cross the water. He spoke of it afterwards: a shout of many voices, then a girl in a white mask crossing the water soon after sunrise. Those who heard this story repeated it in their turn. Because of the mask it began to be said that the girl was Iphigeneia, that she had escaped or been rescued. And in the course of time a standard version found its way into the repertory of the singers. Iphigeneia had not been sacrificed, she had been saved at the last moment by Artemis and spirited far away, as far as anyone could imagine, to the northern shores of the Euxine Sea, to live among the barbarous Taurians and be their priestess.

But all this was much later, when sensibilities and habits of thought had changed, and it was no longer considered desirable that such an ugly thing as the sacrifice of the innocent for the sake of prosecuting a war should feature in the songs of the kings.

Selected Bibliography

Lord William Taylour, *The Mycenaeans*

John Chadwick, *The Mycenaean World*

A. J. B. Wace, *Mycenae*

Michael Wood, *In Search of the Trojan War*

James Hall, *Dictionary of Subjects and Symbols in Art*

Andrew Dalby, *Siren Feasts*

G. S. Kirk, *The Nature of Greek Myths*

Robert Graves, *The Greek Myths*

Edward Tripp, *Dictionary of Classical Mythology*

Racine, *Iphigénie*

Euripides, *Iphigeneia in Aulis*

SELECTED BIBLIOGRAPHY

Aeschylus, *The Oresteia* (translated, with an introductory essay, by Robert Fagles)

Homer, *The Iliad*

M. P. Nilsson, *Minoan-Mycenaean Religion*

Walter Burkert, *Greek Religion*

Hugh Lloyd-Jones, "Artemis and Iphigeneia" (*Journal of Hellenic Studies*, 1983)

E. O. James, *The Ancient Gods*

M. I. Finley, *The World of Odysseus*

A NOTE ABOUT THE AUTHOR

Barry Unsworth won the Booker Prize in 1992 for *Sacred Hunger*; his next novel, *Morality Play*, was a Booker nominee and a bestseller in both the United States and Great Britain. His other novels include *After Hannibal*, *The Hide*, and *Pascali's Island*, which was also short-listed for the Booker Prize and was made into a feature film. He held the position of visiting fellow at the University of Iowa Writers' Workshop, and lives in Umbria with his wife.

A NOTE ABOUT THE TYPE

The text of this book is set in Cochin, designed in
the early 1900s by Georges Peignot and based on
eighteenth-century copper engravings. Cochin has
an unusual mixture of stylistic elements. It is large
and wide and was an especially popular typeface at
the beginning of the twentieth century.